GA

∅ **W9-BZV-210**

DRY BONES
IN THE VALLEY

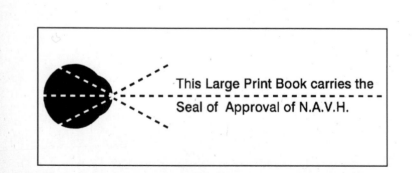

This Large Print Book carries the
Seal of Approval of N.A.V.H.

Dry Bones
in the Valley

Tom Bouman

THORNDIKE PRESS
A part of Gale, Cengage Learning

GALE
CENGAGE Learning·

Farmington Hills, Mich • San Francisco • New York • Waterville, Maine
Meriden, Conn • Mason, Ohio • Chicago

GALE
CENGAGE Learning®

Copyright © 2014 by Tom Bouman.
Thorndike Press, a part of Gale, Cengage Learning.

ALL RIGHTS RESERVED
Thorndike Press® Large Print Reviewers' Choice.
The text of this Large Print edition is unabridged.
Other aspects of the book may vary from the original edition.
Set in 16 pt. Plantin.

LIBRARY OF CONGRESS CATALOGING-IN-PUBLICATION DATA

Bouman, Tom.
  Dry bones in the valley / by Tom Bouman. — Large print edition.
    pages ; cm. — (Thorndike Press large print reviewers' choice)
    ISBN 978-1-4104-7318-9 (hardcover) — ISBN 1-4104-7318-X (hardcover)
  1. Police—Pennsylvania—Fiction. 2. Murder—Investigation—Fiction.
  3. Rural life—Pennsylvania—Fiction. 4. Social conflict—Pennsylvania—
  Fiction. 5. Large type books. I. Title.
  PS3602.O8923D79 2014b
  813'.6—dc23   2014025672

Published in 2014 by arrangement with W. W. Norton & Company, Inc.

Printed in Mexico
1 2 3 4 5 6 7 18 17 16 15 14

For Ma

The night before we found the body, I couldn't sleep. It was a mid-March thaw. The snow that covered everything, everywhere since January finally released its grip, filling ditches and creeks, dripping from my eaves, and streaming out of my gutters as meltwater. Over the horizon, three ridges to the southwest, a gas crew was flaring a well. I shivered barefoot on my porch with a cup of coffee, looking up at the clouds as they flickered bruise-purple from the fireball below. The old farmhouse I rented had been sinking untroubled into the hillside for years. Then came the procession of colossal machines to knock down trees and strip them of their tops and roots, to build access roads, to haul equipment, and to drill. Compared with the undertaking of clearing a well pad, the drilling and fracking was almost quiet. I could almost say it was a strong wind through the pines, if not for the stop-start and whine of machinery contending with the earth, the glow on the nighttime horizon, and the tanker trucks hirpling up and down our dirt roads newly widened to let them pass, so many headlights and taillights strung over the winter hills like Christmas decorations.

At four a.m. I accepted that I wasn't going to get back to sleep. And at dawn, when the sun rose magenta in the east, I was relieved.

About seven I ate frozen waffles with peanut butter, tugged the snarls out of my beard, dressed in my uniform, and headed over to the office. The township stationed me in the garage with the plows and fire truck and other vehicles, near the pyramids of gravel and sand, across from the fairgrounds in a quiet valley among the dwindling quiet valleys in northeastern Pennsylvania. The garage is cinder block surrounded by a dirt lot, painted white with neat black letters that read WILD THYME TOWNSHIP VOL. FIRE CO.

The police station is separated from the garage with drywall; you can hear the mechanics and roadmen working and everything they say. My office came equipped with an industrial-sized restaurant coffeemaker but my predecessor evidently lost the pot with the brown spout, leaving me only the orange one meant for decaf, which gave me the low feeling of always drinking decaf, so I replaced the whole thing with a new all-black coffeemaker on my own dime. That, and way back in history someone had put a drop ceiling in the office, but I disliked looking at all the little holes and brown stains in it. So I popped out the tiles and unscrewed the frame. It's still somewhere in case someone wants to reinstall it. Till that day, I like seeing how everything works, the bones, everything plain from my steelcase desk right up to the pipes and HVAC near the ceiling. There's a framed head shot of the governor on the wall, a map, a bulletin board, a vanilla-scented candle in the john that never gets lit.

When I got to the office that morning, my deputy George Ellis had his head on his desk with his face tucked in his arms; he didn't look up when I came in. A scanner was on with the volume low, and the air felt thick. I put my feet up and looked at a couple faxed wanted posters, the same sorry characters from the week before, and the outstanding warrants page, some of which dated all the way back to 1980.

I fielded a call from Alexander Grace, owner of Grace Tractor Sales and Rental.

One of his skid steers had been stolen from the lot several weeks earlier, and he'd called me every day, increasingly irate about my lack of progress. I didn't tell him that for a theft like this, we had about a twenty percent chance of recovery. This past week, without consulting me, he'd placed an ad in the local coupon circular offering a $2,500 reward for information leading to the skid steer's recovery, no questions asked. "I guess we'll see what I can do on my own," he said. I pleaded with him not to be stupid and to call me if he got any takers.

As he often does, John Kozlowski stopped in to visit. The township mechanic was a drinking buddy of George's, a good-time Charlie with a face full of broken capillaries. He declined to sit, citing oily coveralls, and filled us in on a variety of subjects, including the cottage he was building on Walker Lake, plus, he told us, the his-and-hers Jet Skis he had just bought. Walker Lake being pretty small, I asked him where he planned to go on such a contraption, and he said something unkind about my mother, and we went on like that for a bit.

In those early days of the boom, conversations about gas money were guarded. People would never say outright how much they'd signed for, but their cottages and new trucks did the talking for them. At first some landowners leased rights for as low as twenty-five dollars an acre. By the time Penn State made it clear how much gas might actually be under us, the going rate was more like four thousand dollars an acre. People were scooping up windfalls, but they were of different sizes, again depending on how early in the play they signed, and how much land they owned. Neighbors stayed neighborly, but kept an eye on their property lines.

When John left, we passed time in silence until the phone rang. George raised his head and glared at it, but it kept ringing. He cursed it and answered. After a few short words on his end, he hung up and turned to me. "Dr. Brennan down at the clinic. She's been pulling buckshot out of Danny Stiobhard's side this morning, thought we should know."

"All right." I looked at George as if to ask what he was waiting for. He scratched the white skin under his beard.

"Look, Henry," he said. "Danny and I had a run-in last week. At the bar."

"Ah."

"I'd love to take this one, but . . ." he said contritely.

"It wouldn't be politic, sending you," I said.

"That's what it wouldn't be."

"You know," I said, looking into his blood-shot eyes, "this fighting won't do, George."

"I know."

I didn't fault him, not entirely. He and Danny Stiobhard had a long history, and his taking the deputy job didn't help. For reasons I will explain, I didn't want to make the visit either. I put on my hat and coat, took the .40 in its belt out of the locker, got in my truck, and headed to town.

Geography and culture separates Wild Thyme Township and the town of Fitzmorris, which is the seat of Holebrook County, PA. Fitzmorris started as a summer colony for Philadelphia Scots Presbyterians back in the mid-1800s. It has some nice Greek Revivals, big white ones with columns, bigger than they have any right to be. Most have black trim but every ten houses a high-on-life home owner took a notion to paint theirs turquoise or heliotrope, or all colors of the rainbow. I like those, can't help it.

The township is a rural area north of Fitzmorris. After the Civil War, the state parceled off a bunch of hardpan in the surrounding hills to Fenian soldiers who fought for the Union, and those Fenians told a few more of their friends and families come on over; that's how my people landed in Wild Thyme Township, the Fearghails, they fought for the 50th Pennsylvania. And the Fearghails we remained, until, in a moment of World War II Americanism, my grandfather changed the spelling to "Farrell," and there you have it.

Danny Stiobhard's lineage is similar to mine. Our fathers used to hunt together. His last name goes "Steward," if you care to know. However you say it, his clan has been here in Wild Thyme Township for several generations. While the particulars of their enterprise have changed over the years, the approach has remained the same: they sidestep law, object to government, and profit off the land. Poachers of lumber and deer, burglars, rumored to be dipping toes in the drug trade, they believe they are fighting an eternal Whiskey Rebellion. As we don't get too many high-ranking federal officials visiting, they cast me — a mere municipal officer, mind you — in the role of government tyrant.

I pulled into the health clinic's lot, behind Danny's blue flatbed, noting some speckled perforations on the driver's-side door. The clinic is run-down and small, occupying the top floor of a two-family house, with an elderly couple downstairs. We've all been there; Liz does her best.

Nobody in the waiting room but Jo the receptionist. I laid a finger alongside my nose as I passed her; gravely she nodded and didn't say a word.

Down the hall and through an open door I saw Danny Stiobhard shirtless with his left arm raised above his shoulder, twenty-odd holes dotting his side and bleeding; Liz had a shiny clamp dug into a wound just below his rib cage, and when she pulled it out it stretched the surrounding flesh into a bleb. The shot emerged with the tiniest pop, or maybe I imagined that, but the stream of blood that followed was hard to miss. I caught Danny's face just at the moment when his eyes welled over. The left half of his face looked like a movie alien's, purple, blue, and swollen. Evidence of his fight with my deputy, I supposed. I waited for him to wipe his face with the back of his hand before I went in.

"Morning, Danny. Liz." The room smelled of rubbing alcohol and damp clothes that had not been washed in some time.

Danny raised his good eye to the ceiling. "Oh, goddamn it, Liz, you fuckin called him. Sorry, excuse me."

"Sit still," Liz told him. Blood speckled

14

her green scrubs, and her copper hair was pulled back in a ponytail. She prodded another wound with her finger.

"You said you wouldn't," Danny said.

"Sit still."

I said, "What the hell is this, Danny?"

He had been wearing a hat until recently, from the look of his hair. His beard showed gray. His chest hair was matted, and he had several tattoos. The elastic band of his underwear was soaked red. "Accident," he said.

"Oh, all right," I said. "My work here is done, then."

Danny snorted and lowered his arm. "Liz, stop. Wait until he goes."

"Sit. Still." She plucked another ball out. He hissed through gritted teeth and exhaled when the shot was free. His face looked mighty pale.

"Stiobhard, you might as well tell me who the other party is."

As Liz dug in with the clamp again, Stiobhard yelped and started to hyperventilate. Liz made him lower his head between his knees and slow his breathing. When he regained control, he said, "I'll tell you who to talk to. You know Aub Dunigan out on Fieldsparrow Road?"

I nodded. Aub lived on a disused dairy

farm that most passersby would assume was abandoned. There were younger Dunigans in the area, yet Aub was alone in the world as far as I knew. A recluse.

"Like I said, it was an accident, no doubt. He'll tell you himself if he remembers back as far as half an hour ago."

"You provoke him?" My guess was Danny had his eye on a nice cherry tree; they have grown big in Aub's woods.

"Why would I? Over what? He's old. His cousin Kevin hired me to clear his trails. Evidently nobody told him. You have what you need, would you just? Just go check on the old man. Tell him no hard feelings."

Liz pushed her glasses into place with her wrist. She had bright blue eyes. "Let's talk out in the hall." After she'd closed the door to her makeshift operating room she said, "Henry, I've given you all the time I can right now."

"Got it."

"Let me patch him up, then you can do whatever you're going to do."

"All right. Save the shot, okay?"

She nodded. "Hey, we on tonight? Uncle Dave Macon got the ax this morning," she said. "I made coq au vin."

Uncle Dave Macon is — was — a troublesome rooster. Liz is my best friend Ed's wife. We get together Tuesday nights to have dinner and run through old fiddle tunes. I play the fiddle. All you really need to make dance music is a fiddle and a banjo. Liz comes from a traditional family and plays very good clawhammer banjo and passable three-finger. Ed started out as a rock-and-roll guitar player, but he's been learning. Despite his frequent suggestions that we arrange some heavy metal song in a bluegrass style, and drinking to excess when we play, he rounds Liz and me out pretty well. It's nice to have someone to play with.

Liz saved my life when I first returned to Wild Thyme a few years back, which I'll tell about later.

I told her we were on, left the clinic, then called the office on my cell and asked George to go out and park at the foot of Aub Dunigan's driveway and not let anyone up. I decided to call on Kevin Dunigan, Aub's second cousin and nearest relative that I knew of. If the old man needed to be put in a home, best that process started with family.

It was early enough that I could catch Kevin before work. I put on the lights, but not the siren, and stepped on it, easing through one red light and racing into the outskirts. Kevin lived with his wife in a brick ranch house just east of town, and owned an oil-change shop in Fitzmorris. The house is at some remove from the road in the middle of a field, but you can pick it out at a distance by the flagpole in his yard; he flies Old Glory and, just beneath it, a big blue flag with the oil-change corporate logo on. As a result of that flag he's had to turn away some would-be customers who concluded that his house was the shop.

When I got to his driveway I turned off the flashers and pulled in. One of the garage doors was open and at least one car was still there. Kevin, gray and compact and near fifty, stepped out of the door that communicated between house and garage, and onto the driveway. There was a look of mild concern on his face and a mug in his hand.

"Why, Henry."

"Kevin, how you been?"

"Fine. What, ah, what brings you around?"

"You hear from Danny Stiobhard this morning?"

Kevin's eyes widened. "Why would I?"

"Your cousin Aub winged him with a shotgun. He says."

"Come again?"

Kevin's wife Carly joined us outside, wearing a yellow baseball hat and baggy jeans tucked into galoshes. I didn't know her very well; she worked in the little bookstore in town, and had steered it in a Christian direction.

Kevin relayed what I'd just told him. She said, "*Now* look."

"Don't worry about Danny," I said. "He'll live. Just so I have everything straight: You hired him to clear the trails?"

"I certainly did not," Kevin said. "What on earth."

"He said you did."

"What about Aub? Can we see him? What do we do?"

"Well, I have yet to get his side of things. It would be good if you came with me to check on him. I may have to bring him in."

Carly boggled at that. "You 'may'? You haven't got him now?"

Kevin took a couple steps back, saying, "Oh, no. No, you don't."

I held up my hands. "Hey. Please."

Kevin pointed a finger at me. "Do your own job."

"Uh-huh," I said.

He handed his coffee mug to Carly and rubbed his face with both hands. "Sorry, Henry. Since I was a kid, he's . . . it's been difficult, him in the family. Just don't let him shoot me and I'll get my coat." He went inside.

Carly raised an eyebrow at me.

"He won't get shot," I said.

Kevin followed me in his car, a silver sedan. We drove up and down the hills on 37, the sun getting higher in the morning and the roadside ditches rushing with meltwater. Every now and then a beer can flashed blue. Holebrook County is on the western edge of the Endless Mountains region. The term is a poetic one; what people mean is that it's hilly. We're part of the Appalachian Range, which formed almost five hundred million years ago, along with a vast inland sea to the west. Creatures in the sea died and sank, and the mountains eroded, and over a hundred million years this mix of sediment and organic matter was buried and turned into shale, the Marcellus Shale. Because of the once-living things in it, the Marcellus contains a lot of natural gas, all wrapped up in layers of rock like a present to America.

After maybe seven miles we turned onto a narrower route, passing dirt roads where they coughed out onto the pavement. Many were marked with blue and white ribbons put there by the gas operators, showing the way to sites they were probably going to drill. And not only at roads: if you knew where to look in the tree line, you saw the

20

ribbons marking trailheads. I dislike seeing them but I'm out of luck, because they're everywhere.

Fieldsparrow Road led up and to the north. I waited to see that I hadn't left Kevin in the dust and then made the turn, slowing the truck to about half speed. The township paid for new shocks last year and they won't be doing it again soon. We bumped along for a mile or two, past derelict trailers and at the edge of a clearing, a blue swing set grown over with black grapevine. After a long stretch of woods the road emerged into wide gray fields. On the left stood a couple lopsided sheds, and up a long, steep driveway a farmhouse was half hidden by a grove of maples. I parked behind Deputy Ellis's radio car, where he sat tapping ash over the top of his window, hidden from the house by a barn.

We each got out of our vehicles and stood in the road and George said, "Nobody stirring up there. Far as I can tell." He tossed a butt into the ditch, where the water carried it away. "How's Danny?"

"He'll live."

Kevin Dunigan pulled up. George tried to wave him along with some impatience, not realizing who he was. Extending a hand out his window, Kevin introduced himself.

21

George told him to park out of sight of the house, then turned to squint one eye at me as if to ask what the hell.

The barn we were hiding behind was built into a slope, so that half the foundation disappeared underground. A heap of blue shale fieldstones surrounded the barn, along with a set of rusted rotary blades, several empty jugs of wine, and much more broken glass, all covered with briars and deadly nightshade. The structure itself was standing, I'll say that for it; the siding had weathered silver and was full of holes toward the bottom. I peered around the corner to the base of the dirt driveway and was surprised to find a new hatchback. It was blue, on blocks, and its wheels were gone.

"All right," I said. "George, wait here while Kevin and I head up. Keep your walkie-talkie on." I had bought satellite walkie-talkies for me and George a while back; they're good for a mile or two of range out in the township where neither our two-way transmitter nor the county's is reliable, especially since they moved everyone to narrow bands after 9/11. It'd only take two more transmitters planted on summits between the township and Fitzmorris to make radio contact between us reliable, but of course that hasn't been done. If we need to reach town, we use phones, which is inconvenient when approaching a suspicious vehicle in the dead of night, or fighting a drunk on a domestic call. Anyway, I was pleased about the walkie-talkies. They had been handy back in deer season.

Kevin climbed in the passenger seat of my truck and we set off. It was a bright morning and there was more snow left up in the hills than in the valleys where I'd been; my transition eyeglasses went from yellow to brown. The driveway led past an old barn foundation and up to a corncrib; I always liked those corncribs for their back-slanted walls, walls to keep the rats out. There was a line of trees to one side, with barbed wire strung through it, and more wine jugs lying in the remains of a stone wall. And it was from the corncrib that Aub emerged, shotgun in hand, to peer down at us. We were still about fifty yards away. I stopped, put on the parking brake, and stepped clear of the truck, which I did not want shot, as it might not get repaired until next quarter. Kevin stayed in the vehicle. Aub stood stock-still, hadn't raised the shotgun. I took a noisy step forward.

"Aub, it's Henry Farrell. Officer Farrell. Can you drop that? We're here to say hello."

"It's Cousin Kevin, Aub," Kevin called

out of his window.

"Come on up, then." The old man wore a plaid flannel shirt and alligator-clip suspenders over stooped shoulders. His pants hung loose around his middle and were tucked into black galoshes. His pink scalp showed through strands of yellowed hair. On either side of an Irish nose, his eyes were dark and sunk deep. When we got close, I asked him again to set the shotgun down; he opened the breach, with trembling fingers plucked out a shell, and left the gun open in the crook of his arm. The weapon had to have been at least seventy-five years old. I was surprised he'd convinced it to fire at Danny Stiobhard.

"My friend," I said, "you've got some explaining to do."

The old man's voice shook and he had trouble with his consonants; it took concentration to understand the words that tumbled out half formed and angry. What I made out was this:

"He been coming on my land and cutting trees. They stole my wheels. Seen him coming on up again and I let him have one. But I didn't have nothing to do with that boy." He closed his eyes and turned his head to the side.

"What boy is that, now?"

"One you're coming on up to collect."

I turned to Kevin, who was all bewilderment.

I stated the obvious. "We're here about Danny Stiobhard."

"Fellow got killed up in my woods. You got to come on up and collect him."

Kevin put his face in his hands and said, "Oh, my god. Oh, god."

"Aub, are you sure?"

"Found him yesterday. Mountain let go and I found him."

We all three waited in silence a long time before I decided what to do. I'm a patrolman, more or less, no detective. But I wasn't trained to say, this is someone else's mess, someone else will clean this up. I was trained to take care of it.

"Can you show me?"

Aub nodded, turned, and walked toward the tree line. His farmhouse was sided with green tar shingles, and as we passed it I noticed that the ground between it and the ancient outhouse was muddy and well trod. The old man led the way past the west face of his house and into a field covered in snow. A couple sets of prints made a straight line to and from the wooded ridge at the field's edge, and both prints looked like his, or were about his size, I'm no expert. A few sets of snowmobile tracks led from the road at the bottom of his field to the trailhead, merged into one, and led into the forest. Aub pushed aside a few bare branches to expose a logging road dug into the hillside.

Up we went, with Kevin slipping once and landing hard on his knee until he learned to walk splayfooted. The woods were pretty and full of junk. The pièce de résistance was a rusted-out International pickup at the edge of a clearing, its glass all gone and mustard-colored stuffing popping out of its seat.

In our area we have second-growth forest, meaning the wilderness is reclaiming what used to be farmland; that's where the split-rail fences come from, and why rusted strands of barbed wire disappear into tree trunks that have grown around them. On Aub's land, there were still blue shale walls, two feet wide and three tall in most places, some a mile or more long, climbing ridges and descending into valleys, deep into the woods. One wondered at the farmers who broke their backs making them just a few generations ago, what they were thinking — if they were impatient quarrying the stone and then setting them in place, if they were sure their children would always farm the land and be grateful for those walls.

As the walls remain in wooded places, so do trails — not only the main-drag logging roads like the one we were on, but narrow ways through the brush. People call them deer trails now but I have to wonder if livestock made them first and the deer just find them convenient; I read somewhere that cattle and sheep do tend to walk exact paths, wearing them into the ground over centuries. We passed through a break in the wall and cut onto one such trail, departing from the snowmobile track and following Aub's prints up the ridge. It turned into a longer walk than I expected, but eventually we came to a high-up place where the undergrowth was thinner and the trees were bigger and straighter and let in more sun.

Half tucked underneath a car-sized shale boulder was where we found it. A pale-and-dark patch on the ground, it was unmistakable to the prepared eye, out of place even in those woods already full of ruined and discarded things. I told Kevin to stay where he was; he squatted with his head in his hands while the old man and I pressed on. Within ten feet of the body we flushed several turkey vultures from an ash tree. They didn't bother to fly too far away.

It was plain that this was no boy but a young man, shirtless, face down and away from me, right arm tucked under him. The skin on his back was mottled lavender and looked thin as newspaper, as if his shoulder blades and spine would tear through if he were nudged. He had slid partway out from a hollow, the kind animals dig beneath boulders for their dens, and the snow holding him in there must have melted and let him out. He had on jeans and his feet were still buried. At first it looked like his left arm was hidden under the boulder, but as I got close I saw that there was no arm to hide. It, the shoulder, and much of the upper left side of his torso were gone, as if the arm had been ripped away. We were silent and still so long that the chickadees started singing again.

I've seen bodies — dry corpses crawling with flies in dusty streets, an old woman withered in her armchair, dead for weeks. To say they all seemed to belong where they were might not speak too well of me, or of the places I've been. This one didn't belong where he lay.

I took careful steps, looking for signs of what might have brought this kid to that place. The only tracks I saw were on the trail we'd taken to get there. Looking back at Aub Dunigan, I came to myself, put my hand on my weapon, and told him to lay the shotgun down. He snapped the breach closed and set it stock-down against a tree trunk. Once he'd done so, he didn't know what to do with his shaking hands. "This is none of me," he said.

I got George on the walkie-talkie. He was pretty faint at that distance but I told him to find a spot where he could radio the county, or call.

"What the hell for?" George said.

"Found a body up here."

"What?"

I gave him the code and said, "Raise the sheriff. We'll be down the hill soon as we can."

Kevin had joined us and stood staring at the corpse. Aub turned away and walked toward a nearby boulder. I told him stay where he was. He looked back at me and gestured to where he was headed, as if to explain. I said, "Jesus, Kevin, get him to stay put."

"Aub," Kevin said.

The old man seized a fallen branch and pulled; with it came a piece of cloth and another branch of the same size. He'd made a stretcher by tying a blanket between two tree limbs, must have brought the blanket up on a previous trip. Demonstrating it to me by pulling the blanket taut, he said,

"Take him on down."

For some reason this made me sad. "No, put that down. Just set it down. We'll get him later." I put Aub's shotgun over my shoulder and we walked down to the house without speaking. It took a while.

This was too much for me and George alone. Seeing the body and putting my own tracks everywhere around it gave me an unreasonable feeling of involvement, even complicity. When we made the last turn on the trail down, and there was just a screen of trees between us and Aub's house, which was now flanked by two county sheriff's cars, George's radio car, and an ambulance, it felt like we three were coming out to surrender. As if thinking the same thing, Aub broke our long silence: "He wasn't my doing."

Out we came, me and Kevin and a stooped old man wringing his hands. Out of the woods and into light so white you saw colors in it.

Sheriff Nicholas Dally stood waiting by his car. He's got fifteen years as sheriff of Holebrook County versus my couple serving Wild Thyme Township, and this has always made him seem not only wiser than me, but taller. When he speaks it carries the weight of pronouncement. Good qualities in a policeman. He's a clean shaver but that morning he had a small cut on his chin, a tiny seam of red on a white field turning black. They say he plays the trombone but I can't imagine it.

He touched the tip of his campaign hat, and without a word placed a gentle hand on Aub's elbow, steering him toward a waiting county deputy, who led the old man into the farmhouse. Dally turned to Kevin Dunigan and said, "Would you keep Deputy Ellis company while Henry fills me in?"

Kevin ignored the request. "What's going to happen to Aub?"

"I need to speak to Officer Farrell. I'd appreciate it if you'd stick around, though. We'll need you."

Kevin moved off toward my deputy's car, rubbing the back of his neck.

Dally turned to me. "What's it look like up there?"

"Young man, nobody I know, no shirt, stuffed under a boulder and missing an arm. No tracks other than Aub's. We didn't touch him but we'll need to get up there soon if we're going to beat the vultures."

"Holy Christ. Coyotes make off with his arm, maybe? But how'd he get up there with no shirt."

"No animal sign either. Strange."

Dally shot a look at the house.

"Aub says he had nothing to do with it. I believe him. But the reason I'm here in the first place is he took a shot at Danny Stiobhard this morning."

Dally raised his eyebrows, but all he said was, "Best someone stays with him."

We stepped onto the porch, which was missing only a couple boards. After wiping his feet on a welcome mat made of old tires, Dally headed in. Kevin followed him, leaving my deputy George on the porch smoking a cigarette. I could feel a line of nervous sweat down my ribs. There wasn't much to do but listen to the snow melt, and to think about the vultures up the hill, and worry. I was needed to lead the coroner and sheriff back to the body. My deputy was free.

"George," I said, "got a job for you." He sniffed. "Why don't you bring Danny Stiobhard in for us?"

"Come on."

"I'd try the clinic first. If the doc says you can't have him, tell her I said it's important."

"What if he ain't there anymore?"

"You know, find him."

George trudged off to beat the bushes, grumbling.

Not ten minutes later a maroon extended-cab pickup joined the small fleet of vehicles in the dooryard. Wy Brophy stepped out of the driver's side. The county coroner and medical examiner was long-limbed and tall, with frameless hexagonal spectacles and a camera dangling from his neck. He hitched a camouflage backpack over one shoulder and raised a hand in greeting. Brophy's arrival coaxed the two EMTs from their ambulance — a tall overweight boy and a short plump blond girl, county EMTs with ALS training and good equipment. The boy had a large pack on and between the two of them they carried an orange spineboard.

Their names were Julie and Damon. Sheriff Dally stepped out of the house, and soon I was leading the four of them back up the ridge, leaving the Dunigans with Deputy Ben Jackson.

The coroner walked like an old-timey explorer, addressing the ridge in long, confident strides. He never did slip, and still had breath to ask me questions, sheriff listening all the while.

"How long had the body been out here, did Aub say?"

"He didn't."

"And you saw it?"

"Saw it a little. Didn't touch anything."

"Good. How bad was he?"

"You know. Dead as a mackerel. And he's missing an arm."

"Jesus. No sign of the arm, I gather. Any footprints, anything?"

"Just saw Aub's, and now mine and Kevin's, to and from the farmhouse. Could have missed some, but I didn't want to muddy the waters. Let's slow down a minute." The EMTs had taken a number of falls; connected as they were by the spine-board, if one of them slipped, the other couldn't help but follow suit. They had wet patches on their knees and Damon was sucking wind.

While we waited for them to catch up, we heard a woodpecker knocking for his lunch. Brophy raised his camera and searched the surrounding trees, stopping on a big gray beech. With a click and whirr he took his shot, then turned to me. "Downy woodpecker."

By the time we got back to the scene, a turkey vulture had removed one of the corpse's eyes and eaten it. A red string trailed out of the socket. Taking his first glance, the fat EMT said, "Oh, dog," half to himself, while the monstrous birds flapped up into a tree to wait us out. I could feel them watching.

The sun kissed the forest floor, turning snow into a fine white fog, waist-high. We all stood back while Brophy tied police tape in a rough circle about fifteen feet in diameter, winding it around a series of tree trunks to encircle the body. Then he pulled latex gloves on, removed his lens cap again, and took a bunch of pictures, saying nothing, pausing often in contemplation. Once he called for me and pointed to a series of footprints, asking, "Yours?" I said I thought so. I couldn't help but glance back at the sheriff, and he was looking right back at me. Brophy stuck a blue pencil in the snow next to where my prints doubled back on themselves and moved on.

Eventually the coroner got around to the corpse itself, taking angle after angle of the body as it lay. "We've got to turn this guy over," he said. "Nicholas, you want to come in here, please?"

The sheriff thought a second and said, "Henry, you go. Let's not make any new footprints."

Brophy looked around him. "Don't worry about the footprints, that horse is out of the barn."

One of the EMTs handed me a body bag and I ducked under the tape. The corpse was thawing and I caught a whiff of roadkill as I squatted next to Brophy, who passed me a pair of rubber gloves. Up close, you could see every one of the kid's vertebrae and ribs.

"Okay," said Brophy, "we don't want to disturb any wounds. I'll take him by the neck and abdomen, and you take his left leg, and we'll ease him over onto the bag." I spread the black bag out and zipped it open next to the body. "Okay? Carefully."

His leg felt like wet deadfall. He was still frozen to the ground on the underside where the sun hadn't reached, and he came up with a peeling noise and a flood of rot smell. I tried not to look into the mess where his arm and chest used to be, or his empty eye socket. We laid him on the bag and I took a few steps back into my own tracks.

Brophy photographed the body and the empty space where it had lain, at some length. Then he squatted, blue pencil in hand. With the eraser end, he pulled open the kid's mouth and peered in. Then he turned to the torso. First he moved the pencil over the remaining half of the kid's chest in an arc, then bent down to look into the frozen meat and bone. After moving his hands down the remaining arm, he stopped at the fingers and pried them up for a better look. It was then I saw that the fingertips were gone. He took a glance at the legs and feet.

"This kid's been shot."

This was news to me. Brophy looked about him, making angles from various positions in relation to where we stood. Then he put his face up right next to the boulder's visible surface, moving across and down the horizontal layers of shale as if he were reading fine print. Circling out from where we had been squatting, Brophy scrutinized all the neighboring tree trunks in much the same way, pausing at an old antler scrape but ending by shaking his head.

He pulled off his gloves and let them drop. "Wish we had the rest of him," he said. Producing a small tape recorder, he began to speak into it. "Evident powder burns on anterior chest and abdomen consistent with an intermediate-range gunshot wound. No visible spatter on any likely surfaces around the deceased. Left arm, shoulder, heart, and portion of left lung not present at scene. Marks on body and cuts to the ribs and clavicle suggest trauma by ax or similar sharp tool. Fingertips on right hand severed. Extensive dental damage, likely with a heavy, sharp tool. Left eye scavenged by a" — at this he looked up into the tree — "turkey vulture." Brophy put the recorder in his pocket, lifted his camera, and took a snapshot of the black birds where they lurked in a nearby beech. "Let's zip him up."

On the walk back down the ridge, four of us each took a handle of the spineboard and didn't drop it once. Julie pushed aside branches and guided us as needed.

As the EMTs and the coroner got the body in the ambulance, Sheriff Dally pulled me aside and kept a firm grip on my arm. "So he was shot," he said.

"Guess he was."

The sheriff looked over to the house. "I don't think we have a choice."

"Sheriff, I don't think he has it in him. Something like this?"

"And this morning?"

"Yeah."

"You see how he's living."

"Yeah."

"Tell you what," said Dally. "I've got to bring him in. I'll have Jackson clean him up, keep him as long as I can. Maybe Wy turns up something in examination that rules him out. That seems simplest, and we're doing what we know we have to do. Meantime, I talk to District Attorney Ross and a judge and get us a warrant to search. Yeah?"

"All right."

"Explain to Kevin, would you? Don't say too much, now."

While we were talking, Kevin had emerged from the house. I supposed he was curious. Dally put a hand on his shoulder as he passed to get to the farmhouse, where through a warped pane of glass I could see Aub sitting at the table alone, with Deputy Jackson standing off to one side.

Kevin had half turned to follow the sheriff when I stopped him. "You know Aub's got to go in." At this Kevin opened his mouth to say something but I raised my hand. "We don't think he has anything to do with . . . that up there. But with Danny Stiobhard getting winged this morning, the sheriff needs to get everything straight."

"Jesus."

"Look. He'll eat well, get cleaned up, and they'll figure all this out, and in the meantime you and Carly can look into care for him. Could be a good thing in the end."

The ambulance pulled out of the yard slowly, lights rotating, with Wy Brophy following in his truck. A cloud of diesel smoke hovered in the air for a moment, and then the breeze carried it away into the white morning. Soon after, the farmhouse door slapped shut and out came Aub, pinned between Deputy Jackson and the sheriff, who held the old man by the upper arm. Aub yanked it free; the sheriff seized it again; Aub yanked it free once more. He wasn't cuffed. As they approached Deputy Jackson's patrol car, Aub said, "I won't go. I won't go," sounding as if he could have been saying, *I don't want to go.* Looking around in anguish, as if he'd never see the place again, he met my eyes with his, just for an instant, and disappeared into the back seat.

Dally turned to me. "Nobody in or out."

"Nicholas, there are trails all across this ridge. Dunigan's land must connect to six other plots, not to mention the plots those plots are connected to."

"You have a deputy."

"He's out chasing Danny Stiobhard."

"Is he? What for?"

"I don't know," I said. "He had business on the ridge. I'd like to know what it was."

"That's a good question. Here's another: Why did Dunigan feel he had to defend his place with deadly force?"

"I don't know. Look, Nicholas, you can't believe Aub did this."

"Henry. You don't know who did what, or how it happened or why. Next time, check with me before stepping outside your remit."

I nodded but said nothing. I was not answerable to the sheriff, though he sometimes treated me so.

Dally, gazing out at the hills, scratched under his campaign hat and said, "Fuck me. Wait here until we get back, then. I'll get us some staties. Try not to let anyone up."

They drove off, no lights, no sirens. Kevin followed in his own car.

Holebrook County law enforcement is a skeleton crew. Dally had two deputies, two patrolmen, and an administrative assistant

41

— not much. Fitzmorris had a nominal chief of police and two deputies. I was one of five township officers scattered throughout the county; the remaining fifteen townships had decided they didn't need them, and used the state. And I just had George Ellis. Even if they pulled a patrolman or two from Fitzmorris, or even some state troopers from the barracks in Dunmore, we couldn't cover the whole ridge plus Aub's homestead. But for the time being someone had to do what they could, so I headed down to fetch my truck and bring it to where I could watch both the house and the tree line.

As I walked down the long driveway, I peered in the windows of the little blue hatchback with no wheels. Still looked new. The west-facing main doorway to the barn was directly in front of me; it was a legal gray area to check inside, but curiosity won out. The doors were tall and heavy, and slid open and shut on a rusted track. I tugged one open wide enough to reveal a vaulted interior in decent repair, though there were enough chinks in the siding to give a kind of stained-glass effect with the sunlight. Bat and bird shit coated the floor, tarp-covered tractor implements, and disused furniture. I took a quick turn on that floor and headed back outside.

As with any barn of this age, there had been some serious decay; brambles covered the floor sills along the southern side. The bottom-most timbers crumbled in my hands. On the eastern face, wind and rain had weathered the pine siding to a silver sheen. It was one of my favorite colors.

I found another sliding door about five foot high. I pulled it open and caught a familiar bouquet of guano, old wood, and mold. I ducked inside. The basement's floor was packed dirt, none of it disturbed that I could tell. Much of it was hidden by rusted tractor implements, old hay bales, five-gallon buckets, and every other thing. Just above my head, rough-hewn joists, many still bearing the shapes of the tree trunks they had once been, supported the first floor. They in turn were supported by coarse, fat posts at the walls and along the structure's midpoint. And running the length of that midpoint was the largest sleeper beam I'd ever seen. It was a full forty feet long, about twenty inches square, and perfectly straight, disappearing into darkness at the far end of the cellar. The oak tree it came from had to have been old growth.

As I picked through the basement, trying

not to leave any trace, my Maglite chanced upon something flash-orange up against the south wall. It didn't look of a piece with the other junk. Pushing aside a coil of wire fencing, I found four traffic cones fixed diagonally tip-down in a wooden frame. I realized what it was, and felt a slight creep when I saw the splatters. That method of slaughtering chickens is much more common in this area and among Aub's type of people, do-it-yourself people I suppose is what I mean. Trying to get to a chopping block with an ax in one hand and an upset chicken in the other just isn't sensible; you only see it in movies. This way you take a sharp knife to the jugular and the chicken stays put. That's how Liz and Ed do it, too.

I shut the barn door and drove the truck up to the farmhouse yard, fishtailing once in the slush. I parked. The sun had to cut through the whitest mist you ever saw. When I closed my eyes I saw the corpse and felt its weight in my hands.

I stepped out and approached the corncrib where we first ran into Aub that morning. This type of outbuilding is rare now, but would have been an ordinary sight as recently as thirty years ago, when I was just a little kid and the world hadn't sped up. I turned the white porcelain doorknob by the

44

stem — so I wouldn't smear any fingerprints, or leave any — and opened the door.
A scent of sawdust, mixed with gas and oil.
Near the door a chain saw sat ready for use,
yellow dust caked around its oil cap and air
filter. Sharpened chains hung on nails, and
beneath them, three splitting mauls and a
single-bit ax leaned in a row. I squatted to
peer at their blades: there was no blood that
I could tell, and they were all dull and rusty.
Empty plastic jugs of oil were strewn about
on the floor, and there was a pile of junk at
the back.

I stepped outside. Beneath the wooden
stairs there was a little gap in the stone
foundation. I knelt and shone my light back
there, and caught a glint of color. The entire
south-facing foundation was lined with
domes of turquoise glass about the small
size of bell jars, the ones they used for
insulating power lines in the old days. They
were nestled into the stones, must have been
about thirty of them. In my flashlight and
with a few thin beams of light shining
through gaps in the stone, the glass shone
like cats' eyes.

Out behind a huge old lilac bush, Aub had
about a face cord of firewood that must
have been split that fall, and several rows of
seasoned stuff, one of which had taken a

break and sat down in the snow. As I was walking around out there, I heard an approaching car — a rarity on this dirt road — and my instinct was to duck behind a woodpile. My truck was partially hidden from the road by the stand of maples. A gray-silver compact sedan passed slowly, as if the driver were taking a long look at the farm. I couldn't tell the make. Could have been Kevin's. It slid east from behind the big barn, picked up the pace, and then disappeared into the woods.

In the farmhouse's kitchen doorway, I stood looking in, not daring to enter. The outbuildings were one thing, a domicile quite another. I wanted to see inside, to make sense of this predicament, to act. I stayed outside where I belonged.

I heard cars pull into the yard, doors open and shut. Sheriff's Deputy Jackson rounded the corner along with two state troopers. Jackson handed me a Styrofoam cup of gas station coffee. There were several police vehicles lined up in the driveway, including three all-white Crown Vics belonging to the state police, and two county cars. The two troopers had been borrowed from Dunmore. They were a bit younger than I, and much more squared away; each had a little bath mat of hair atop his head, nothing but pink scalps on the sides, reddening in the cold along with their ears. I'd had to call in troopers for help on domestics involving weapons. You sometimes have to step in there on your own and pray the staties won't take an hour to join you. I've had fights lasting three minutes that seemed like two hours. Anyway, I didn't know these guys — they looked new. Robertson and Zukowski were their names. Turned out they both lived in Clarks Summit, well to the south. We stood drinking coffee and watching as across the yard Sheriff Dally stood talking and pointing about the property with a third state trooper. This one was older, paunchy, his uniform a little more decorated, his campaign hat tucked under his arm.

"Who's that one? He with you?" I asked Zukowski.

"Detective Palmer, Forensic Services," the trooper answered. "We loan him out to rural departments. He's out of Scranton."

"He's here to make sure us local woodchucks don't dick it up," said Deputy Jackson.

I've mentioned our manpower struggles, which go double in the poorer rural municipalities. Our people don't want taxes, naturally, and tend to believe they can fend for themselves. The township supervisor who hired me was a Brylcreemed old-timer who knew roads and maintenance — and everyone in the township over fifty — and left me to my own devices. Last year a newcomer named Steve Milgraham unseated him. Pudgy, personable, and inclined to wear salmon-colored pants, Milgraham inherited a flourishing construction business and knows everyone in the township under fifty. Broadly speaking, I don't care about politics. I figured that, with the sheriff's support, I would continue to enjoy the blessing of the local, largely Republican, base. But with Milgraham's arrival I began to hear rumblings from the distant right: Why does a small rural community need not one but two law enforcement officers? Are the DUI checkpoints legal? Can't Officer Farrell cut my cousin a break? Why should we pay taxes for a service we don't want, when there's a state police barracks nearby? And so on. Once, after a township meeting, I overheard Milgraham say that having a policeman in Wild Thyme Township was like putting a silk hat on a pig. Who is the silk hat, and who is the pig, I want to know? Privately I began to refer to him as the Sovereign Individual, or just the Sovereign.

We watched from a distance as the sheriff

and Palmer from Forensic Services conversed in the yard.

Trooper Zukowski turned to me and said, "So, you found the body, huh?"

"First on the scene."

"Did he fall out of your beard?"

Soon enough, Dally approached us, handing me a small can of pink spray paint and asking me to show the way once more, blazing trees as I went so that any police could find his own way henceforth. I was to leave one statie up at the site of discovery and another stationed somewhere on the logging road that led through the woods to Aub's farm. I didn't see the use in mentioning that that wasn't the only trail leading to Dunigan's land. We didn't have the men anyway. Jackson and I were to return to help exercise the search warrant as needed.

Leaving the staties at their posts up in the woods, Jackson and I tromped back down the trail. I asked him how Aub was holding up.

"Aw, man, it broke my heart. You ever have to help an old man like that take a shower? He's skin and bones, Henry. Our cells ain't so bad, but leaving him there, he started singing. Half moaning, half singing. I don't know if he can hear himself much."

"You think he's going to be charged?"

"We'll see what turns up, I guess."

We met Sheriff Dally and Detective Palmer of PSP Forensic Services in the dooryard. Detective Palmer shook my hand and introduced himself as Bill. "And you've been keeping an eye on things here?" He asked me. "Everything undisturbed?"

"It's a big spread, as you can see. I took a look in all the buildings to make sure we weren't missing something that wouldn't keep." At this, the sheriff gripped the bridge of his nose between thumb and forefinger. "Oh, a car," I said. "A silver car passed slowly but never stopped."

"Well," said Palmer, "with a place like this, we can only do our best. Deputy Jackson, come along with the sheriff and me. Officer Farrell, you want to resume your post down at the foot of the driveway?"

I returned to my truck feeling a little let down. The ridge was where they should have started; I was sure of it. Aub didn't kill and chop up that young man any more than I did. I ran the blue hatchback's license plate through JNET: it was registered to Aub, with no violations. Nothing but fuzz on the police radio, so I turned to the hot country station and listened to the commercials and syrupy songs.

Around two, Deputy Jackson drove down,

took a lunch order, and brought me back a roast beef sandwich with red onions and mustard. Every so often I'd get out, get some air, and see if I could see anything with my binocs. When they hit the corncrib, I watched as they brought out all the mauls and axes, labeled, with their heads taped in plastic. Then Dally emerged holding a piece of cloth in his latex-gloved hand. He spread it out and held it up to the light: a cornflower-blue dress shirt, stained everywhere brown. That's when I began to worry for Aub.

Deputy Jackson bagged the shirt and they disappeared inside Aub's house for what seemed like a couple hours. My mind was in different directions. The sun just kissed the western hills when I heard all the vehicles start up and head my way. Deputy Jackson was last out, and he paused by my truck long enough to tell me about a meeting tomorrow morning at the sheriff's office, to go over the coroner's report and what they'd found at Dunigan's farm.

Time passed slowly. Around five I heard cars coming up the road and wondered was it George with something to tell me, but instead it was two more staties to spell Zukowski and Robertson. I convinced one of them to take my post at the foot of the driveway and that two troopers on the ridge was one too many; they'd never be able to cover it all, so best just keep one of them where we found the body, and one by the house. By the time I left the farm, the sky had begun to darken.

Back at the station, I turned up the radio and flipped back and forth between the nothing on channel one and the nothing on channel two, listening for George. All I could see was the body lying there. I tried thinking of other things but the body always returned, an afterimage floating blue on black.

In a morgue the size of a walk-in freezer, Wy Brophy was opening up our John Doe. The sheriff would be briefing the DA's office and the judge, and dealing with Aub. My deputy was wandering the Heights, and it had been too long since I'd heard from him.

I picked up the phone, intending to dial Liz Brennan at home, as the clinic would have closed. Calling her made me nervous, and after a few calming breaths, I shook my head and told myself, idiot, she's just your best friend's wife. I dialed. When she answered I could hear her boy and girl in the background — they're five and three — and some kitchen noises.

"Listen," I said, "don't . . . this is between us, but I sent George to pick Danny Stiobhard up today, and I —"

"Yeah, he stopped by. Danny had already left."

"Yeah."

"I left him lying flat for two minutes and he found the back door, I guess. Jo never saw him leave till his truck started up. Should have known."

"He say anything to you that might be useful? Too much to hope for."

"No, nothing important. Kevin Dunigan came by, also too late."

"What shape was he in?"

"Danny? You saw him. Walking wounded. He said Aub tagged him as he was stepping out of his truck, kind of through the door and window. He told me he never even set his foot down, just closed the door back up and drove straight to my office. Listen, it's almost six. We can talk in person."

"Yeah. I doubt I'll make it over tonight."

"Come on."

"No, sorry, I —"

"How many times is this? I'd let you off the hook again, but I'm tired of it. We take it personally. I'm going to stop asking."

Into the silence on the other end I said, "I can't find George. I'm sorry."

"You don't know your own deputy, even. He'll be at the bar. Hey, what's going on today? Been seeing a lot of cops. Not locals either."

"Can't say right now. It's been a busy day." We said goodbye and hung up.

I keep a drawer of maps of the county. Topo maps, the kind that show the shape of the hills with concentric lines, and give elevations in feet. Maps from the county office divided into parcels of ownership. I pulled out the whole sheaf of them and found the ones I wanted. My route this morning from 37 to 189 to Fieldsparrow Road had led me progressively into the wilds — fewer roads, and narrower, between ridges of higher elevations. If you squinted you'd be hard-pressed to tell a road from a creek on those maps. There were fewer landowners and larger parcels out there, though in recent decades some had been subdivided and built upon. Little ranch houses plopped down in lawns the size of football fields.

I found Aub's spread on the county map, and matched it to his ridge on the topo. The scales weren't exactly the same, but close; I took a ruler and measured out the old man's land, then scaled it down and drew it in red pencil on the topo map. Wrote *Aub* in the middle of it. It was a huge L-shaped plot taking up much of the ridge where we'd found the kid, and the eastern half of the next ridge to the south. From there I moved concentrically out, marking off parcels. The plot westerly-adjacent to Dunigan's belonged to the Gradys, a family that had been in the area several generations. Mrs. Grady and and her son's family lived side by side. Their place was all hills, some field, mostly forest. From there the ridge tapered off to the west and we had a subdivided piece of real estate; three parcels of about ten acres each radiated out like fingers, belonging to Wild Thyme families of long standing — Heslin, Moore, Loinsigh ("Lynch").

Continuing south, I marked off what used to be the Regan dairy, and was now a horse farm belonging to people named, evocatively, Bray. Their place fit into the crook of Aub Dunigan's L-shaped land and was bordered by Route 189 on the southern edge. To the southeast, three fifteen-acre plots got us from the southern border of Aub's land to Route 189. I wrote the names: Nolan, Weatherall, Sawicki.

To the east of Dunigan's plot was an

impassable swamp at the foot of the steep ravine. The summer camp owned that. Camp Branchwater owned hundreds of acres in the township, including a lake and everything north of Fieldsparrow Road for at least three miles in either direction from Aub's house. The boys who went there came from wealthy, conservative families up and down the East Coast; they sailed and fished on a private lake, played tennis and baseball, shot skeet and target. The manly arts. I marked Camp Branchwater off on my topo map. It was a start, and I had something to bring to Sheriff Dally in the morning.

For a while I strained to decipher cautious talk on the county's radio channels, what I could hear through the static. I looked through missing person reports in neighboring Pennsylvania counties, but couldn't find anyone close. Even though I saw the JD just about every time I shut my eyes, it was the position of his body, the frozen mess of blood, bone, and tissue where his shoulder used to be, the missing eye. When I tried for details I could summon only a vague idea of what the boy actually looked like. He had been tallish, skinny, pale, and had black hair — could have been white or Latino, Asian a remote possibility. After a while it felt like a waste of time. I wondered what the sheriff was up to, and how Aub was faring. A few times I flipped through our radio channels and listened. I dialed my wayward deputy's cell but it went straight to the message.

I locked up and got in the truck and headed out. My first stop was the High-Thyme Tavern.

The High-Thyme is a two-story inn on Walker Lake Road. It's old, isolated, and was likely built where it was to distance it from the piety of the county seat. The dirt lot was muddy and rutted with tire tracks. The radio car wasn't there, and neither was George's crappy yellow pickup among the many other spattered, rust-edged vehicles. When I pushed open the heavy wooden door and stepped inside, I heard someone say, "Aw, shit." I had to laugh. I took a stool next to a wrinkled old lady, who smiled at me. It took me a moment, but I eventually placed her as the seamstress who had reversed the collars on my uniform shirts when they got frayed the year before. I ordered a beer and everyone went about their business. The bartender hadn't seen George all day. I took a turn around the bar to see if I could find any of George's buddies before I pressed on.

The tavern is still technically an inn. The

upstairs rooms are occupied by one dead poltergeist and a collection of living ones, poor semi-itinerant folks. I assume some crank gets smoked up there, even crack, for all I know. Downstairs in the public area there are three large connected rooms — a dining room on one end, a big U-shaped bar in the middle, and a dance floor with a stage in the back on the other side. It was a good happy-hour crowd and each room was occupied. Around the corner I ran into the township mechanic, John Kozlowski, who also hadn't seen my deputy and had heard nothing from him.

The next place to look for George was his trailer park on 37. It was a ten-minute drive from the bar. As trailer parks go, his was pretty nice. That may have been due to the Seventh-Day Adventist church next door, a corrugated steel warehouse painted white, with a steeple cobbled on. It was full every Sabbath. I didn't know whether George was a member of the congregation there, and if so, whether he believed as they do. We never talked about it. The church and trailer park are both tucked in an open valley with a tree line marking where January Creek wends through. As night deepened I bumped to a halt in front of my deputy's trailer. His yellow truck was there. On either side of his front door, two wooden half barrels contained devastated geraniums, a collection of cigarette butts, and a crushed tallboy. I knocked, but no answer came. I got back in the truck.

Driving down 37 toward the part of the county where the Stiobhards lived, I was kept on the path by the skeletal trees to my left and the steep black hills to my right. A handful of stars spread out above me in the gap, looking like a watercolor painting because of the mist — white mist that I caught in my headlights when I passed through gullies, and collected as droplets on my windshield every mile or so. The snow was still melting. It would be gone by morning. The radio offered no opinions.

I had the feeling of things getting carried away from me. The worry took many forms and faces, moving in and out of recognition and time. Polly made a cameo, Polly, my wife, who died in Wyoming, when there was nothing we could do. And that let the black dog in.

If you're in a mood, turning onto Old Account Road won't cheer you up. It's little more than a dirt track that the township doesn't maintain in the winter or any of the other seasons. Why, I don't know. I guess there are probably a lot of people below the poverty line living on it, and people who don't pay taxes. The road was like a creek bed; that night, you could see great ribbons of muddy water cut through it, right down the middle, exposing fins of blue shale. My shocks whined, even at ten miles an hour. While Fieldsparrow Road meandered through wide-open spaces and rounded ridges, Old Account Road gave access to territory that felt compressed and crowded and too steep to live on. There wasn't a place in the township that wasn't hilly, but everyone referred to this particular area as "the Heights." I knew from hunting there that every second step you took, you might also be ankle-deep in a stream. Even with the knife-edge ridges and the hollows in between, some of the blue and white natural gas ribbons fluttered optimistically on trailheads either side of the road. The whole Heights were interconnected with trails used with as much regularity as the county routes. Trails leading from home to home, spot to spot, hidden places you'd never see from any road. A decent outdoorsman with sympathetic neighbors could run me around for weeks.

Around the third bend was a gritty driveway marked by a mailbox in the shape of a tractor, with one of those blue plastic cubbies beneath it to get the *Pennysaver;* behind a thick wall of woods was Michael and Bobbie Stiobhard's place, the most fixed abode that the Stiobhard family had. Their two sons and a daughter revolved around this little homestead perched on a slope and found themselves semipermanent situations nearby. I weighed my options: it was unlikely Danny would be here, knowing I would be looking for him. Yet, he was hurt and in need of care. It'd be foolish not to at least check. I continued past the driveway like I wasn't going to stop, rounded a curve, killed my lights, and pulled over.

Closing my car door softly, I stepped off the road and into the woods. Yes, I had no warrant, and I hope you can forgive me. The ground was soggy, but a carpet of snow and wet leaves kept me from squelching too much in the mud as I walked, taking irregular steps to throw off anybody listening. Heel-toe, heel-toe, taking my time. There was a light on in Michael and Bobbie's house. I approached it along the clearest and driest path I could find. As I got near, I reached a patch of prickers that seemed to have no end. I did my best to move quietly, but a thorn caught and then popped out of my uniform trousers, sounding like a firecracker in the stillness. I heard the abrupt chain-rattle of a dog going to red alert in the yard. I froze. When I heard the chain clink again, that's when I moved away from the sound, toward the front. It wasn't as I remembered: not only was the house itself different, but when I was a kid the Stiobhards had sedans up on blocks, appliances saved for parts, mysterious crates, and so on. Now it was a pale empty expanse, save for the camper set up behind a modular log cabin, a prefab home replacing what had been a ramshackle farmhouse up until about ten years ago.

As soon as I reached the edge of the yard, white light blinded me. They caught me with a high beam, the way unsporting hunters spotlight deer at night. And just like a deer, I was rooted to the ground for a moment. Long enough for a woman's voice to call from the house, "I see you, motherfucker!"

I tried to step out of the beam but couldn't move fast enough. When I turned to run, Danny Stiobhard was there in the woods, not six feet away. I had never heard him. The spot cut off and I was blind, Danny's afterimage moving with me as I turned my head and waited for my eyes to adjust. A gun barrel pressed into the side of my neck. A hand grabbed at my holster, undid the snap, and my .40 was gone.

He said, "I have to show you something."

"Danny, Jesus!" I said. "Think about this."

"No need to talk. You'll drive us."

I walked toward where I'd left the truck. Danny followed close behind me. I slipped once and steadied myself against a narrow tree trunk. My hand came away wet and coated with grit. We hopped over the rushing water in the ditch and stood by my truck. "You got one chance," I said. "Return my weapon. Christ, you can drop it in the ditch, for all I care. Just give it back and walk away."

"You drive," he said. "It's not far."

In the truck's interior light I got a look at the snub-nosed revolver Danny had pointed at me. It was a black .38. When he adjusted his gun hand I caught a glimpse of yellowing athletic tape on the handle. It wasn't a beautiful weapon. It did look practical. He was dressed in a waterproof hunting coat and a camouflage cap. In the close confines of the car, his strange scent was in every breath I took.

I wanted to talk, as if to remind him I was a human being and maybe steer him away from whatever he had planned. "Where are we going, man?"

The knuckles on his gun hand whitened. I

chanced a look at his face and saw desperation there, his good eye raw and troubled.
We bumped along in the dark, deeper and
higher into the hills. He pointed me to an
old logging road about five miles in, and I
turned onto it, bare branches scratching at
my windshield and the sides of my truck. In
my headlights, I saw fresh tire tracks in the
mud and snow.

If it happened in an instant, it wouldn't
be bad.

No, I didn't mind dying; what I didn't
want was to die after fighting Danny Stiobhard and losing. I'd have to win. My blood
raced as I pictured the ways it might touch
off — if he raised the gun to my head while
I was still behind the wheel, if we stepped
out of the truck, and so on. I thought about
spinning inside his arm and getting control
of the weapon. I thought of the mousegun
in my pocket.

Danny knew what was on my mind. "I
don't want to kill you, Henry."

"That's nice to hear."

"I'm not going to hang for this."

"Hang for what?"

We continued in the dark. The logging
road descended into a cavernous clearing, a
hollow. In one swift motion Danny was out
of the car and around the front. I braked so

65

as not to hit him. He kept his pistol on me the whole time, came around and opened my door as I was 'putting the truck in park. The parking brake handle was close enough to the butt of the tactical shotgun holstered behind the passenger seat — something I wasn't sure Danny had noticed — that I considered reaching for it, but dismissed that as a quick way to lose the fight.

Metal and glass reflected in my headlights. We were standing in the neighborhood junk-yard: automobiles and appliances, bottles and cans, mounds of full trash bags, and my deputy's patrol car. I started toward it, but Danny stopped me.

"Just listen, Henry," he said. "I didn't have to bring you here."

"I'll make sure they put you down like a dog. Step aside."

Danny considered this and the air went out of him. Never taking his eye off me, he backed toward a rusted oil drum with several bullet holes in it, took my .40 out of his pocket, and dropped the weapon in; it splashed in the standing water and thumped when it hit bottom. Never letting me out of his line of vision, he stepped out of the yel-low high beams. Then he was lost in the dark. I heard movement in the brush, then quick footfalls in what sounded like water.

In an instant, those sounds were gone too.

I pulled out the shotgun and my own spotlight from the compartment under the passenger seat and made a slow circle, holding the light in my left hand, the handle of the shotgun in my right with the barrel crossed over my left forearm. For all the good it did, it also made me a perfect target. I killed the spot and my headlights too. When I knocked over the oil drum to retrieve my weapon, a few gallons of water rushed out. Had to upend the barrel completely for the .40 to tumble out. I holstered it wet, twisted on my Maglite, and walked to George's radio car.

Whoever had laid him on his side in the back seat had done so with care, but he was dead, his weapons gone. The back of his head was matted and bloody, as was the rolled-up uniform coat somebody'd tucked under him as a pillow. His eyes were half open and there was an exit wound through his cheekbone.

Where Danny Stiobhard had disappeared into the woods, a narrow stream emerged from the earth. Stones covered in bright green moss marked the springhead, and the stream continued down into the dark. I followed it until it branched, then stopped to listen: heard the water at my feet, burbling onward to wherever it went. Condensation dripping from trees to a saturated forest floor covered with wet leaves. In the distance, a car moving fast and steady on what was probably 37, and a little closer than that, what could have been a four-wheeler. I headed back to the hollow. Had to drive about ten minutes in the hills before I could find a clear enough spot to radio the county.

Hunting deer since age eleven, I've gotten my share, but Father was a nose-to-the-ground dog when it came to the red menace. Need made him that way. A few years back, he and Ma packed it up for North Carolina to be near my sister Mag's family, bringing his dominion over the whitetail population of Wild Thyme Township to an end; at the time he left, the number of deer he claimed to have shot was in the two-hundreds.

As I have mentioned, one of his hunting partners was Michael Stiobhard, Danny's father. Hunting deer isn't usually a solitary pursuit. Depending on the season, it takes at least two men but preferably more: one to sit still and wait in a tree stand or some elevated, downwind spot, and a couple more to drive the buck to where the sitter is. You want your partners to have sense and focus in the woods. If you're lucky you'll have a good tracker — a guy who can read a place's changing story every day, the story of where the deer is that you want. You want a guy who knows the buck personally.

Mike Stiobhard and Father had both worked for the same machine shop in Wild Thyme, burring the edges off steel and aluminum parts that would then be shipped away to become pieces of something, nobody knew what. Every day Father's hands came home laced with fine scratches from the parts' edges, scratches filled with black dust that wouldn't ever wash completely clean. He took me into the shop once when I was about six and let me try the sandblaster — the fingers of the rubber gloves were clammy from the guy using it before. It was thrilling to press the trigger and feel the force of the sand, heavy and permanent, and see it put a shine on a small aluminum square. He let me keep the square and I still have it. But the shop closed, and hunting changed from a pastime to a necessity.

I'm not sure Father and Mike were friends, exactly, but they were cut from the same olive drab. Good trackers, full of methods. Mike used to be able to stand stock-still under a tree, camoed to the eyelids, and call a deer in by whirling a white sock around, moving only his wrist.

Father had a trick of confusing deer with balloons that he hasn't shared with me yet. They had their secret ways, but mostly they were patient and determined.

About twenty-five years ago Mike and Father had got a beautiful eight-point, and the Stiobhards were cooking a roast and asked us to dinner to share it. I knew Danny from school but we weren't friends — you'd think the other children calling us both woodchucks would have brought us together in solidarity, but I regret to say it didn't. Still feel bad about it. But when I was ten years old I saw things differently, and wasn't thrilled about dining with the Stiobhards; stepping in their house would be a for-all-time exclamation point on what everyone had been saying I was. I might as well have accepted it back then and saved trouble. Thankfully, Ma and Father had whacked enough manners into me so I don't think my true feelings showed to my grown-up hosts, though Danny probably guessed how much I wanted to be there.

Upon entering, Ma and Father were handed cans of beer and Mag and I were dragged into the kids' bedroom lair. The room was so small that even a few objects could crowd it, especially with the two sets of bunks, one of which had a sheet hanging over it, an illusion of privacy for Jennie Lyn, the daughter. After a show-and-tell of scuffed toys, we thumped outside to a rope swing where, in failing November light, Mag and I watched as the three Stiobhard children took turns swinging each other around and trying to pull or knock the one on the rope down. I was too chickenshit to join in and nobody asked Mag. No grass grew on the ground below the swing; the dirt was hard-packed, and knobs of oak root jutted up. Jennie Lyn, the youngest and also a girl, was thrown to the ground no less than four times. The fourth time, she got up crying. But she didn't run back into the house, she just stood there huffing until she stopped, and then jumped back in the fray, popping an older brother neatly in the teeth.

We were called in to supper, and I remember tucking my legs under a tablecloth with floral embroidery around its edges. There was a feast on the table. Mag and I had eaten plenty of game at home, including squirrel pie and, in lean times, brown stew I suspected contained real woodchuck, but we had dreaded this meal the way kids dread most cooking that's not their own mother's. Still, it looked and smelled good. Venison roasted brown, surrounded by copper-colored potatoes. Pickled green beans provided a suggestion of a vegetable, and in a basket, probably fifty yellow rolls that magically looked both baked and fried; I'd heard Danny refer to these as "overnight rolls." We bowed our heads for the blessing and then Mike Stiobhard took up a fork and knife to carve. Danny, sitting one away from me, grabbed the basket of overnight rolls and made to pass them to me — doubtless they were his favorite, a special treat that he wanted to share. Mike saw it and clouted his son on the ear with a sound like a branch snapping underfoot. The basket of rolls fell to the table, dislodging a spoon from a bowl full of mustard. A silence settled as Danny rubbed at the side of his head. We stared at our plates for a moment. I cut my eyes right to Father, who had not looked away, but instead held Mike in a gaze that wasn't embarrassed or hot, but perfectly cool. Turning to Danny, he said, "You all right, bud?"

Danny was confused for a moment, as if he knew he should say nothing and keep his eyes to himself. But Father was a guest and an adult, and manners required an answer. He managed, "That wasn't nothing."

The table began to murmur again once dishes were passed, and we soon found conversation again. But nothing tasted as good as it looked after that; we Farrells never went back there, and though Father continued to hunt with Mike, Danny and I still weren't friends at school.

Sheriff Dally had met me in darkness where the trail to the junkyard joined the road. He was trying not to look tired. Patrol cars continued to scream along 37 and then lurch up Old Account. He suggested I go home; someone would be by to get my statement. I said no. He attempted to order me away but I dismissed him with a wave.

"We've got our K-9 unit on the way," he said, "and part of a SERT team. I understand you wanting to stay, but we don't need you."

"A dog won't help. He's covered in liquid fence." Dally looked blank, so I explained. "Coyote scent, probably. My truck still stinks of it. I know you've got to try, but he may be long gone by now and a dog won't help. We can't wait for people to get their stories straight. We should knock on doors and try to find a witness."

"All right," said the sheriff, as a black E350 pulled up. "All right, stay. Find Jackson out by the Stiobhards' place. Do nothing until you hear from me, you follow?"

The sheriff left my side to speak with the

van's driver. I took the opportunity to head back down the trail to where Palmer and a couple forensic techs were combing the area around George's patrol car; a generator thrummed, powering construction lights. I sat still on the hood of an abandoned car, well outside of the perimeter, and watched. In just a minute or two, a group of black silhouettes entered the floodlit area. Four men in all black, with vests, knee pads, and trousers bloused into high boots approached Palmer. Two of them carried what looked like M5s, and one had a tactical shotgun. As Palmer led them around the junk heap to where they'd marked my last sighting of Danny, the man with the shotgun, taking the measure of his surroundings, stopped short when he saw my form, peered closely, and nudged his neighbor. By the time they turned my direction I was back in the woods and out of sight.

I gave the SERT team a good head start in case they were using NVS, and followed their tracks into the vale. If Danny was still in the area, he could avoid them, but he might not expect me following. The officers' tracks headed west, so I pushed a little east of them, back toward the Stiobhards', listening for the little snaps and wet footfalls that told me where their four-man line was to my right.

A whitetail buck is going to see and hear and smell you before you know where he is. You can push him down into a white pine patch. He won't like it if you follow him in, so he'll move up into some tag where he thinks you won't want to go. With luck and patience you'll push him to where your partner can take a shot. Four men weren't going to cover much ground compared to what Danny could do up here, and they were heading toward habitation. I followed them across a dirt road and caught up outside a single-wide, where they were pulling out a family — a long-haired man and his wife stood with their hands on their heads as the team leader addressed them, and one of the SERT guys had a struggling boy of about ten by the elbow, chicken-winged up. The remaining two made entry into the trailer. I gave up following them.

The Heights concealed much besides Danny Stiobhard, and the sheriff certainly knew that. An opportunity to kick a lab or two down — without papers, without consequences — might not arise again for some time. Dally would never have admitted to this agenda but I'm sure that's what he was thinking.

My attention was undivided. I slipped

through the woods to my vehicle and drove back on Old Account. Deputy Jackson had parked his car on Mike and Bobbie's lawn, leaving deep muddy tracks; he had kept his lights spinning, and stood glowering at the house. I pulled up in the yard and got out, pausing long enough to ask him to turn off his flashers. Before he could stop me, I was knocking on the aluminum screen door and pulling it open all at once.

It was not the original house I remembered, but it contained what looked like the same hook rugs and religious watercolors. A prefab log cabin had been set up on the original stone foundation, and two garden sheds were tacked on the side, with mismatched windows installed, aftermarket. Glancing back out the front door, I could see red-and-blue lights through the trees; I counted six so far. Mike and Bobbie sat side by side on a black leather couch that could only be secondhand. They had a couple worn chairs in there, heaped with folded clothes.

Mike started to rise, but the effort subsided into a gesture. I touched the brim of my hat and asked who else was in the house.

"Just Jennie Lyn," said Bobbie.

"Jennie Lyn," I called. "Come out where I can see you, please."

A floorboard in the kitchen spoke and a ropy woman in her thirties appeared in the living room doorway, hanging her hands on the lintel. She was dressed in camo, same as her brother, and her narrow face was shadowed by long sandy hair. "Evening," she told me, and there was something ugly in the way she said it that I can't explain.

"Coffee, Jennie-girl," said Mike. His hair had turned from black to silver since the last time I'd seen him.

I turned again to look out the window. County and state cars bumped by. In the yard, Deputy Jackson's top half had disappeared into his driver's-side window; doubtless he was raising Sheriff Dally on their two-way and telling him what I was up to.

"We just have a short time here," I said, turning to Mike and Bobbie, and speaking loudly enough that Jennie Lyn could hear me in the kitchen. "Jennie, come on. Come out." Danny's sister refused to join us in the living room, but met me halfway by sitting down at the kitchen table in my sight, hands wrapped around a coffee mug.

"I'm going to head you off a moment, Henry," said Mike. "If you mean to go after my son, you've got it wrong. Danny and George weren't friendly, I grant, but their

78

problem is with a woman named Tracy Dufaigh, nothing to do with this. Danny is no killer."

"I can't take that on faith. Tell me. Anything that can help, anything you'd prefer to keep from the county. What happened to my deputy: that's my concern. I'll get there with or without you, but if I get no help, I swear to God I'll tear down everything I see."

Their storm door squeaked open and Deputy Jackson stepped in, removing his hat. "Evening," he said. He gave me a look that everyone in the room must have caught. "Officer, you are needed elsewhere." He held an arm out to lead me through the door.

I made him wait. "Jennie Lyn, I'll take that coffee. Don't worry, I'll return the mug. You know where I live if I don't."

Jennie emerged from the kitchen holding a chipped mug with a band of yellow roses on it. I took one last look at my hosts Mike and Bobbie, hoping to see something in their faces. Bobbie wore thick glasses with large frames, and that didn't help. The Stiobhards weren't like most people I knew, but some things are universal; they didn't behave like parents whose son had just killed a man. Maybe that's what Danny had made them believe. Or maybe it hadn't sunk in yet. "Anything you can tell me," I said, and left.

As Deputy Jackson and I watched, the ambulance carrying George Ellis swayed back and forth as it descended Old Account Road. "Go home," Jackson said. "Write your report. Dally told me to tell you."

I got in my truck but I didn't go home. Old Account Road climbs the south side of a ridge and, once it hits the top, teeters along the summit for several miles west. I knew the road well, so when I rounded the last curve before the long straight, I turned off all my lights — my flashers and my headlights too — and downshifted to avoid using brake lights. At a dairy farm near the western border of Wild Thyme Township the road makes a Y. I descended the south slope and passed through woods into a swamp, pulled off to the side, and cut my engine. Checked was the shotgun loaded and stepped out with it. My door clicked shut quietly but it was still too loud; every noise I made down there was going to be.

All around me, ragged pine trunks, softened by decay, strained to stay above the water's surface. The swamp spread for acres, its edges choked with pussy willow and reed. The beavers always found a way to dam it so that every spring the road was submerged, and the township had to wade in and break the dam up. Local hunters knew that deer favored the swamp for its ample cover and access to water. But if you knew that, you also knew that though the Stiobhards didn't own it, they considered it their personal grounds. I'd received a couple calls in past years from fellows who'd been cursed and chased away from there, wanting to know what could be done about it.

I knew of one way to get where I wanted to go: a stone causey leading through the rushes. Father had taken me once. I pushed down a strand of barbed wire strung between two red pines and hopped into the shadows. Strange how ground covered in pine needles always sounds hollow. I skirted the swamp's bank on the northern side until the scant light caught the pale branches of a black alder cluster, trees that grew only man-height and no higher so close to the swamp, and produced bright red berries you shouldn't eat. I ducked under the thicket of branches, snapping only a dozen or two. Finding my footing on the rubble that formed the causey, I began a slow crouching progress into the depths of the swamp, switching the shotgun from hand to hand.

A smear of snow lingered where the sun

hadn't hit the trail that day, some boot tracks in it; to my left and right clumps of bulrush had gotten a head start on spring, bright emerald even in the dark. I crossed channels of water, and they ran deeper and clearer and faster than you might imagine, feeding the rusty belly of the swamp. The water moved much faster than I. Up ahead there was an island where a stand of old-growth pine remained, too difficult for farmers to have reached; I was headed there.

There was no red glow of an open fire ahead, no hiss and pop, but the smell of woodsmoke told me I was close. Willows got so thick I had to crawl on my belly to get past them, shotgun out front. My heart was thudding, I tell you what. It seemed impossible I wouldn't be heard. I made myself slow. All the stars in the sky might have passed over me while I dragged myself over those stones. My front was soaked, and my elbows too from digging in with them. The light on the island was small and uneven: a flame in a lantern. It made the night's blackness appear deeper as I emerged from the brush and lay flat against a bank covered in pine needles. Not sixty yards distant stood a hunting cabin the size of one of those garden sheds that come in a kit; a metal chimney puffed smoke into the pine canopy. A window on each side of the cabin let out that flickering light I'd seen on my way in. How they'd got the thing to where it was, I don't know. I listened for voices and heard only a hush of wind in the pines.

A round whacked into the tree next to me, some six feet above from my head, and I heard the shot slap out after the fact. Some instinct had already curled me up tight to the ground. I called out, "This is Officer Henry Farrell! You shoot again, I'll shoot back."

After a pause, a distant voice said, "Didn't know it was you."

If you've been through a shitty little deployment like I have, you learn not to appreciate being shot at, even if the round wasn't meant to hit home. I stood and strode onto the island, not knowing whether I was shaking from anger or fear. Other than the lantern pulsing, it was black under those big trees; I stepped high to avoid the roots crossing my path, and strained my eyes for movement. I thought of how George had been shot, how it could come from anywhere. When I got to within ten feet of the cabin and the cabin's occupant still hadn't revealed himself, I stopped and turned slowly in a circle. To my right a fire ring was surrounded by logs for sitting, and everywhere else was pine trees, some of them toppled into the swamp, with their root systems turned on end like colossal circular saw blades half buried in the earth.

The voice murmured to my left. "You wouldn't be trying to bring me in for something?"

"Looking for your brother."

Part of a fallen tree moved. I twisted my Maglite on and just caught a glint off Alan Stiobhard's glasses before he said, "Please cut that."

When I did as he asked Alan approached me in silence. He stopped about ten feet off, clad in camo and a boonie hat, his deer rifle cradled sideways in his arms. Looked like maybe a .243. Alan was the eldest brother. He stood about six-six and was both taller and narrower than Danny. He had a beard longer than mine, and you rarely saw his eyes unprotected by thick square glasses with black frames. The other thing was, he almost never visited town. His retiring nature invited rumor and blame-laying: that he was a poacher and a house thief who sought ammunition, cash, and liquor, in that order; that he fathered a kid on a teenage dropout and sometime prostitute fifteen years his junior outside of

84

Rosedale; that a few years back he'd slit the throat of a meth-dealing thug named Wesley Crummy and sunk his body in the swamp. Wesley was before my time. He had never been found and it wasn't my intention to start looking that night.

"George Ellis has been shot," I said, nodding at his .243. "What the fuck you think you're doing?" Alan pulled the bolt open, and the spent shell pinwheeled into shadow. I pointed my shotgun to the side.

"Poor George," Alan said, his voice soft and slight. "I'm sorry about that."

"So you heard."

" 'Twasn't Brother Danny who let George in on the big secret. I can tell you that."

"Danny's been here, then." Behind me, footfalls dropped as gently as water from an icicle, moving through the dark toward the causey. As I turned, I heard Alan slide the bolt of his .243 home.

"You go after him, I'll cut you in half. Now hold that difference-maker out at your side." I did as told, and he took the shotgun and slung it into the darkness, where it thumped and skidded across the bed of pine needles. "Pull out your sidearm there. Drop it and I'll keep it safe for you." I did so. He approached.

When he slung his rifle up and bent to

retrieve the .40 I drove an elbow hard as I could into his face. He toppled onto his back and just had time to chamber a round and point the handgun up at me when I landed on him, whanging my own head against his and tasting copper. The .40 never went off, and I had it pinned between my arm and side, my other forearm under his chin. I could feel him trying to reach his hands together to transfer the pistol behind me, so I put all my weight on his throat and he made a desperate sound, a high gurgle, and I felt the .40 drop.

The world went white and silent. It took me a moment to know I'd been hit upside the head with something and that I no longer had control of Alan. I reached into my pocket and found the .22 mousegun. When Alan reappeared in the glow surrounding the hunting cabin, the little pistol snapped in my hand, startling me. A stone the size of a rabbit dropped from Alan's grasp. He swatted at his shoulder as if stung, then reeled a bit.

"Jesus Christ, Henry. You could have killed me."

"What'd you . . . what'd you do?" I reached up to the side of my head, expecting to find blood. There wasn't much. I kept the .22 pointed in his direction and we glared at each other, each heaving for breath.

"Might as well come in, have a drink," Alan said. "Danny's got enough of a start by now, and I've got to take care of this." I picked up the .40 and holstered it; he didn't stop me, so I didn't stop him taking his rifle along.

We approached the cabin and I fought an urge to kneel and vomit. The cabin wasn't fixed to the ground, and stood on wooden runners, presumably the easier to tow it. Something about that seemed wrong, and though the correct response to the wrongness would have been to vomit, I held it in. Hanging from the doorknob was a two-foot northern pike, gutted, its crooked jaw full of fangs. "Breakfast," said Alan, hooking the fish with a finger through the gill. At that, I did puke. Alan stepped inside and let me do it alone.

In the cabin, the potbelly stove was warm and leaked smoke. Alan gestured to a folding camp chair near the stove, and I took it. He swept a sleeping bag aside and sat on the cot. There wasn't room for hardly anything else: a couple pairs of waders, a change of clothes hanging from a nail on the back of the door, a rod and tackle, a couple old books missing jackets. Racked above the door, an over-under shotgun and a muzzle-loader. There was one empty rack where presumably the .243 went. Alan set the deer rifle beside him on the cot. "I'm not going in. You understand?"

I nodded. His voice sounded distant; he was probably in shock and I knew I could arrest him if the world weren't diagonal and trying to slide back into place. He produced a bottle of top-shelf vodka — no doubt liberated from someone's lake cabin — from beneath his cot, pulled on it, and shook it in my direction. "You need to visit the doctor's office?" I declined. He splashed some of the liquor on the small wound in his shoulder, diluting the stream of blood into a wash that coated his chest. Then he felt for the .22 slug where it rested between bone and skin, and popped it out the same way it went in, tossing it in a dark corner when he was done. Pressing a rag soaked with alcohol to the wound, he gave me a look of quiet accusation. All he said was, "You going out for turkey this spring?"

"Is that what you're asking me?"

"Farrell, I'm sorry about George. Like I said: Danny's not the one. Chasing him all over the county would waste your time. You know that."

"It looks bad."

He smiled. "That's right. Everything we do looks bad." Alan flipped open the door of the stove, broke a few dry branches in half, and placed them inside. "Leave Danny. You won't find him unless he wants to be found, and he ain't the one anyway. I know, those two scrapped. When did you ever fight someone who didn't matter to you? I don't guess you ever did."

I considered explaining to Alan that the only things worth fighting over were things you couldn't have or couldn't help. Everyone comes to know that at some point in his life. Some people know it all their lives. And I'll bet that those who know, but don't know that they know, make the killers of this world.

When the kindling caught, Alan swung the stove door shut and said, "Not to change the subject, but who did that fellow up on the ridge?"

"Pardon?"

Alan nodded. "That boy's been up there since January at the least. Seen sign of him months back."

"And said nothing?"

"And said nothing about none of my concern."

"Who else knew?"

"That's the question. The answer is, I

couldn't say. Reach up behind you and open that window, would you, Henry?"

To do so I had to turn my back. I told myself he'd have found a way to shoot me already. Smoke curled out of the window in a gauzy sheet, and the heavy night silence joined us, mixing with the sighs of the woodstove and the medicinal stink of vodka. Not far to the southwest, I heard a motor kick off, sounded like a dirt bike or a four-wheeler. It revved three times even, then three times again, and pulled away. Over the hill and gone.

"Okay," said Alan. "Talk's over."

We limped along toward where the causey met the island; in an unspoken agreement, neither of us trained his weapon on the other. When we reached the waterside, I said, "Going to need my shotgun back."

He swung his .243 to waist height and, without exactly pointing it at me, said, "I only mean to be helpful. I'm sure you see that. Please don't press your luck."

"Well. Thanks for all your help," I said. He backed away, turned, and headed for the darkness at a trot; by the time I'd made my fingers close around the Maglite, he had disappeared. It took a few minutes rooting around in the pine needles to locate the shotgun. I turned to find his lantern snuffed out and the island gone silent.

I drove the dirt roads for hours, looking for light in the trees. Met a total of three cars, two of which I waylaid by flashing my brights. One contained a rueful man who expected me to DUI him. He promised me he lived just half a mile away, and I let him go with a warning. Another car contained a teenage couple. The third was Trooper Zukowski doing the same thing I was. We leaned out our windows and talked awhile, not mentioning George except when we parted and he said, "We'll get that shitbag," meaning Danny, I supposed. I kept my hands down so he wouldn't see them shake. We each pressed on. It got late and I knew I wouldn't pry anything out of the houses or the places I passed. By the time I got home it was after three and I was too tired to eat, just pulled off my boots and set my .40 on the table. Took it apart, cleaned it, and left it to air on the thinnest of my three towels. I held an ice pack to my head and got down my bottle of single-malt from atop the fridge, a present from Ed and Liz. I poured myself an inch and sat. Forgot to splash some water in, so all I tasted was burn.

Even in the farmhouse with the windows closed, you could hear the drilling a few ridges over. I stepped out into the yard, not bothering with my shoes, and looked up at the clear sky with the wash of stars disappearing into the flickering purple to the southwest. I knew I wouldn't sleep and likely shouldn't with my head the way it was. Went back inside, got out my fiddle, and rosined the bow.

I read where the jazz pianist Thelonious Monk used to spin around in circles while he waited for the band to get the tempo just like he wanted it. Sometimes he'd spin for minutes. The man who taught me fiddle had a different approach to the same end. John Allen was his name, an oldster who'd walk or bicycle over to my parents' house on Wednesday evenings to give me lessons. One of the first things I had to learn was that fiddling wasn't all sawing back and forth with the bow, it was patterns, you know, down-up-up-down-up-down-up-up-down-up and so on. You fit the tune to the bowing pattern. Because I was nine and it took me a while to build the patience for this, at John's insistence we'd often spend even ten minutes at a stretch just down-up-up-down-upping in a particular key, until John could recognize that neither of us was thinking about it anymore but just doing it and all of a sudden he'd call, "Red Haired

Boy!" or "Edward in the Treetop!" and we'd be off.

Another thing I learned from John Allen, when I got halfway better at the fiddle, was the virtue of slowness. There were times when, justifiably proud at having practiced that week, I wanted to whip through a tune, to show off. If I did get out of hand, John would set his fiddle on his knee and smile and say, "Too fast for me! Can't keep up." Which you knew wasn't true, just a nice way of saying slow down and let the tune work through you, not vice versa.

Down-up-up-down-up-down-up-up. You get the pattern and the rhythm right and then wait for the tune. I needed something I could rip into. "Bonaparte's Retreat" found me. Most versions you hear give you whiplash, even the older ones. It's best slow. I'd heard that it's not as triumphant a tune as you'd expect, but originated with Irish soldiers hired by Napoleon, heading home in defeat. In the case of that tune, slowing it down is the only way something so familiar can still live and breathe. It was always a good one with Polly on the bodhran, she always had steady rhythm but indifferent pitch.

By the time I got to the modified part B Copland had made so famous, I had to stop and breathe. I thought of George Ellis. Got a piece of paper and curled it into a funnel, poured the rest of my whiskey back into the bottle, and went to bed, but never to sleep.

It's not hard to get up if you never go down. Dawn brought a hint that the weather might get clearer. With enough pain pills, my head would too. The eastern sky was bright as a wild rose as I walked stiff-backed from my woodpile with an armload for the stove. The snow had melted, and my boots left prints on a field that, newly bared, crackled underfoot and shimmered silver; it was a beauty that would not last another ten minutes, so I dropped the firewood and stood and watched the night's frost dissolve into morning mist. Somewhere in the tree line, a bluebird burbled a tune, but I couldn't pick him out. It was the first songbird I'd heard that spring, other than the wisecracking redwing blackbirds, and the chickadees who never leave. Before long the wheezy timing belt in Ed Brennan's pickup joined the choir. The truck jounced along my driveway and backed up next to the tumbledown

95

shed referred to as the "Big Garage." There is no Little Garage, far as I know.

My place belonged to Ed Brennan's Aunt Medbh, who died. The farmhouse stood snug against a gentle slope of a hill, with a view down a wooded valley patched with yellow fields. It was once a small dairy farm, as the slumping post-and-beam barns and a milk house attest. Barbed wire, vanishing into the earth in spots, marked the border of the thirty-acre plot. Ed had bought it from his cousins following Aunt Medbh's death of old age. When natural gas arrived to the area, his cousins kindly offered to buy the place back, but Ed had plans to improve the farm and preserve it all in one swoop. He doesn't love the idea of hydro-fracking, Ed, and will sign no leases. I live there rent-free with the understanding that I'll help improve the place to his specifications, and will also have right of first refusal when I can get the money together, provided I agree never to allow drilling once I own it. Until that day, Ed pretends the house already belongs to me. I'm of two minds, surrounded as I am by landowners who have already signed. My misgivings won't keep gas away any more than Ed's will.

I gathered my firewood and walked back inside, dropping it by the stove in the living room, then went out to help Ed with whatever he was doing. In the truck's bed were about thirty rough-cut boards. Ed was in the shed, setting risers for the lumber. By way of greeting he called out to me, "I don't know anymore."

"I don't know anymore." This covered a lot for us.

Exhaling a long plume of marijuana smoke, he held out a one-hitter to me. "Safety meeting?"

I declined, and sprang the ratchet on the nearest strap holding the load down. The lumber's grain swirled orange and yellow. "This cherry?"

"Milled it myself. Tree fell across the road out in Midhollow and I got there first." Ed reached into the pickup's bed, lifted a board, and examined it. "How about a new kitchen floor?"

You could see even at that early stage how the lumber would make a handsome floor, a braiding grain that would deepen to red over years in the sun. "Beautiful," I said, and popped the other ratchet.

Ed waved me away. "I don't need help. You got work. Go."

I was more tired than I knew. Suddenly the thought of being alone with everything was too much; I fell to my knees and sobbed as I had not done for years.

"Jesus," he said, and patted my shoulder for a while as I heaved and tried to catch my breath. "Come on, now." When I slowed down, he said, "Up. Up's a daisy, Officer," and pulled me to my feet. The world spun a couple times.

I dragged my sleeve across my eyes. "George Ellis was killed last night, shot. I shouldn't be telling you."

Ed's face hardened. "What?"

"Shit." I shook my head. "Please keep it to yourself, will you? You can't even tell Liz, not yet."

"But *who*?"

I didn't answer. It wasn't only George upsetting me; I'd shot a man. He was fine, and I was justified, but still. My head was out-of-round and I was exhausted. Ed drew me in — he hugged frequently and all his hugs were bearlike — and told me he'd help however he could. He wiped his own eyes with a canvas glove and returned to his task. We stacked the lumber neatly in the garage, laid a couple of sheets of steel roofing on top, and weighed them down with heavy rocks that had fallen loose from the foundation. When we were done, he straightened and blew a long, contemplative breath out. "You'll need company. I know you don't think you do." He opened the door to his truck and put a foot in. "You all right?"

"Just tired. Keep it to yourself?"

Ed drove away. I stepped inside and sat at my kitchen table where the view down the valley was best. While my fresh mug of coffee got cold, I just kept looking down at the kitchen's narrow uneven floorboards, painted periwinkle, and dotted with white from when someone repainted the ceiling years back. I decided to use them whenever we tore them up, make a table or maybe a bench for outside. I drained my coffee, slapped my face, got dressed, and drove to the courthouse.

The Holebrook County Courthouse sits atop the high end of Court Street overlooking Fitzmorris's downtown business district. Dollar store, consignment, a late-run movie theater, two bars, two restaurants, and a sandwich shop. Carly Dunigan's bookstore is around the corner somewhere. Many of the other businesses have moved out toward Route 488, where they can spread out and build themselves new boxes to be in, or they have been replaced by chains.

The courthouse is a dependable structure, with pillars, a cupola turned green, and a working clock. It was built in the 1850s. The sheriff's department and holding cells are on the basement floor, along with Wy Brophy's office and the tiny county morgue. In an all-purpose chamber whose high windows look out on budding trees in the adjacent square — the kind of government room where corrective driving courses are given, and juries deliberate small-time fates — the coroner and lawmen had gathered, along with District Attorney Ross and Wild Thyme Township Supervisor Steve Milgraham. There was a sour smell of coffee. We took seats around a scratched oak table. At the center of the table were several evidence bags, large and small; I took note of the bloody blue shirt found in Aub's corncrib, a misshapen bullet which I assumed had taken George's life, and other sundries. A whiteboard stood at the front of the room, clean. Dally stood and drew a black line down the center of the board, writing *John Doe* at the top of one half, and *George Ellis* on the other.

The sheriff cleared his throat. "Last night was as bad as it gets. George was a good policeman. Let there be no doubt: we'll hit back harder than anyone ever thought of. Every one of us in this room is here to . . . to do so." He glanced at me.

The sheriff continued. "But we can't spread too thin yet. We've got not one homicide, but two, and not quite enough men for one. Anybody remember John Doe?" He tapped the board with a marker. "We know how George died. But I'm afraid this JD puts us out of our depth. So, let's stay on his side of the board until we can touch bottom."

I was sure the line between those two deaths would fade before this was over. The extent of its blurring was the question that interested me; in that border zone down the center of the board, I hoped there would be truth enough to fashion meaning.

Deputy Jackson let out a mighty yawn and looked around, eyes wet, to see if it was noticed; he hadn't slept; no one had, except Milgraham and the DA. I caught the deputy's yawn and pushed it shivering out my nose.

Wy Brophy cleared his throat and opened a manila folder. "Guess I'll start." He passed around some photos of the body, his octagonal glasses perched on the very tip of his nose. "The guy had been out there a month or two at least. Absence of insect life in the body means, A, he was packed in the snow pretty well, B, it was a cold winter and he never thawed, or C, both. You'll note that he'd been wedged under that boulder facedown. The lividity on his back suggests he'd been lying dorsal for some time before winding up that way. On his back, then, not on his stomach, is how he started out dead." He handed another photo around, a close-up of the corpse's chest and the wound. "See here, this speckling like cinnamon in a semicircle pattern, this is a powder burn. He was shot, most likely at a distance of twenty feet or less. More burn than I usually see. And" — Wy produced a red plastic baggie — "I found this. A lead ball that bounced up into his neck, right snug against his jugular." It looked like a .50-cal lead ball to me, slightly flattened by its journey through the body. "Making the likely murder weapon, what?"

"Jesus," said Jackson, coming awake.

"A muzzle-loading musket," I said. "Most likely a flintlock." In the seventies, flintlocks came back in fashion. Hunting with a flintlock was a celebration of frontier life long gone, a way to stand apart from the modern world. The brief season between Christmas and New Year's allowed you to add a doe to your freezer if you couldn't get a buck in the fall. That is, if your ass didn't fall off from the cold and if your musket actually shot when you pulled the trigger. Some of the firearms were handed down, some bought new, some converted from replicas. More hunters own them than use them.

"Are you sure?" Milgraham said. "Hoo."

"Someone tried to dig it out. Probably couldn't find it and gave up trying." Brophy passed the baggie to Deputy Jackson. "It's got something on it, could be human fat. It felt greasy. A musket, I'll bet that's right."

"Aw, shit," said Dally.

I said, "A lot of hunters have one in their locker. Season's in late December." Deputy Jackson handed the baggie to me and I hefted it between thumb and finger.

Detective Palmer grunted respectfully. "Farrell's probably right. Tough shit for us, though: no rifling in the barrel, no ballistics."

"And it's probably not registered anywhere," I said.

"Maker's mark on the ball, anything?" said the sheriff.

Palmer held the musket ball in a pair of tongs and peered at it. "Looks homemade."

Dally turned to me. "Anybody even know anyone who uses these things?"

"I probably do," I said. "And we can check who bought a tag for this past season. Let me look into it." That would pick up a few owners in the area for sure, but still I guessed that would only account for a quarter of them, if that.

"I'll have Krista contact the common-wealth." Dally made notes on the board.

Brophy picked up where he had left off. "His missing fingers and teeth and the . . . other wounds, and absence of any visible spatter at the site of discovery, suggest he didn't die up on the ridge. He was killed elsewhere, prepared, and brought there."

Dally and Palmer nodded at this. Dally asked, "The fingers: that's not a defensive wound?"

"No, Sheriff." Brophy raised a hand against an imaginary blade. "Imagine that." He then drew his other hand across the fingertips. "No, the cuts are too regular. The fingertips were probably lopped off after the fact. Very soon after." There was the briefest pause where we all imagined this happening. "Anyway, the rectum was inconclusive, nothing in the pubics. No nonmatching hairs, no nothing on the body but some blue fibers in the shoulder wound and in the waistband of his jeans that almost certainly match that shirt you found." He turned to Detective Palmer. "I take it this case won't be made on DNA, even if quality material were available."

"I doubt it extremely."

"The rectum was inconclusive?" the sheriff

asked. "What does that mean?"

"He's far gone." Brophy opened his hands in resignation.

"What race is he?" I asked, and the whole table turned in my direction.

"White, Latino, or a mix. His face is decayed. I looked at the hair and it's closest to Latino, but it's actually hard to be sure."

Detective Palmer asked Sheriff Dally, "You have many Latinos in this area?" Holebrook County had remained overwhelmingly white even as the small cities in northeastern Pennsylvania and over the New York border had drawn African-Americans, Asians, South Asians, and Latinos into their citizenry.

"A couple families," Dally said. "Nobody reported missing."

"Out my way we have some temporary workers," I said. "New arrivals, out on the well pads and pipeline cuts. The other week I gave directions to a Mexican truck driver dressed like a cowboy. He was living in one of those Lincoln Log barracks up by a well."

"Some of 'em in the Super 8," said Jackson.

"Most spend their downtime over the border in Elmira," said Dally. "Fewer roughnecks actually living in the county than you might think, and they tend to stay up near the pads, working long shifts. Still, we should see if any have gone missing. This guy could be anybody, from anywhere. We need to know. If we knew that . . ."

Palmer said, "Someone can check NCIC for look-alikes." Nobody volunteered for that duty. It wasn't going to be me. "In the meantime, we can continue working from the other end. Starting with our guest down the hall, who happens to favor ancient firearms. Mr. Dunigan submitted to a gunshot residue test yesterday, which I'll send down to the lab in Scranton with a trooper today."

I cleared my throat. "He submitted, did he?" Dally fixed me in a look, and I backpedaled. "Well, I'm sure you explained things to him. At any rate, we know he'll come back positive."

"I considered," continued Palmer, "swabbing John Doe to see if I could match elements, but decided that was a fool's errand. Whatever we get off that body will be so full of noise that it could actually harm your case. And these tests take money and time, so. Additionally, we found four bladed tools on the Dunigan farm, any one of which could have done the damage we see here. But again, to test them all for blood residue, or god forbid Doe's specific DNA . . . best you be reasonably sure first, then decide whether to test. Especially given your budget constraints. The shirt we found in Dunigan's shed. There could be a clean sample to be had, and that may be worth sending down with the gunshot residue swab."

"Seems awfully convenient, don't it?" said Jackson, yawning once again despite himself. "Finding it where we did."

"Could well have been planted," Dally admitted.

"That's not the simplest explanation I can think of," said Palmer.

"Look," I said. "I don't know Aub. Nobody really does, not what's in his head. But just look at him. He's old and all alone. People run all over his land, race their ATVs, pull out lumber because they know he won't be able to stop them. Jesus Christ, did you see someone stole the fuckin wheels right off his car? I mean, you're talking about the most vulnerable citizen we have. And everybody knows he is."

"Well," said Palmer, "it's true we didn't find much else in Dunigan's house or curtilage. Obviously we couldn't douse the whole place with Luminol, but we found no spatter in any of the places we deemed likely — the barns and sheds, the house basement, the porches, the doorways, all clean."

Above us, the courthouse was coming to life. Hard shoe heels tapped down a marble hall, a banister creaked in duet with a staircase. Outside, car engines hummed and a sliding door opened and slammed shut.

Sheriff Dally sighed. "This doesn't leave us with as much as I'd like. Is it possible his arm's still out there somewhere? God knows. I'll continue interviewing Dunigan, though that's nobody's picnic, I tell you what. I'll need his mental health evaluation for any of it to count. And an interpreter for my own sanity. He's talking, just not making sense."

"Anybody find representation for him?" I asked. "He see a judge yet?"

"Carly Dunigan was by," said Deputy Jackson. "Bought him a set of new clothes, said Kevin was looking into lawyers. Seemed like they'd let us keep him awhile, not sure how long that'll last with a lawyer in the mix." District Attorney Ross shifted in his seat and looked uncomfortable.

"Anybody . . ." Sheriff Dally said, "anybody have anything that should go on the board not already there?"

I thought of Alan Stiobhard, and decided to keep that encounter to myself. "Well," I said, pulling my topographical map from an

108

inside coat pocket, "this might be useful. I know Aub's ridge some. But we should know every inch. There's something Danny Stiobhard needed to get to up there; could have been John Doe or something else. I'm curious, don't know about you." Reluctantly, heads began to gather over the map where it was spread on the table. "Right here we see all the adjoining properties; there are trails and old logging roads criss-crossing and connecting everyone near this ridge. Once we learn who John Doe is, I bet you anything he'll lead us to one of these plots. And we may get something to point us to Danny Stiobhard in the bargain."

DA Ross nodded. "You're warranted for Dunigan's land only. You have a week."

Dally fixed his eyes on the ceiling.

"That won't be enough," I said. "We'll get permission from the landowners."

Dally broke in. "Right. Henry, you want to knock on a few doors?" He peered at the map. "Wait a while before you visit Barry Nolan," he said, pointing to an eastern plot abutting Aub's. "Camp Branchwater is right next door to all this; Nolan's the caretaker and I want to call Pete Dale first. The camp has a little history with Dunigan. He'll want to know." Branchwater's original owner had sold the boys' summer camp to Pete Dale, a former camper himself. He was an affable, fiftyish millionaire who smoked cigars, knew about wine, and painted landscapes. Though he lived in Westchester County most of the year with his wife, he was a regular presence in Wild Thyme in the summer, and we'd spoken once or twice.

"What kind of history are we talking about?" Milgraham asked.

"This was some years ago, before your time, before Henry's too," the sheriff said, "when Pete first took over the place. Aub had walked to their lake to fish early one morning, and he spooked a couple campers. Pete called me, I visited with Aub, and it turns out he'd had long-standing permission to fish and hunt from the previous owner. Anyways, I sat the two down and everything worked out.

"Pete'll want to keep the camp out of it. Enrollments are down, lake rentals are down, everything's down. Leave it to me," said the sheriff. "I'll put in some calls to the gas operators too, see what I can find out. Meanwhile?"

Palmer said, "We wait for lab results."

"Yes. And Krista and Deputy Jackson will search NCIC," said Dally. "Moving on to the other side of the board." He rubbed his face to cover a yawn. "As you may know,

110

Detective Palmer was good enough to supply us with a SERT team out of Scranton last night. And while we didn't turn up Danny Stiobhard, I am pleased to report we discovered a lab in a derelict trailer off Westmeath Road. It's not a priority until we find Stiobhard, but you may as well know that the owner is one Pat McBride." Dally distributed a mug shot of McBride; a pissed-off slouch with his hair buzzed close, a blond goatee half covering a weak chin. "He's a transplant from Williamsport, set up shop here last year. He wasn't at home to receive us last night. If any of you happen to see him, we have a warrant. Don't be shy."

McBride looked like someone who needed to be arrested. Some people do; it's a fact. I guessed his story, even if I didn't know him — he'd probably been a dealer in Williamsport until something drove him into the country. Out in the Heights, he set up his business and looked around him and found almost no police to get in his way. His friends would follow from the city like ants in a line to a chewed piece of gum.

"Okay," said the sheriff. "To more pressing matters."

Wy Brophy turned to Detective Palmer. "You want to . . . ?"

"You start."

Wy gave me a fleeting look that seemed to ask was I ready. I nodded. He produced photographs from another folder. "George Ellis was shot point-blank in the back of the head with a .38. So close it burned a patch of his hair completely off. Here's an exit wound through his cheek. And in the department of small favors, he was shot where we found him, in the junkyard. Someone had tried to wash away spatter not too far from the patrol car, but it wasn't a clean enough job for Detective Palmer here."

Palmer said, "We were able to dig the bullet out of the ground." He picked up the slug in its plastic bag and let it clunk on the table.

"There's something else," Brophy said. "When I peeled away his scalp, I found a fracture that travels across his skull and meets the entry wound. It could be from the impact of the bullet, but some bruising on what's left of the scalp tissue raises the possibility of antemortem blunt-force trauma."

"Aw, shit," Dally said.

"So he might have been clubbed," I said.

"Yes, with significant force, from behind. With something heavy."

Dally turned to me. "Henry, you know

Stiobhard best. How do we go forward?"

"He's like a wild animal. I mean that actually. He'd sooner avoid you than take you on, and he can avoid you for a good long while. If we're clumsy we'll be in a gunfight, and nobody wants that. We need to surprise him. Overwhelm him." I shook my head. "He'll be tough to find. We need to settle into his area and wait for our chance."

"That may be a more leisurely approach than we're allowed. There are some complicating factors," said Dally. "I assume nobody notified George's next of kin?"

"He's got a brother in Florida. And no."

"We need to get on that. The local news caught wind of John Doe, and you can bet they'll have heard something about George too. I've stalled them by promising a statement this morning, but we need to get his family word. More than that, it's his friends I'm worried about."

I knew what the sheriff meant. George had drinking and hunting buddies throughout the county, men who would be riled and hard to calm. Unless we managed information and did our best to divert what could become a mob, a SERT team wasn't going to be the worst of it for the Heights.

"Let me make an appeal to John Kozlowski," I ventured. "Start a phone tree or something. Last thing we want is twenty drunks tearing up the county with .30-06's."

As the conversation continued, I had the unsettling sensation of someone slowly turning down the volume. My vision closed in.

A blank.

Dally said, "You all right, Henry?"

"Fine, fine," I said, opening my eyes and rubbing my face, frustrated. My mind was like a handful of water. I willed myself to focus. The sheriff regarded me with suspicion.

As the meeting drew to a close, I remembered one more thing. "Anybody know a woman named Tracy Dufaigh?" Nobody did. "She may have been close with George."

The sheriff stared at the whiteboard and sighed, aggrieved. Then he stood with some effort and scrawled *Tracy Dufay* on George's side of the board. He looked at his watch. "Listen, Henry. If you can leave by the back steps? Ben will show you. In about forty minutes I've got to hand these goddamn reporters something. Henry, I'm relying on you to reach the brother in Florida. Nobody talk to the press. Stay in touch."

Bill Palmer stayed behind with the sheriff.

Deputy Jackson held the door open for me, and we stepped into the hall. Wy passed me on the way to his office, patted me on the back, and disappeared. We passed a metal door that led to the holding cell and to Aub.

"Ben," I said, "what's he been saying in there?"

"Not much about the JD, except it wasn't his doing. The kid isn't even on his radar; he has to be reminded before he'll even mention it. He keeps bringing up a woman; mostly it's just 'she' and 'her' but maybe Ellen? Ella? Hard telling, not knowing." Jackson met my eyes. "His mind's going, Henry. It ain't . . ." He shook his head rather than finish the thought aloud.

"Can I visit him? See him, maybe?"

Deputy Jackson craned his neck in the direction of the room containing the sheriff, the DA, and Detective Palmer. "Don't you have a phone call to make? Quick, now." He unlocked the heavy door to the holding cell and let me in.

The walls were Baker-Miller-pink up to about five feet. Above that, pale green paint was flaking to expose the cinder block beneath. The lights were fluorescent, of course. I heard a formless muttering coming from down the hall. That and a high-pitched man's voice that began screaming obscenities soon as we stepped through the door. In a whisper, Ben Jackson cautioned me not to look at or respond to its owner, whom I soon saw rocking on a cot in the first cell, his wrists still bound with a black plastic tie. He was a long-haired lost soul in an Eagles jersey two sizes too big. Sensing he had an audience, he screamed, "The bitches in Fitzmorris got nice asses!" He said it again, looking deep into my eyes.

I said, "No, they don't. Shut up."

"Fuck you, fuck you, fuck you, pigs. I fucked your mother four times."

"Henry, meet Kyle Leahey."

"Fuck you, too," he said to Ben.

We continued on. "SERT team picked him up in the Heights late last night near that lab they took."

In the third cell of three, Aub Dunigan sat on his narrow bed. There were still creases in the new work pants his relatives had bought him. One thing about the old man, he did not make himself at home in a jail cell, but sat with his hands on his knees like he was in a waiting room and his name would be called any minute. Deputy Jackson hung back while I stepped into Aub's view; he raised his eyes to me with an unreadable expression.

"Coming to take me on home?"

116

"Sheriff needs to keep you a little longer, Aub."

"Got to feed my birds."

"You haven't got any chickens right now. That I know of."

The old man waved dismissively. "Ask her to do it, then."

"Her? Who?"

Aub didn't answer.

"Do you know where you are?"

"In the fuckin jail."

"You know why?"

"Henry," Deputy Jackson warned.

"Something about her?" Then, upon reflection, "No. Yon sheriff, he coming in and talking about that kid you collected. That ain't my doing. No."

"You keep telling him that," I said.

"Henry," said Jackson.

"Just hold tight. Cousin Kevin'll be along to get you out."

The mention of Kevin prompted another impatient wave. Deputy Jackson gripped me by the arm and steered me out of the holding cells. At the back steps to the courthouse, he bid me goodbye. "Look, I don't feel good about it either," he said.

I escaped the courthouse without incident and drove the few blocks to the clinic. I parked next to Liz's station wagon and hopped up the steps. In the waiting room, the country station was on and an old lady sat enthroned in a wheelchair with an inflatable splint around her ankle, which was raised, the foot naked and outraged as a newborn baby. A man in a parka sat beside her. I guessed he was her son. The receptionist Jo waved me through; as the door closed behind me I could hear the old lady voicing objections.

In her private office, Liz had most of an orange peeled and in sections on a napkin. "You look like shit," she said, and handed me two sections of the fruit. I ate them and, after looking in vain for a garbage can, spat the seeds into my hand and put them in my pocket. "You ever find George?"

"Yeah."

"At the bar, was I right?"

"Uh, nope. No. You still got that buckshot somewhere, I could use it."

"Oh. Yeah." She disappeared and came back holding a baggie containing a small handful of shot. "I didn't know —"

"Nice, Doc, thanks much." I turned to go. "Listen, you may see some things on the news today." Liz's cheerful demeanor faltered at this, and I didn't see the sense in keeping from her what she'd find out anyway. "Well, okay. We found a body in the

118

woods off Fieldsparrow Road. Nobody knows who he is."

"Holy shit, man."

"We also . . . George was killed last night. I can't say more right now."

Her eyes misted behind her glasses, and she said, "Oh, honey," and pulled me into a hug. I hate to admit how quickly thoughts of George were pushed from my mind.

She's my best friend's wife. I have a wife, even if she's gone. There are feelings you can't help, but you can't chase after them either. No, never.

In my truck, I fished out a piece of the shot Liz had plucked from Danny's hide and rolled it between my finger and thumb. It was crumpled, dark, and dull — lead, common from before Fish and Wildlife made a big push for the steel shot that doesn't poison the ecosystem so much. I pulled away.

Irving Sporting Goods, owned by the Irving family, is one of the few mom-and-pops that still does a brisk business in town. They're in a renovated, windowless barn a couple miles away from downtown, in South Fitzmorris. Though I find the ownership a bit prickly, I do shop there out of civic feeling. I parked out front and stood rapping on the door; the store wasn't quite open, but one of the Irving boys stood in plain view inside, smoking a cigarette behind a glass counter. When he saw who it was, he put out the butt and let me in, returning to his post. The radio news was turned up.

The store carried new and used firearms. I reviewed the weapons lined up behind the counter and saw no muskets. Irving eyed me as if waiting for an explanation. When he didn't get one, he said, "Help you, Officer?"

"Wonder if you can. I'm curious if you've sold any flintlocks lately?"

Irving stared at me and made no response, so I asked again.

"Don't carry them anymore," he said. "Not unless we get one used."

"No?"

He shrugged.

I pointed to the ammunition on display. "How about musket balls? I see you still carry them."

He gave another shrug.

"Tell me something," I said, "how about .38s?"

"Let's see," said Irving, running his eyes over the handguns in the glass case below. "Come back with a court order."

"Listen," I said, "later today you're going to find out why I asked. If you change your mind and want to share, give me a call. That's if it doesn't offend your principles too much." I gave him a card. "Right now I need a list of all the muzzle-loader and flintlock tags bought here this season."

"Talk to the Game Commission."

"We are talking to the Game Commission. Me and the goddamn sheriff's department. Right now I need your list because I don't have time to sort through their fuckin list. Do it now, Irving."

"Easy," he said. "Easy."

He stepped out from behind the counter and edged past me. In the back of the store there was a desk surrounded by plastic child gates. He stepped in, slumped into a swivel chair, and contemplated his ancient state-issued computer equipment. I leaned in to try to look over his shoulder, and was startled by a girl, about three, seated behind the partition. She was combing the hair of a doll that had one eyelid shut. I waved, and she looked blankly back. After some muttering and tapping on the keyboard, a printer on the floor made a bleat and churned out three pages of data. I took them, nodded thanks, and left.

George Ellis's brother in Florida, name of Tim, turned out to be the least of my worries. My grief training came through for both of us. I let a handful of bare facts and boilerplate do the work. Tim was incredulous at first, then enraged at the killer, and then angry at us for not finding him yet. By the end of our conversation he had quietly accepted his brother's death, even to the point of wondering how much of the burial would be paid for by the township (not any). He asked would I see to his cremation, and he'd find the time in the next few weeks to arrange a small service. It wasn't a big family and I hung up with the impression George wasn't tight with them.

I closed George's personnel file — which contained one sheet — and filed it. In one of his drawers I found a bottle of bourbon with two inches left. I set that on George's desktop. John Kozlowski came in with a look in his eyes that told me the news was out. He shook my hand, took the whiskey bottle, and made to leave.

"John," I said. "We'll get it done."

"I should hope."

"I don't want you to worry."

He kept his back to me. "You think we don't know who you're after?"

"No, I think you think you do. That's why I'm talking to you now."

"Well, Officer. I'll do what I can to help." He took a drink. "At this point, the race is on." He pulled the door shut behind him when he left. I cursed quietly.

Before me sat an electric typewriter and a small pile of blank incident reports. Tough to separate the events of the previous day into distinct moments with beginnings and ends, but I did the best I could, leaving out my encounter in the swamp altogether. One, Aubrey Dunigan's alleged assault on Daniel Stiobhard with a shotgun; two, the discovery of John Doe on Aubrey Dunigan's land; three, George Ellis. I struggled over the last one most, and not just because the letters kept rearranging themselves and going unfocused. In the process of writing it, I composed a sentence on a separate sheet of paper — *As I surveiled the property of Michael and Roberta Stiobhard, Daniel Stiob-*

123

hard disarmed and held me at gunpoint — and left space for it on my incident report, but didn't add it in just then. You've got to write these things up basically as soon as they happen. It's not only the litigious era we live in. As ever, the Sovereign would be looking for a way to call me on the carpet, and whatever it was going to be, he could get me for the paperwork as easily as the thing itself.

I filed the reports deep in a desk drawer and examined the printouts from Irving Sporting Goods. There were about eighty names on there, mostly regular tag holders including the muzzle-loader season, and not the flintlock. Fourteen people bought tags for the flintlock season at the local store; two from over the border in Apalachin, New York; several from as far south as Scranton; three or four from nearby townships had bought them. Mike Stiobhard had bought one for himself and one in his wife's name, though it was reasonable to assume he'd be the one out in the cold. Danny Stiobhard had one, too. Of the eighty or so names, three more caught my eye: Grady, Nolan, and Bray. All of them lived in the township. Grady had only bought the standard tag, which made him less interesting. Bray and Nolan both had flintlock licenses, and in fact, Nolan had bought two — one in his son's name. All three men were neighbors, and all three had land abutting Aub's.

I opened the weapons locker. A uniformed policeman is asked to carry many things on his person, I say on his person, but it's his belt, really; try a day of carrying around the .40, two extra magazines, the Maglite, pepper spray, jackknife, telescoping baton, two sets of cuffs, and so on. I never carried all that. It reminded me too much of lugging around a ten-pound rifle and sweating through my gear in Somalia. The thing about Somalia was the dust, everywhere. If you took your rifle out, you had to clean it when you came back. Every time. It wasn't an empty exercise, and I got in the habit with all of my weapons back home. If I took something out in the field, I cleaned it. In my quiet township with minimal supervision, I often left everything in the locker and carried only a set of handcuffs and the Maglite. The mousegun had been my wife Polly's to ward off bears while camping. It was far too small to bother a grizzly, but it had made her feel better, and I always took it along on the off chance I would need something in a pinch. Never had until last night. Now I contemplated all that standard-issue equipment and it almost looked like not enough.

I spent a little while filling magazines and tucking everything back in its place on the belt. I checked and cleaned a second .40 and strapped it under my left arm in a cowhide shoulder holster. Armed to the teeth, I sat at my desk in my sleepy station and listened to the garage on the other side of the wall and thought.

I had always sought rural postings because something in me needs the wide-open space and the boredom. Some people need to be surrounded by other people. Some love talking; I don't. That was one thing I liked about George, he never required conversation. And the station, the station itself was just the kind of place I could keep neat and functional; it had never asked much of me beyond that. Now things were getting worse by the hour and it felt like I was dragging my heels in the dirt, getting pulled after a train.

When the knock on the front door came, I knew it meant trouble. Usually people know to walk right in as if they own the joint. I Indian-crept to the window adjacent to the door and stuck a finger in the venetian blind. The TV reporter standing there looked shorter and older than he did on the five-thirty news. He was from a local station over the border in Binghamton; Holebrook County didn't have enough news to warrant a daily paper, let alone a TV station. Behind him stood a cameraman fiddling with a digital camera, a long fuzzy mic tucked under one arm.

I opened the door, cleared my throat, and before the reporter could start talking, I held up a finger as if I'd be right back. Then I closed the door on him. After pulling on my coat I stepped through the inside door to the garage and found Kozlowski.

"John," I asked, "where can I find a girl named Tracy Dufaigh, do you know?"

He nodded as if he knew why I might be asking. "Don't know exactly where she lives, somewhere in the Heights. Last I knew she works up at the horse farm that used to be the Regans's."

That gave me a little shiver. The Bray place was on my list already.

"She and George were on the outs, just so you know," John continued. "Even if someone's told her, she may appreciate hearing it from you all the same."

I glanced out of a portal in one of the garage doors and was dismayed to find the news team between me and my truck. "Listen, you got something for me to drive?"

Kozlowski loaned me a three-quarter-ton

diesel pickup from the eighties that the township had bought from the National Guard and painted red; you could still see camouflage paint on the insides of its doors. There was no tape deck but someone had bungee-corded a little boom box to the dash; cassettes were scattered about the cab, some good ones, an Alan Jackson. As the truck roared to life, John opened the garage door for me and I drove away without a second look from the news reporter, who last I saw was still at the station door patiently waiting for me to emerge.

After a deafening ten minutes on 189 I turned up a dirt drive at a sign that read BRAY STABLES and showed a silhouette of a prancing horse. Didn't know the Brays, but I had known the Regans a bit. Did odd jobs for Philly Regan one summer in high school, clearing trees and splitting wood. I'll always remember the advice he gave me the first time he handed me a chain saw: "Try not to cut your dick off." He keeled over with a heart attack two years ago and his grown kids finally sold the place a year later, just before natural gas started handing out lease money.

As I pulled into the yard, I saw that the Brays had kept the farmhouse much the same, white with hanging flowerpots on the porch, now empty. Up the hill they had kept a one-story structure that used to be part of the dairy operation, and converted it into stables. The rest of the post-and-beam barns had been replaced by two colossal window-less buildings made of corrugated steel.

I stepped out of the truck still feeling the vibration of its huge engine through my body, my ears ringing in the sudden quiet of the farmyard. Figuring nobody could have missed my arrival, I just kind of stood in the mud, looking around, until a screen door creaked open and slapped shut, and a woman approached me from the house. I summoned a smile and waved. She couldn't have been over five-two, with dark hair clipped back and blue jeans tucked into high boots. She smiled in a way that gath-ered her whole face around her eyes; I guessed she was in her forties. I found her attractive, and that made me awkward and shy.

"Wondering when we'd meet," she said, extending a hand. "Shelly. Bray," she added, gesturing about her.

I nodded and shook her hand and fumbled through my own name and title. "Sorry to come by unannounced," I said. "We've had some trouble up here on the ridge and I thought I ought to visit."

Her smile grew wary. "Please come in."

We passed a small sign on the lawn that showed the word FRACK crossed out. The house we entered was furnished with antiques. The walls were white, and plastic kids' toys had collected in the corners and on the staircase. Shelly led me to the kitchen, where she offered me a glass of water and we sat at the table.

"I do kind of wish my husband was here for whatever it is. It's not too serious, is it?"

"What's he, at work?"

"He's an engineer. BAE Systems."

"We'll need to talk to him, too. And you have kids, I gather . . ."

"Yeah, boy and a girl. At school now, of course . . ."

"Ah." I looked around the kitchen at the ornate flatware on display, probably from Italy or France. "Listen. Yesterday we found a body. A young man up on the ridge, on Aubrey Dunigan's land."

"My god, what?"

"Hard to believe, I know. He'd been up there some time." I waited but she stayed silent. "No, no sign of him on your end, nothing?"

"Um. No." I watched her move from shock to something like bewildered acceptance. "What happened? Who is he?"

"We're looking into that, of course. There's some we still don't know."

"I'm — I don't know what to say." She stared into her water glass, unseeing.

"Can I ask you something, you see much of your neighbors? Aubrey Dunigan, I'm mainly curious about?"

"From a distance. We lead trail rides up on the ridge. Not in the winter, of course. Sometimes you see him puttering around his house. It was on his land?"

"Yeah, but it was near enough to your plot, and some others besides. Felt it best to let you know."

"Naturally."

I had been watching her for signs of prior knowledge, nervousness, deceit. There was nothing like that. "Mrs. Bray, have you seen or heard anything unusual this winter, had any trespassers, maybe trying to come in from 189?"

"Officer —"

"Henry."

"Henry, how did this man die?"

"We're trying to figure that out."

She nodded, a tentative, unconscious motion. "We're not in danger here?"

"I don't think so. Couldn't hurt to lock your doors at night."

"Jesus, he was *murdered*?"

"Like I said, we're determining that."

She looked at me in silence for what felt like a long time. "Did Aub do it?"

"No. I highly doubt it."

"Well, no. I haven't seen or heard anything."

I gave her a description of John Doe. "Does that sound familiar, maybe someone who had been riding out here?"

"No," she said. "Of course, we have more day-tripping riders than regulars, people who come out for a onetime experience, so I might not remember. Or I might not have even been here."

"You have regulars?"

"Yeah, little girls taking lessons and a few rich old ladies. I stable several horses that aren't mine. Listen, is there . . . is there someone out there?"

"We've had state troopers on the ridge. Actually, part of the reason I'm here is to ask your permission to walk your land."

"Yes. Of course. Please."

"Shelly, I don't think you or your family is in any real danger. The man died for a reason. Nothing to do with you."

"Uh-huh."

"And there's something else, a separate matter." I took a deep breath and looked away and wished that I didn't have to say it.

"I had a deputy, George Ellis, who was shot and killed last night."

"Are you . . . my God. I'm sorry."

"It wasn't anywhere near here. It . . . but Tracy knew him, Tracy Dufaigh works for you?" You could see the nearness of all this violence affect her. I expected she was ready to gather her children and run to the nearest civilized county.

"When she shows up, yes. She's here now, out at the stables."

"This will be on the news this afternoon but I want her to hear from me as soon as . . . as soon as can be managed."

"I understand." Shelly led me to the front door and pointed to the stables.

"You didn't know George?" I asked.

"No, I didn't."

"He never came here to visit Tracy, or . . ."

"Not that I know of, Officer, sorry."

"It's Henry." I left her a card.

Shelly made me promise to stop and see her once again before I left, in case she thought of anything. I strode up the hill to the stables, my boots slipping in the muddy driveway. Over top of the hill, I was taken aback by something I hadn't seen from the house — a silver compact sedan, its sides splattered with mud, parked in a dirt patch. I made a note of the license plate. The interior was strewn with cracked CD cases and fast-food bags.

By the stable door, you could feel the horses inside, a thick presence almost like sound, almost like scent, separate from the smell of their hay and shit, and the gentle explosions of their breath. I have never been big on horses since a nag, drunk on rotten apples, bit me on the stomach when I was a boy. When I slipped through the partway-open door I heard a woman singing, but couldn't make out the words; it was a nice, alto voice that avoided blue notes, the kind you hear in sixties folk records. There were about six horses tucked in shadowy stalls. I could feel their big eyes on me. Soon as I saw Tracy, I recognized her from the bar, a brawny girl with a lip ring, and short hair dyed jet black. She was brushing a chestnut mare. She startled when I called her name, spooking the horse a bit. After soothing the horse she held a hand to her heaving breast in a theatrical way.

"Sorry," I said. "Tracy Dufaigh, right? You got a moment?"

"I got a choice?"

I smiled and knew it looked false. "I can come back in a few."

She tilted her head forward and gave me a look from under her brow that said it all.

This was not the first time she'd spoken with a cop. There was a hint of defiance in her that suggested a hard upbringing, like she mistrusted authority not taken by brute force. And a ready resentment of the world because it works that way. I know; I'm a little like that myself. She being younger was nearer to it, and it showed fresh in her stance and in the look in her eye. I'd have hated to be her high school teacher.

"No, no, it's fine," she said. "What's up?"

I filled her in on John Doe first. She stood staring up at me in the semi-dark. When I'd said my piece she blinked twice and said, "That's unusual. We don't get many murders around here."

"I didn't say it was murder."

She rolled her eyes at that and said, "Well, I sure didn't do it and I don't know who did."

"Good. But you're up on the ridge a fair amount with the horses, aren't you? Seen anything I should know about?"

"Not this winter, haven't been taking them on the trails much. Snow's too deep and crusted over; they bloody their shins punching through the ice. Looks like they might finally get some trail work, though."

I nodded. "That your car out there, the silver sedan?"

"Yes."

With John Doe out of the way, I sighed and rubbed the back of my neck. "There's something else, honey. You might want to sit." She didn't sit, and I told her about George. I forced myself to watch her face change as I broke the news. Actually, it started when I called her "honey," a quizzical look verging on indignation that vanished with understanding, and then crumpled into grief, almost all at once. But she didn't cry.

"What the hell. Oh, George." I watched her process the information. "Hey," she said, "come out back. I don't want to upset the horses. They pick up on this." We passed between the horses and stepped over some hay bales half covered in a blue tarp. Toward the back of the stables, a collection of hand tools hung from the wall on spikes.

Outside, she lit a cigarette, betraying a slight hand tremor. Away from the horses, I caught her scent: stale cigarette smoke mixed with sweat and something chemical, even metallic. I let her get about a quarter of the way through her smoke before picking up the conversation again. "You know anybody who'd want to kill George?"

"No. Everybody liked him." She shook her head and grimaced, exposing her stained lower canines. "You probably know he and Danny Stiobhard didn't get along."

"Yeah. Why is that, do you think?"

Her face and neck turned red.

"So," I continued, "there was a fight at the bar last week? You involved in that?"

She shook her head with a hint of impatience. "You have to understand, I haven't been with either of those fools in over four months. When I was . . . when I took up with George, I wasn't quite through with Danny, and that started some shit. In the end it wasn't about me at all, just . . . something that wasn't going to stop on its own. Stupid fuckin George, it's his fault for falling too hard in the first place."

"Is it possible that this is where it led?"

"Is it? Anything's possible." She smeared her cigarette out on a flagstone. I noticed for the first time that she wore low-top canvas sneakers, her bare feet stuffed into them and looking like water balloons about to burst. Her fingernails were chewed. "I really can't say."

I thanked her and asked for a number and address where she could be reached should I need her again.

"I work here most days. I don't have a cell right now, but you might find me at 1585 Upper Sloat Creek." That was a Heights address; I made note of it. "There going to be a service for George?"

"Yeah, I'm working that out with the brother." I thanked her once more and walked past one of the big steel barns to a field that stretched back to meet the forest. My plan was to bushwhack up to the site where we'd found the corpse, to see how determined one would have to be to make the journey, lugging a body, in the snow.

I followed a well-trod patch of lawn to where an old logging road led into the forest, blazed by a flash-orange ribbon; it was as good a place to start as any, though it wouldn't be the only way. The slope was steep and the logging road switched back three times before I crested the ridge. I hit a crossroads of sorts at a windy clearing scattered with boulders and bordered on the east by a stand of hemlocks. Trails wandered away from the clearing in five directions. Stopping to mark where I had been on my map, I continued in the general direction of Aub's place.

The ground had turned spongy, and even my waterproof boots couldn't keep my socks dry. I passed from the shade of second-growth forest to a clearing that was on its way to being choked out by white pine and red maple. The trail narrowed and

I was raked by beech tag on both sides, brush so dense and brittle and full of secret animal paths that I almost missed the turnoff north, which I took instead of continuing east. Though I wasn't conscious of why at first, I spent a lot of time scanning the ground in front of me and shuddered a bit when it dawned on me I was looking for John Doe's missing arm. Soon I was back in the woods, where the logging road widened once again.

The hot pink blazes I'd spray-painted the day before led me toward the site, and I followed them until I heard voices. Expecting to see two staties, I was taken aback to find three old people, dressed head to foot in expensive microfiber walking clothes, inside the perimeter. One of them, the only man, had flipped the floppy brim of his hat up in front, the better to take pictures with a large camera.

"Stop right there," I called. All three of them jolted. "Nobody take a step."

"Ahoy, Officer," the man said.

"Don't . . . don't ahoy me. You know you're trespassing?" The three of them stepped back under the tape, looking guilty. "Seriously, what in hell you doing out here?" I hadn't any sleep in a day. "Goddamn it, I should fine you." Two days, actually. "In fact, I will."

As I took names and addresses, it dawned on me who these people were, and that maybe I shouldn't be too hard on them: Mark and Freida Moore, and Mary Loinsigh. Leading citizens of the township, always busy with preservation societies and parks, they were neighbors to each other and, more distantly, to Aub. Mrs. Moore ventured, "We were trying to help."

"You were?"

Mr. Moore lifted his jaw. "You've got a dead body, a missing arm, and a lot of acres to go through."

His mention of the arm surprised me. I gave him a look and said, "You want to be a good citizen, try the volunteer firemen. I see you or anyone else who doesn't belong out here again, they're spending a night in jail." I didn't know if I could make that happen. But they seemed to take me to heart, and when they turned tail and loped southwest, I believed they wouldn't be back.

As I sat there on a rock, my thoughts turned to George and what he might have seen in Tracy Dufaigh that I couldn't. Maybe it was just like she said, that she was just who she was, and George and Danny ended up two old bucks locking horns over her, neither one giving ground. But I didn't think that was entirely true. Not that she'd outright lied to me, I can smell a lie, but there was almost definitely something she wasn't volunteering.

The walk back to Bray Stables was shorter because I knew where I was going. The sun was climbing already and I had much to do that day, so I didn't plan to linger there. I made my way down an open trail, my vision swimming among the shadows. Because I had been hearing a lot of echoes that morning, and things sounded far-off, I didn't trust my first impression that someone was in the woods with me, to the east, to my nine. I stooped as if I were tying my shoe and listened: silence. When I walked again, the extra set of footfalls continued with me.

I reached the trailhead and a man was there waiting at the edge of the field. He was dressed in business casual and had a pair of hiking boots on, with the cuffs of his woolen pants rolled and pegged. There was a cell phone clipped to his belt. I approached him with some wariness; he smiled and extended a hand and introduced himself as Joshua Bray.

"Your wife said you were at work," I said.

"I came straight home," Bray said. "I'm sorry to hear about . . ."

"I appreciate it."

"Listen," he said, "I know what you told Shelly, but can you give me anything more? My family is here. Right here."

"I understand. All I can say is, the . . . the deaths don't seem random. They're not motivated by money, at least not by robbery. You don't have any history of a bad element on this ridge, or any too nearby. I'd lock my doors at night and just don't let the kids wander alone."

He sighed. "So there is someone out there." Before I could respond, he continued. "What do you recommend as far as protection?"

"You have firearms in the house?"

"Yes."

"Keep them locked up?"

Bray nodded.

"Mind if I have a look?"

"What for? Oh, Jesus, you've got to be kidding."

He led me to a side door in their house, and down a set of stairs to a carpeted basement. There he pulled open a desk drawer and began to rummage through it.

"Get a deer this year?" I asked.

"Nope."

"But you did go out."

He turned to me with some impatience. "Yes." He leaned over the desk drawer.

A flat-screen television sat, monumental, in an entertainment center loaded with speakers and electronics. Posters of models in swimsuits hung in frames here and there — from the eighties, judging by the hairstyles. I found it an odd way for a man of Joshua's age and circumstances to decorate his walls, and particularly odd that he had bothered to frame them. The whole basement felt awfully neat.

What Bray was looking for turned out to be a key; he led me to an alcove, where a five-foot gun safe stood against a wall. He opened it to reveal a row of rifles, shotguns, and muskets. Among the deer rifles and over-unders I saw an AR-15, the country cousin to what I carried in the 10th. Five handguns were mounted on the inside of the safe's door, including a .45 revolver, a six-shot .38, and three automatics. Bray shifted from foot to foot as I cataloged everything in my mind.

"Can I handle them? Pick them up?"

"If you must."

I hefted a couple of the automatic handguns for show, then the .38, which I examined for signs of recent use and, with my back turned, sniffed. Gesturing at the rifles, I said, "It's a lot."

"Yeah."

"Anybody else have access to the safe? Know where the key is?"

"No."

I picked up a Thompson muzzle-loader that looked expensive and unused and had a scope — I held it to my shoulder as if in appreciation, and the lens was dusty. Next to it was what I was most interested in: a .50-caliber Hawken with brass fixtures in the stock; I guessed it was about thirty years old. "Oh," I said. "Beauty. You go out this year?"

"Not for flintlock."

"Do you usually?" I picked the musket up, cocked it, and set the frizzen, scraping a nail along the pan. Clean, far as I could tell. I pulled the trigger and the hammer snapped down.

"I'm beginning to think I need a lawyer."

"Hey, come on. You got a kit for this? Patches? Balls? Powder?"

"No."

"How can you go out if you don't have a kit?"

"I just told you, I didn't. Last season I went out with Barry Nolan, our neighbor over the way. This past one we didn't get around to it."

"Ah."

"He's got everything. We get a deer, he

processes it, gives me the backstraps and a loin, and keeps the rest."

"Get one last season?"

"He did, not me."

I set the flintlock back down, saying, "I appreciate it."

Before closing the safe, Joshua Bray stroked his chin and contemplated the handguns. He selected a 9mm, put it in a vest pocket, where it sagged halfway down his thigh. Then he locked the safe and led me back outside.

"All right," he said. "Nice meeting you. Let us know of anything. I'm off to walk the property line."

"Mr. Bray, please don't go up there now. There's an ongoing —"

"See you, Officer." He turned his back and headed into the woods.

Shelly Bray must have been watching for me; as I approached the old pickup she stepped out of the stables and cut me off at the pass. She produced a little card with the stables' logo on, good for one free horseback lesson. On the back she'd written what I took to be her personal number.

"It's selfish of me, I know," she said. "With all that's going on, I'd feel so much better if you'd check in on us from time to time. And who knows, once this is all over with, you may want to take me up some lunch hour." She nodded toward the card in my hand. "Horses are good for you, you know."

"Yes," I said, "thank you, Shelly. I may." As I stepped into the truck, I said in farewell, "It's a nice place."

"We're trying to keep it that way." She returned to the stables, and I drove away in a thunderous cloud of smoke and noise.

Sometimes I suspect I am not good company. In fact, I know I'm not. My natural response to an invitation is quiet disbelief and I often decline in order to spare the other party my presence. But sometimes you have to say yes or you wind up like Aub Dunigan. I said yes to Ed and Liz when I moved back East, because they wouldn't take no, and thank God I did. It helps me to have something other to do than talking. I couldn't, for example, sit across a table from someone and drink coffee at a coffee place and talk about life. Even though I disliked and feared horses, I'd rather ride a horse than talk.

I turned onto 189. Barry Nolan was a friend of George's I'd often seen at the horseshoe pits in summer, but I never had much to do with him myself. Even among the dedicated boozers at the bar he was considered something of an alcoholic, slow, ill-tempered, and not a man to cross. For gainful employment he worked rotating shifts at a precision machine shop in Kirkwood and served as caretaker of Camp Branch-water. Nolan lived on a slim parcel of land that abutted Aub's ridge to the north and the Brays to the west. An avid hunter and tracker, he was one of the breed who work just as much as they must in order to fund their real lives outdoors. Sheriff Dally had asked me to wait before sitting him down, but that seemed wrong to me. My instinct was to get as many people as I could unawares.

I pulled onto a driveway leading past a row of fir trees and drew up beside Nolan's olive split-level. His truck was there, and so was he; as I climbed the stairs leading up to his back deck, he pushed open the storm door and gestured me inside. He was a big guy, and tall. A short beard covered the wattle of his neck. Without asking, he poured me a coffee and set it down on the kitchen table, where it slopped out and pooled around the mug. By the door there was a mountain of empties — liquor and beer — rising out of a recycle bin, and several more on the floor ringing the receptacle. The refrigerator was layered with photographs and newspaper clippings. Most were about Wild Thyme High School sports and Lehigh University football. My eyes settled on a portrait of Nolan's son, about age ten: the kid's hair was buzzed and braces spanned his upper teeth. In subsequent pictures he had grown into a bruising defensive tackle. Now a college junior playing D-1 ball, he — and the town — had some expectations of an NFL career.

The house was cold, and Nolan wore a brown work vest with threads escaping from the armholes. His hair was damp. Leaning on a counter, he rubbed his swollen, bloodshot eyes.

"Fuck me," he said.

"Yeah. So you know?"

"I know. Tell me this motherfucker's going to get his."

"He will."

"Yeah," Nolan agreed, "he will. One way or the other."

"Can I ask how you found out?"

He yawned and shook his head. "I'm all off schedule, late shift, I can hardly think. Koz called this morning. What he knows, I know."

"So you, you aren't aware of . . . the boy we found yesterday? Up on the ridge?"

He blinked, almost expressionless. "What?"

"We found a young man dead on Aub Dunigan's land."

"That can't be."

"I know. But . . ."

He shook his head again, bewildered. "I know everything that goes on up there. No way." He saw I was serious. "What happened to him?"

"We're figuring that out. Looks like he may have been shot. Best keep that to yourself."

"Course I will."

"Can I ask you about Aub? You see much of him?"

"Not too much, considering we're neighbors. He a suspect?"

"What about at the camp — I gather he visited there sometimes?"

"Not in recent years. He fuckin loved baseball; I'd let him know when the boys were scheduled to play. Sometimes he'd get a free lunch from the mess. But he's getting old, you know. Non compos."

"So he was welcome there?"

"More or less. Harmless, far as I know."

"Barry, you're not going to like this. I need to see your gun locker."

His expression darkened. "They've been saying on the radio this day would come." I caught the briefest glint of humor in his eyes, but it disappeared. He led me to a side room and opened a closet door. Tucked behind a row of camouflage and flash-orange outfits he had a .30-06, a .240, and a .22, a newish in-line muzzle-loader, and a Browning twelve-gauge, all in good repair, plus a compound bow and a quiver of evil-looking arrows. High on a shelf, a black case was nestled among boxes of ammunition and spray bottles full of scent. Nolan retrieved the case and showed me the chrome .44 automatic inside. "Never had much use for this, but I guess it's good to have one around."

"Where's your flintlock?"

"What?"

"Sorry, you didn't go out this year?"

"No, flintlock, I gave that up. Can I tell you, it's just a bitch? Last year I had a doe dead to rights, a beautiful young one. Crossed right in front of me on the trail up there. So I pull the trigger and the pan flashes, and nothing. Hang fire. I stand there, the doe stands there, and she jumps just as the musket goes off. Got her somewhere on the haunch, and she limped off into the swamp to die. Couldn't get to where she was. The worst thing was, soon as I shot, out comes her little one I hadn't seen. With the double-lock triggers it went off early just as much as late, or never. I sold the damn flintlock."

"But you bought tags this year."

Nolan regarded me with suspicion. "Jesus, you got my phone tapped too? You look through my trash? Yeah. My son loves the season, god help him. It's when he's home from college, you know. He wasn't interested this year."

"Huh."

"Look, and I got bills. Obviously. Between a kid in school and the . . . the divorce. Something had to pay for Christmas, and keeping the lights on, and, you know. Everything. Getting by."

I hadn't known about his breakup, or what his wife's name was, hadn't ever even seen her. It had seemed like there was a marriage still in the house. I was embarrassed, and only nodded.

"So," said Nolan. "That all?" We went back to the kitchen.

"Who bought the flintlock?"

"Some New Yorker. I forget his name."

"If you think of it, let me know. So, Josh Bray, you two hunt together? He an all right neighbor?"

"Yeah, okay. Far as hunting, useless. I help out here and there. The wife gives me ideas — wouldn't kick her out of bed for eating

151

crackers. You ever get a look at her?"

I didn't answer that. In the silence I became aware of the television that had been on in the background: a talk show with a loud audience had been replaced by the studied concern of a local news anchor. When I heard "Wild Thyme," I rushed to the living room. The local news had just switched to a shot of Dally in the basement hall of the courthouse, his head inclined toward several microphones. The sheriff mentioned "a local officer" but not my name. The unidentified corpse was "maimed, and in a state of advanced decomposition." He admitted the difficulty in a case as cold as this, but expressed confidence all the same. Since he had not named Aub, I was taken aback to see the wide shots of his farm that followed. There appeared to be nobody stationed to secure the scene. A reporter stood before a yellow police line that jerked in the breeze, giving the image of Aub's place — beautiful, if dilapidated — overtones of horror.

About George, Dally was more guarded. When asked the inevitable question, which you couldn't hear in the broadcast, you could see his expression move from deadpan to stormy while the reporter was talking. His answer was short. He named Patrolman

George Ellis as the victim and me as his superior, and concluded with a warning that the investigation was ongoing, and to respect the family's privacy. They showed a blurry picture of George in uniform, and that was that. Grim news from over the border in Wild Thyme.

"Guess it's out there now," said Nolan from the kitchen. "I can't watch."

You could see how, with the information that had been doled out, the two deaths would be connected in a much grislier tableau than they might otherwise have been. Was George the officer mentioned who discovered the first body? Did he encounter the murderer out there in the woods, or in the bloody basement of some tumbledown barn? And so on. You could see.

I bade Barry a quick goodbye and drove to a hilltop where my cell worked. The phone in the sheriff's department rang thirteen times before Krista answered, sounding harried. She put me on hold, where I stayed for ten minutes, waiting for the sheriff or Ben Jackson or anyone. In the end it was Dally himself who picked up.

"Henry, what is it?"

"There's nobody stationed at the Dunigan place. The press is out there. I had to chase hikers away from the site on the ridge. Where are the goddamn staties anymore?"

Dally sighed. "A couple got called back, a couple are up in the Heights. We had some trouble up there. Ben was conducting some interviews and came back to the car to find two slashed tires and his lights busted. Changed one tire before rocks started flying from the woods on both sides of the road."

"Jesus. He okay?"

"He took one on the ear but he'll live. We've got to put a foot down on these people."

"I could pay a call or two this evening, try to mend some fences."

"Mend fences." There was a pause on the line. "Well, we'll be out there making what arrests we can."

"Can you send Lyons or Hanluain over?"

"They're busy, sorry."

"What about Fitzmorris PD?"

"Over budget on overtime already this quarter. We're just as screwed as always, Henry."

I sped down 189. Though it was against my nature, I turned the truck onto Field-sparrow Road and eased it through the gauntlet of TV cameras and reporters at the foot of Aub's driveway, snapping the yellow police ribbon like I'd just won a race in slow motion.

You ever have your vision close in around you, that's what it felt like with all those eyes on me. The left side of my head began to throb once more. I parked inside the perimeter, on the blind side of the barn. Taking a deep breath, I walked the twenty paces to the clutch of newspeople. As I attempted to retie the police ribbon, a blond reporter in a fake-fur-lined hood put a microphone in my face.

"Could we have your name, Officer?"

"Officer Farrell."

"You found the body?"

"No comment." I stood helpless, staring down, willing myself to complete a simple granny knot. My fingers wouldn't cooperate. The microphones and voices came at me too fast.

"Officer, how did George Ellis die?"

"No comment." My voice sounded small; I could barely hear it over my pulse.

"Are the deaths related?"

"I have no comment."

"How does it feel to lose your deputy? Were you close?"

"No comment. Please."

The knot tied, I left the reporters and stalked up the driveway, pretending to have some business in that direction. The farther up the hill I got, the easier I breathed. When I reached the dooryard, I caught a slinking movement on the far side of the farmhouse. A photographer was poking his camera into Aub's privy. He was youngish and thin, with long hair in a bun on the back of his head. I watched as he snapped a string of photographs. *Jesus, not again,* I said to myself. As he stepped inside the little shack, I crept up behind him, stood in the doorway, and said, "You're under arrest."

Seeing the kid jump improved my mood slightly. I took his right wrist and cuffed it to his left, behind his back.

"You're serious?"

By way of an answer I half dragged him down to the truck and helped him inside it, saying, "Don't touch anything."

"This is never going to —"

I shut the truck's passenger-side door and stepped to the yellow line, where all those eyes — human and mechanical — waited for me. A hush of anticipation settled over the small crowd. Trying to bite down on my anxiety, and at the same time think of what to say to dampen curiosity and let us work in peace, proved difficult. "We are in the middle of two ongoing investigations, so . . ." A camera clicked. The silence

156

deepened. "*No comment.* This line? Imagine that it extends all the way around Dunigan's property. Cross it and you will be arrested. Everything there is to see, you have seen. Thanks for your cooperation."

Inside the parked pickup, I took deep breaths and gradually loosened my white-knuckle grip on the steering wheel. The photographer introduced himself as Galen, and asked me a couple questions before understanding I wasn't going to answer. Little by little and then all at once, the news teams flew their perches. Finally only one red hatchback remained, parked half in the ditch; without a word I got out of the truck, opened the passenger-side door, helped the kid out, and unlocked his cuffs. He thanked me.

"Listen," I said. "You invaded an old man's privacy."

He nodded his head like a turkey. I didn't quite believe his contrition but I had to credit his effort. "I'll just keep whatever shots I took from the road."

"Tell your friends: don't come around here."

The afternoon proceeded quietly. Apart from a few cars that slowed down as they passed the farm, then sped up when they saw me, we had no visitors. It was warm enough that I unzipped my coat and loosened my shoulder holster. Where the extra .40 pressed against my side, a patch of wet cooled in the breeze. After squeezing out my socks and attempting to dry them on the truck's hood, I gave up and pulled them back on and took to the trails. The ridgetop caught a lot more sunlight that day, and after stopping in at the site, which looked emptier every time I saw it, I cut due east on a trail, hoping to connect with the smaller plots south of the Bray place. It took a few miles before I began to hear tires passing on a paved road somewhere below me. I slipped down a steep decline into a piece of land grown so marshy that even youngish trees were falling over. The larger ones — beech, mostly — had been diced up by a chain saw, leaving gnarled root systems and a stump on one end, tops on the other, and here and there on the soggy forest floor a spray of sawdust.

I climbed the other side of the ravine and found a riot of orange POSTED signs, one to every tree, along a dry stone fence that slumped into piles. Through the bare gray trees I could see dwellings or maybe barns. If my map was right and I wasn't out of my mind, these places belonged to the Grady family — Grady the Elder and Grady the

Younger. Choosing a dry boulder some distance from the yards, I surveyed both spreads for signs of activity, and in maybe fifteen minutes I saw none. A squirrel forgot I was there and traipsed along the wall not far from me. I stood and approached the clearings.

At the border marked by the orange signs, I was able to pick out which household was which; in a corner of the yard to the left, or north if you will, was a small trampoline sagging from a pool of water in its middle, and a little soccer goal for practice. The newer home was a split-level ranch sided in vinyl. Next door, separated by a line of trees and undergrowth, was the original Grady farmstead. A pea-soup-colored farmhouse blended in to the wet gray of March almost as if it were camouflaged, along with a timber-frame shed that had fallen to its knees, several apple trees, and a few lines of firewood. Here and there rotting canvas tarps were becoming one with the earth, seeming to pull their contents down with them.

Any sensible person would have chosen to begin with the tidier place, so I did too. As I clambered over the wall into the neater property of Grady the Younger, my foot caught on something; I looked down and saw a silver wire stretching the length of the stone fence. I was able to disentangle myself before the shock arrived, for it was an electric fence, the kind you use to keep cows in and deer out. I stood in the shadow of some trees and tried to devise a way to get around front that wouldn't seem skulking. While I was thinking and getting nowhere, a raspy woman's voice called from off to my right.

"You there!"

I stood still.

"You!" she continued. "In the trees. Can I help you?"

"Mrs. Grady?"

"Yes, and you're on my son's land." Evelina Grady stood in her back doorway, her bulky body propped up by a medical cane.

"Officer Henry Farrell here. We've, ah, had some trouble on the ridge."

"No kidding."

"Well, I was hoping to speak with your son, but it doesn't look like he's home."

"Nosir, he isn't, but I'm free. Come over."

When an old lady gets me in her clutches, as happens down at the station about once a month, I figure, oh, well, at least we're running at the same speed. I get along with them. I hopped the wall and waded through the tall grass in Evelina's backyard.

She ushered me into a parlor whose every surface was covered with something — magazines, sewing patterns, medical supplies, and so on. A series of fancy dolls stared out at me from a glass case. The window curtains were closed and it was quite dark inside, and smelled of cigarettes and cat litter. Several portraits of Jesus hung on the walls, and photographs of an old, fleshy man abounded. Ron Grady, I surmised, felled by cancer a while back. Though Evelina was probably pushing seventy, her curly brown hair showed no gray. She wore thick glasses with a chain to keep them around her neck, sweatpants, and a sweatshirt with a large butterfly embroidered on it. Pointing me to the couch with her cane, she took a low easy chair herself, settling into it with a groan. I put on my listening face.

"Well, now I know what it takes for the law to check in on an old woman," she said, not unkindly. "Two in one day. Lord."

"All you ever have to do is call." I cleared my throat. "So I gather you saw the news."

"Yessir, and I'm hoping everything's all right over there." She leaned forward a fraction as if to continue, but her train got delayed.

"Meaning over at Aub's?"

"Yes, at Aubrey's is what I mean. Arriving the back way as you did, you may have noticed some signs? That's a way to upset my son, coming through the woods. Why didn't you come by the front, like a normal man?"

"Just out walking. You know. About Aubrey . . ."

"About Aubrey. He, my son, he put up those signs because of him."

"Yes? You have trouble?"

"Yes and no. Now, I've been knowing Aubrey since I was a young woman and we moved here. He don't talk much, but he's harmless. Shoveled my drive when I was pregnant with that one" — she inclined her head in the direction of her son's house — "and helped get wood in. I'd feed him every now and then. He came and went as he pleased; sometimes he had an old car, more often he was on foot.

"Now, my son Ron's got two girls. His wife come out early one morning to find Aub sitting in the passenger seat, waiting for a ride to town. It was something he used to do with me, and I warned her about, but still, she run in screaming like there was a rabid dog on the loose. Ron come running out, asks him what's he doing. He says can

162

you give me a ride. Ron says no, and don't ever do that again. Well, sure enough a month goes by and Aubrey" — she patted her knees with a flourish — "sits right back in that passenger seat. I need a ride to town. Now, that got Ron mad."

"How old are the girls?"

"Ten and twelve. Eight and ten at the time." She showed me a picture: pretty, gap-toothed little girls on a summer day, making a show for the camera.

"And Aub never . . . showed any interest in them?"

"No. No. I can see why you might ask that, him being alone all these years." She coughed and lit a cigarette. "No, there's a lost love in his past, a woman many years ago. She threw him over and he never married. I don't guess he had as many chances to *get* married as we do now."

"I'd never heard that about him."

"That's all he ever told me. I asked him once. Pressed it out of him. There was a time I might have known him better than anyone." Frustration crossed her face, and it seemed she made an effort not to look in the direction of next door. "Yeah, he didn't always smell fresh or have nice manners. But he was a good neighbor. His mind started to wander some years ago. I wouldn't be surprised if it was permanently lost by now. A shame, the way he got. Not many like him left."

"He got what, forgetful?"

"Yeah, forgetful." In a motion that seemed to include the house, or maybe just the room we were in, she opened her arms wide and then brought them in close, making a little sphere with her hand. "It was as if his world had closed in on him. You couldn't reach him. He didn't know you. He'd talk about something made no sense, you couldn't tell what. This had started maybe eight, ten years back. But between the time Ron shut him out and the next time I saw him on the road, he was about gone."

"What about Kevin and Carly? Anyone around to help him?"

"They were never close. They did what they could, I think. The state helped a bit, my church helped a bit."

"Let me ask you something. You don't think —"

"Nosir. Don't know who that fellow was you found on the ridge. I'm reasonably sure Aubrey don't either."

"Seen anything unusual up there? Or down around here, for that matter?"

"I don't walk much anymore." The old lady gave me a litany of health issues. I commiserated wordlessly until a pause came long enough to break in.

"Well, there's one last thing," I said.

"Surely you're not leaving yet?"

"Any firearms in the house?"

"Yes," she said, "and no. Ron Junior took his father's collection off my hands. I said I'd be happy to hang on to them, I can shoot and we do get an occasional bear, but he, he felt he should have them. He left me a little revolver, the size you put in your boot, you know. A five-shot pistol."

"May I see it?"

"I haven't seen it myself in some time. When Ron left it, I said, what am I going to do with this? It won't but tickle a bear. He says, you get an intruder, you don't need to shoot him, just shoot the couch. Shoot the couch? I wouldn't like to."

She rose and took her time getting up the stairs. I heard the sounds of boxes being taken down and opened, and some muttering. When she came back a few minutes later, she was empty-handed. "I — it's not where I thought it was. I'll turn it up, and bring it around to you."

"Do you know the make? Caliber?"

"I don't know the make. It's a .38."

We continued to talk for maybe ten minutes. She asked about George; I shut that topic down quickly. I sensed she was getting weary of me, but didn't want to let me go, either. When headlights swept the house next door, I saw my chance and stood.

"Oh, Officer."

"Henry."

"Henry, you can't leave yet?"

"Evelina, I must. I'll check in on you."

"I'll be waiting. I'll hold you to it. Come by the front next time, won't you?" She patted my shoulder. "Here, I'll introduce you to my son." Through the thin line of trees that separated the Grady yards she hallooed an SUV in the driveway, its doors open. "Ronnie?" Nothing. She called louder, and that time a man answered, terse. "Ronnie, honey," Evelina said, "Officer Farrell is here about . . . about what-all's been going on."

I heard him mutter something before saying aloud, "Good. Why don't you send him over."

I slipped through the line of trees to Ron's front yard. The family was unloading plastic tubs and cans of food in industrial sizes from the back of the vehicle. Over an armload of groceries, Ron's wife gave me a thin smile and introduced herself as Dot. She hurried herself and her daughters into the house. I didn't see or hear them again. Ron Grady turned to me with a plastic barrel of

166

pretzels under one arm and cheese puffs under the other. He gestured with his head to the open SUV door. "Close that for me?" I did, and followed him inside, noting a lawn sign that read OUR WATER QUALITY IS FINE. NO TRESPASSING.

Grady the Younger's house was tidier than his mother's. Shoes were lined up in a stone foyer, presumably to avoid staining the beige wall-to-wall carpet; I bent to take mine off but Ron stopped me. "Don't worry about that. Just wipe them."

As I sat in a floral-print wingback, he disappeared into the kitchen and came back with two light beers, one of which he handed to me. Short but muscular, and fidgety, Ron appeared more distracted than nervous at the prospect of talking to a policeman. A long drink seemed to focus him, and he listened quietly as I went through the story of the previous day. When I was done, he whistled through his teeth but said nothing, as if waiting for me to continue.

I said, "Your mother said you had words with Aub Dunigan?"

"You have to understand I have daughters. I can't have him wandering around, getting in my cars." He seemed defensive, so I held up my hands as if surrendering. He nodded, satisfied.

"So when you had these run-ins —"

"It was a couple years back, and I was clear the first time he tried it, or so I thought. When it happened again, I took measures."

"Ah."

"Yeah. Look, say what you want about Aub Dunigan, he's an old coot, but I doubt he's got it in him, doing away with an able-bodied man like that. Ma thinks he's a gentle soul, a child of God. Me, I couldn't say. Except it don't make sense, this. He's too far gone to kill anyone."

"Do you have any idea what may have happened up there?"

"No."

"And the young man we found. He doesn't sound familiar to you?"

"Nah, no idea. Him, now, George. You think" — he leaned toward me — "we got someone doing this for fun? How worried should I be? My girls will be spooked. Too much TV."

"The kid died for a reason. We're just not sure what it is yet." Ron raised an eyebrow at that, and I knew myself it was thin. I continued. "I mean, don't go wandering around up there, don't send your kids up there or anything. But live your lives. You're safe; we've got police up on the ridge." I didn't mention that it was only me.

"Shit, my kids don't go anywhere without my knowing. Appreciate the visit." My host stood as if to end our talk. I returned my beer to him unopened and stood.

"One more thing," I said.

Ron Grady, Jr., kept his father's firearms in a tall oak cabinet with red stained glass in the door. I examined them all, including the middle-aged muzzle-loader that Ron claimed hadn't been out in several years. When asked about his mother's handgun, he shrugged. "That's why I kept all these others."

"Okay," I said. "I'll be checking on your family until we sort this out."

"I appreciate it but there's no need. I'm here all day and night. Unless I find work. If you hear of anything . . ." He was edging me toward the door.

Last I knew, Ron Grady had been employed at the garage that Kevin Dunigan owned. Normally I would never ask, but since he brought it up, I said, "How long you been out of work?"

"Since November. Merry fuckin Christmas."

"Dot works, though?"

"A teacher, thank God. Third grade."

He seemed rueful, but I wondered. Maybe the windfall of a gas lease had something to do with his sudden unemployment. Maybe the promise of one. Neither he nor his mother seemed to be living extravagantly, but you saw that sometimes, newly wealthy people who didn't change. The thing was, the Grady plots were on the small side, and any drillable lease including them would have been bundled with a larger landowner, such as Aub or the Brays.

Outside, Ron was determined to see me off, so I admitted to him that I'd come on foot. On our way around back, I said, "It'd be helpful, having permission to cross your land." He gave it, but it was slow in coming. He made a show of unplugging the orange extension cord that led to his electric fence, thanked me once again, and stood watching as I stepped back into the woods.

As I tromped toward the ravine, I glanced back at the two homesteads, following the slanting evening sun as it passed through bare trees. In the long dappled light that now struck their stone fence dead-on, something gleamed. Though by now I knew what it would be, I went back to confirm. Crouching on the forest side of the wall, I pulled out a turquoise-glass line insulator and hefted it in my hand. Had to be ten of them tucked into the stones at intervals.

By the time I got back up on the ridge, I was bone-tired and let my feet carry me back to Aub's farm. The sun was still high enough to warm the west-facing cab of the township truck, and I put my head back and slept two hours without feeling a bit sorry. Woke up shivering in the dark with my hands between my thighs.

Clouds had rolled in and the dark was the kind it's hard to argue with, and the beam of my flashlight showed me very little of the farm as I walked a final round. I needed to eat and I wanted a word with Sheriff Dally. Thought about exchanging the township pickup for my own official vehicle, but it was in the wrong direction and I didn't see the point for a radio that wouldn't have the reach anyway.

In town, I bought two warmed-over pieces of Mama Rose's pizza for dinner. We have square pizza in our area; it's pretty good. I ate driving to the courthouse. There remained a news crew out front, and one in the rear lot, someone having figured out where the courthouse's back door was. Entering, I kept my eyes low and passed through a flurry of questions without speaking. Pushed a microphone aside in a way that seemed gentle to me, but maybe not so much to the reporter holding it.

In the fluorescent-lit hall running the length of the courthouse basement, Kevin Dunigan sat on a wooden bench. His arms were crossed and he was staring at the opposite wall. I crouched next to him and also stared at the wall a moment before I asked him how was everything. He blew out a lungful of air and said, "I don't like this being on the news. I didn't okay that."

Of course he knew it wasn't up to him what went on TV, so I didn't bother to say so. Deputy Ben Jackson came down the hall. He was hatless and had a white bandage over his left ear, and his collar was blood-stained. He nodded to me, unlocked the door to the cells, and gestured Kevin inside. As the door shut behind them I heard Kyle Leahey, the formerly raving inmate, now sobbing in the grip of methamphetamine withdrawal.

It wasn't thirty seconds before the door swung back open again, and Kevin, red-faced, stalked down the hall. I stood and followed. In the sheriff's department, Dally's office was tucked behind a high fake-wood counter, hidden from civilian view; being in the basement, its one high window had bars over it and looked out on the sidewalk if you hopped high enough. While reception was rinsed in fluorescence, beyond it the offices were dark save where light from green-shaded desk lamps gathered. Kevin had vaulted the little swinging door and found Dally at his desk. I arrived just as Ben Jackson was trying to lure him back out again. It wasn't working.

"Nicholas," Kevin was saying, "haven't we been cooperative?"

"Kevin, you see our situation down here. It's not a hotel —"

"Either Aub moves or the crankhead does. I'm not convinced either of them doesn't belong in a hospital."

The sheriff opened his hands as if to ask what hospital.

"Well, you going to charge him? No? Has he even seen a judge? Then I want him out."

"That's not the best idea, Kevin —"

"I want him out."

"Bring your lawyer by in the morning. We'll talk."

Seeing he wasn't getting anywhere, Kevin drew himself up, said, "I will. Fuck yourselves," and made his exit without acknowledging me.

Dally turned to his bandaged deputy and said, "Am I dreaming? I told you to go home, and yet here you are."

"All right, boss," said Jackson.

"Don't wear that bloody shirt tomorrow. You have a clean shirt?"

Jackson turned the light out in his office, wished us luck, and was gone.

"He's a good sport, but he's down to one earlobe. He used to have two, just like the rest of us." Dally had the beginnings of a beard and he looked exhausted. "Don't," he said, "please don't talk yet. I'm going to hide under my desk and weep for a minute."

"In that case, I'm going to the Heights."

I had expected the sheriff to warn me away from there, but he surprised me. "Bless you, young man. Be careful."

I swung by my house to pick up some gear — gloves, a hat, binoculars, a thermos of coffee, and the waterproof cushion I bring hunting. Before I left, the sheriff had advised me that two state troopers and one of his guys were out patrolling the area surrounding Old Account Road, and at the foot of the Heights, I met the first of them. Where a clearing provided a little distance from the woods on both sides of the road, the trooper was running what appeared to be a sobriety checkpoint, but was in actuality a way to search vehicles for Danny Stiobhard without moving himself. The patrol car was so clean it shimmered in the dark, and drew the eye like a shark in shallow water. The trooper — French was his name — waved me down with a flashlight, not recognizing me as police in the township's beater truck. I introduced myself and asked how long he'd been stationed there.

"Close to an hour."

"Checked many cars?"

"Not too many, no."

"Word will be out by now. People will be taking the long way around."

French looked put off. "Shifty people you got up here."

I said horrible hunting to him and continued on my way. Upper Sloat Creek Road ran along top the ridge south of Old Account. A series of trails, steep dirt junctions, and a power-line cut connected Upper to Lower Sloat Creek Roads the length of the ridge. All through the Heights, people had fashioned homes out of whatever they had to hand. Small modular houses dropped onto carved-out ledges was about as nice as it got; there were more trailers, and trailers sprouting extra rooms made of garden sheds and fifth wheels, and at the lowest end of the spectrum, dwellings that seemed at once to rot into the land and to be propped up by it, structures with open wounds leaking pink insulation, homes that seemed to draw no definite line between indoors and out.

My intention was to orient myself to the murder in the Heights, as I had been doing over on Dunigan's ridge. I wanted to experience firsthand the stretch from, for example, Tracy Dufaigh's place to the junkyard where George was killed. Not that I thought she had done it. And though part of me knew it was a fool's errand to try, I wanted an eye on the Stiobhards, including Alan. Though he spent most of his time on the outermost skirts of the county, my guess was that he had a place to keep a truck and get laid somewhere more civilized than the cabin in the swamp. He bore scrutiny, just like the cookers and dealers who kept springing up as soon as we arrested the previous crop.

In hunting, patience is the cardinal virtue. You scout, you find the likely spot, and wait. It can take years to build up the sense of where a likely spot is. But once you're there, with your ass freezing to the ground and your back against a tree, you sink into the rhythm of whitetail life. A line of does and yearlings feeding through an overgrown orchard as the sky turns green in the east, their huffs of white breath and sharp, careful steps in the woods. Walking the same way, days in a row. Then one morning, the buck is there. Maybe the next morning he'll give you a shot. You have to be in the flow. You can't force it. George's death, the SERT team pounding through the woods — all that had jarred some of the natural rhythms of this area, and I hoped to find my likely spot before things settled again. As I said, my intention was only to scout.

I left the truck just off Upper Sloat Creek Road in the power-line cut, hoping one rusty pickup wouldn't excite too much interest. Stepping out into the night air, I smelled the smoke from dozens of wood-stoves below me. It was near freezing again.

Number 1585 was three houses to my west, and I picked my way through the brambles in the power-line clearing until I found the mouth of a trail. What I could see was rocky, narrow, and steeply sloped; farther in it was black as coal. I stood there for a while, hesitating, until a tree stump at the edge of the woods seemed like a better idea and I took a load off. I was beginning to feel I couldn't do it all alone. I needed to sit and convince myself otherwise.

The tree stump afforded a view directly south across ridgetops almost to Scranton, a distance marked by the red lights of radio towers just outside Clarks Summit. All the strange, sad lives in between the ridge I was on and the nighttime horizon seemed to hover below me in a haze of exhaust and woodsmoke. The red lights winked in the south, and somewhere to the southwest, seen imperfectly through bare tree trunks, Chesapeake or Cabot or Encana or whoever was sinking a well in a blaze of yellow light. Orion stretched above me, and I took a moment for the stars overhead, which could be seen very clearly in this black pocket of the county, well pad or no. It may have been longer than a moment that I devoted to the stars.

A far-off ATV growled and barked as it changed gears. To the west, I heard two more ATVs before I saw their lights. When the three of them rounded the bend below, they brought with them the roar of four-stroke engines. They took the straightaway on Lower Sloat Creek at a furious pace as a state trooper's patrol car swung in behind them, lights flashing. The statie was losing ground. The road, with its washboards and widow-making hunks of bedrock protruding through the surface, could not have been an easy ride for a Crown Vic. His siren wailed.

I crashed through the brush heading back to my truck, expecting to catch them somewhere on a road to the east. But the ATVs paused. I could hear their engines idling, and voices, but not words. Then they turned up the power-line cut and headed in my direction. My first instinct was to hide, let them pass, and pursue in the pickup. I changed my mind and fought my way to the center of the clearing, feeling thorns rip into my trousers and hands as I struggled for position. A rocky trail ran steep down the middle of the cut, flanked by stumps and boulders. I set up where two great masses of shale would bottleneck the four-wheelers, drew a .40 and my Maglite, but didn't turn it on. Not seeing me, the ATVs kept cranking up the slope. My mouth got dry. I waited for what seemed like an age, but couldn't have been thirty seconds. The statie's spotlight swept them from behind, catching the Day-Glo decals on their helmets. With about twenty-five yards between us, I shone my light in the face of the first rider, who braked immediately, followed by the other two. I yelled for them to cut their engines. In response, all three revved, and then the hindmost two took their vehicles off the path, turning back down the hill and onto a trail running east. After a moment, the statie took off east as well, following their headlights through the bare woods.

That left the first rider, who hadn't moved. I lifted my firearm, making sure he saw. Though his face was partly hidden by his helmet, I could swear he smiled and cocked back his ears as he gunned his engine. The ATV leapt forward and bore down on me. I stepped behind a boulder, flipped the Maglite in my hand, swung it, and caught him full on the faceguard as he passed. The helmet came partway off his head. He sailed off his ATV and landed like a fish in the dirt, turning over once on the point of his shoulder and winding up facedown. He'd pulled the four-wheeler back with him, and it crunched into the boulder next to me, pinning my thigh between rock and a piece of hot engine. A front tire, still spinning, dug into my shoulder before I was able to lever the thing off of me and shove it to the other side of the trail. When the vehicle had gone over backward, the safety switch had cut the engine off, and after it slid into a resting place in a thicket, the only sound left was a mysterious ticking from somewhere within the hunk of plastic and metal.

The rider groaned, a piteous sound choked by pain. That's when I knew he was a she, and I clutched my head, unbelieving.

Holstering my .40 and taking a quick inventory, I found I was mostly undamaged.

By the time I made it to the rider, whose faceguard had failed her to the tune of a mouthful of blood and a broken tooth, the shock had worn off and the pain had settled in. She hissed as I removed her helmet the rest of the way and tossed it aside.

"Jennie Lyn," I said. "Wiggle your toes for me. Can you?"

"Yes."

"Now let me see your right arm. Move it for me." She did so, and I pulled her glove off and snapped a cuff on her wrist. "Now your left."

Having secured the youngest Stiobhard, I sat down in the dirt beside her and let out a long breath. "Who're the other two? Danny with you?"

She didn't answer.

"I'll find out anyway."

"Henry. We need to go. You need to let me go."

"You been smoking tonight? Got any sharps, anything on you I shouldn't find?"

Grunting in frustration, she said, "Clean sober. Got a gun in the ATV and a knife in my jacket. Folding knife. You going to let me go?"

She spoke between short, shallow breaths. Enfolded in her pain, she didn't wrestle with her restraints.

"Where you headed in such a hurry? You got no time for the trooper?"

"Not for you, either."

"Well. Nice night." I looked around. Jennie Lyn wheezed. I asked her, "You think you might have a broken bone in there somewhere?"

"Don't know yet."

"You ready to find out, I help you up?"

"Might as well."

I lifted her to her knees, and from there she was able to stand. She limped over to a rock and sat. I patted her down, pulling a folding knife from her jacket pocket.

"Jennie Lyn, here's what. We're going to visit your place." Last I knew, JL was living with a small group in a turquoise school bus on a scrubby patch of land belonging to the absentee mother of one of her crank-time friends.

"No —"

"We're going to your place and you're going to search it for me while I watch. And then I'm going to dig up your neighbors, your old boyfriends, your old girlfriends, and everyone you ever thought of, until we turn up your brother."

"Henry —"

"I got you on vehicular assault, Jennie, seriously, on a police officer, with everything

— you fucked yourself here." Jennie Lyn shook her head despairingly. I asked, "Can you help me in any way?" She didn't answer. "Okay, come on." I pulled on her arm.

"Wait, wait. Please." The "please" caught me up short. She moved her tongue around in her mouth, winced, and spat blood. "Ma and Dad's. That's where. It's your fat-ass buddies after my folks. We weren't going to stop for any fuckin statie. It's my folks. Take me anywhere you want, long as we head there first. Now."

I helped her limp to the truck, retrieving a battered Springfield 9mm from a compartment in the four-wheeler on our way.

I drove for Mike and Bobbie's fast as I could, the cab smelling like blood and burning plastic and a hint of gasoline. JL had time to talk. "I don't know who killed George. If I did, I'd tell you," she said. I didn't buy that. "But you might like to know it was kids who stoned the sheriff's deputy."

"Oh? That makes sense."

"Yeah, you heroes dragged a lot of people out of bed last night. Moms and sisters and little fuckin brothers. You made insults to the people here. Anyway, they're just kids, so I'm not saying their names."

"As your conscience dictates." We turned on to Old Account Road. "I'll tell you what:

any more attacks on police up here, I'm coming straight to you."

Jennie Lyn shrugged. "Just you play fair, Officer."

"Always." We had a minute or so left in the drive. I looked at JL sidelong. "You hear from Alan lately?"

"No, why?"

I couldn't tell whether to believe her. "I don't know." Another silence fell. I said, "That kid we found up on the Dunigan ridge."

She didn't meet my eyes. "Aub probably did him."

I wasn't expecting that. "Why Aub?"

But Jennie Lyn's face had closed. I sensed a different kind of anger in her, slower and colder — didn't know what it was about, but it was clear I wasn't going to hear any more on that subject, not then.

We rounded a bend and saw several trucks parked half off the road on either side of Mike and Bobbie's driveway. "Motherfuck," JL said. "You got to uncuff me, Henry."

"You need to stay here."

"You kidding?" Hands behind her back, she twisted toward me, displaying a dark bloodstain — chin to chest — that almost disappeared into her camouflage jacket. "You can't leave me cuffed, Henry! I heard

something about George. I did hear something."

A rifle shot cracked, followed by two more.

"What? Be quick," I said.

"You'll uncuff me?"

"You'll stay in the fuckin truck if I do?"

"I'll stay here. I swear it." Jennie Lyn
turned, presenting her shackled wrists,
which I freed against my better judgment.
"Brother Danny said he had an idea who.
Someone close."

"That's it, 'someone close'?"

"Someone George was fuckin, some girl?
I don't know, I didn't know George."

"Lock the doors and get down. I won't
bring you in tonight, but I need to hear
more. If you want to help your brother —"

"I'll be waiting."

It was dark on the road. The raised voices
I heard changed the night into something
smaller. I made for the lights of Mike and
Bobbie's house through the trees — electric
lights and something flickering like a torch,
but brighter, what looked like a road flare. I
didn't trust my eyes. Since Alan had
whacked me one on the head, my relationship to light had changed. Sometimes I saw
too much, and it felt like I was seeing my
own pain. Other times, what should have
been plain before me was shrouded and

confused. As I trotted up the driveway, a shadow stepped out of the forest and into my path. A man — a large one — asked me who I was. I took note of the rifle barrel over his right shoulder.

"This is Officer Farrell," I said, stepping closer, and put my hand to my hip. "Lay it down."

"Oh. Just got this deer rifle. Ain't got the magazine in. It's Barry," he said. Up close Barry Nolan's eyes looked more pink and puffy than ever before, and I smelled a barley scent of beer on him. "Jesus," he said. "Glad you're here. This is turning into a goddamn mess. It ain't what I had in mind. Anyway, you caught me on the way out."

"How many of you are there?"

"The five of us went out looking for Danny Stiobhard. Then we got two wood-chucks just pulled up on ATVs behind the house. It's somewhat of a standoff. Shit, I came in — I came in someone else's truck, but he's about to get left."

"Just wait right here," I said, and continued up the drive.

Nolan shrugged. "Like I said, it wasn't what I had in mind."

From the house, two shots thwacked out. They sounded close enough that training and instinct kicked in and I hit the dirt.

I stood, and when I reached the edge of the yard, I saw that I had been right, that the pulsing light was a road flare, bright white and searing a black patch in the middle of Mike and Bobbie's lawn. Nearer the perimeter of the woods, there were fresh sprays of dirt in the half-frozen grass. Something didn't look right about the house; all the lights in the living room were out, and it took me a moment to realize that where the flare should have been reflecting on the big picture window, there was only darkness.

A voice in the woods to my right called out, "Listen, fuckhead, just give us John and we'll go."

Another rifle shot erupted from the dark window, and was met with curses from the trees near the edge of the yard. Someone whispered loud enough for me to hear, "Shut up your mouth. You're giving him a target."

I walked to the middle of the lawn and stood close enough to the flare that my eyes stung. I held up my badge and turned in a slow circle, announcing myself. "Everyone lay your weapons down and come out of where you are," I called. No answer came from the woods. And then I heard several men crashing through the brush toward the road. Keeping squarely in Mike's field of fire, I turned to chase them down.

From the house, Mike called out, "Henry-boy? Got a friend of yours in here."

I stopped before I hit the tree line. As the pickups' engines started, I made my choice. "Okay, Mike. Coming in. Better lay your weapon down."

As I climbed the steps, a movement to the right caught my eye. Without having made a sound, a gaunt young man dressed in camo emerged from the trees on the east side of the house; not looking at me, but not exactly looking away, he returned a blade to his boot. As he did so, another face, hollowed out by drug use and hard labor, emerged from the darkness in the trees and stared at me frankly. The two young men turned and melted back into the woods. I reckoned they had been a minute away from giving the county several more bodies to keep cool. I stepped inside, giving the dog straining against its chain a wide berth.

Mike met me in the living room, looking regal in a tartan bathrobe that almost reached his knees. A gently smoking .30-06 stood up against the wall near the busted window. The living room was dark, but the kitchen was lit, and framed in the doorway I saw township mechanic John Kozlowski sitting at the table, a picture of calm.

"Move slow, now," Mike said.

As I stepped into the kitchen, I saw why. Pressed up against the base of John's skull were the barrels of a shotgun; at the other end of it stood Bobbie Stiobhard in bare feet and a patched nightgown. She looked stern and matronly as ever, but her arms were shaking.

Somewhere behind the house, two ATVs kicked off; through a window I watched their lights meander into the trees and gone.

"Bobbie," I said, "I'm going to sit here across from John, and you can lower that."

She looked at her husband, who reached out and gently pulled the shotgun away from her. She excused herself to find a sweater to cover up.

"Now," I said, "what's all this?"

Here is what happened: Mike and Bobbie were settled in and watching a movie when a stone passed through their front window. Mike sent his wife to the rear of the house, while he retrieved his .30-06 and the road flare. Lighting and flipping the flare out of where his window used to be, he caught the forms of several men lurking in the yard, and sent warning shots in their direction. The men retreated to the trees, and from relative safety began to fight with their mouths. Bobbie was able to reach a friend of Jennie Lyn's on the phone. Meanwhile, John Kozlowski, emboldened by drink, tried a flanking maneuver to see inside the house, and wound up sitting at the kitchen table. Without Bobbie's shotgun barrel improving his posture, he looked defeated.

I asked Mike, "Did anyone fire at you, fire at the house, show any weapons?"

"I like to not give them the chance," he said. "They seem to think Danny shot your deputy, too. How'd they get that, I want to know?"

"Not from me." In the kitchen, a birdsong clock struck ten with a cheery recording of a nightingale. "So what do you want to do?"

Mike pondered his prisoner, while John sat, arms folded, and wouldn't meet his eyes. "I can get a man up to fix the window. He don't work for free, though."

"Send me a bill," John said. His tone turned plaintive. "The rock, it wasn't me . . ."

"But we got you and we don't got them." Mike leaned over the table so he could force eye contact with Kozlowski. "Surely you had some rifle with you when you came, a custom Weatherby, maybe, big hunter like you? I don't see one here. You leave it in the backyard, maybe?"

It took John a while to answer. "No," he managed, "no rifle."

Mike looked pleased. "Don't come up here again or you may not come down. I'm easygoing but I can't speak for my sons or them they run around with." Bobbie reappeared in the kitchen. "You find some cardboard for the window? Where the hell is Jennie-girl, anyway?"

As it happened, Jennie Lyn had disappeared from the truck where I'd left her, and the only sign she'd been there was a wadded-up paper napkin soaked in her blood. She could have been anywhere in the Heights by now. And Nolan had evidently connected with his friends on their way out and found a ride, leaving me and John Kozklowski to limp away in the township truck. I got behind the wheel and we began the long process of leaving the Heights.

After a period of silence, John said, "You going to arrest me? Charge me?"

"I would have if Mike had wanted it. You dumb shit."

There was another silence. John said, "My truck's probably at the bar."

"I don't care where your truck is. I'm going to the station. You can get home from there however you want."

We encountered the two state troopers assigned to the area; they had rendezvoused at the initial checkpoint and looked a bit befuddled. I leaned out the window to talk to them. The smile on my face did not come easily.

French asked me, "You hear any shots fired? We couldn't find the place."

"I checked; it wasn't anything. A celebration." I turned to the other trooper. "You ever catch up with those four-wheelers?"

"That was you up in the clearing?"

"Yessir. Henry Farrell. Sad to say, I let mine get away."

"No way we're catching them up here."

"Suppose not. Good night."

French gave John Kozlowski a funny look, but let us go.

John and I drifted over country roads and eventually fetched up at the garage. The reporters had given up on me and gone home. I kept the truck idling and John slid under the wheel. I said, "I saw Nolan out there. You going to tell me who the others were?"

Before closing the door and pulling away, he said, "Sorry, Farrell. You can probably guess, so I don't really need to say, do I? Couldn't believe my luck when you showed up."

It comforted me to be back at the station, and before I knew it I'd taken off my boots and socks. I found a plastic bag and dropped JL's pistol and knife in it, labeling it with her initials and the date, and stowing it in the gun locker. There was a phone message from the sheriff asking me to check in the next morning, and letting me know that one of the roustabouts on a well pad near Midhollow had not made it home to Texas for Christmas, and neither the company that employed him nor his family had had any word since. The tremor of excitement in his voice was unmistakable.

In the process of putting my shoes back on, I slipped into a dream of an upside-down tree in a river; the dream alarmed me, and I decided to just put my head on the desk for several hours. I woke up at three, got in my truck, and headed for home and bed.

I met my wife Polly some thirteen years ago, hiking in the Wind River Range. After my tour in Somalia was up and I got discharged, I was wandering America with some notion of becoming a mountain man. I'd heard that when they gathered, they gathered in Pinedale, Wyoming. Do-you-know-how-to-skin-griz, pilgrim?, Wyoming. With bear spray and a backpack with my fiddle strapped to the side, I was making for a place deep in the mountains called Scab Creek. I chose the destination in hopes that its name might discourage casual tourists and campers. In my mind, at that time, I was a serious frontier man.

I was two days into my journey, having camped the night before by a small hilltop pond that looked inviting, but was alive with giardia from the cattle that were allowed to graze there part of the year. I'd made it up into the real high country, where the air was cooler and much thinner, the light much more white. I hoped to outrun both cow shit and people. One thing I wanted very much was a freezing-cold mountain lake all to myself, but I knew to be careful. I'd had parasites in Africa, inside and out, and I can tell you it's nobody's picnic. A bear or two, I felt, I could handle. Well, I never did see a grizzly but one that trip, prancing in a tributary of the Wind River far below me.

I had been following knife-edge ridges for some time, and had descended into a lodge-pole forest so that I could ascend once more into the cold solitary air on the next peak. The climb was tough, over roots and stones, and my head was pulsing from the altitude, which may be why I didn't hear Polly's bodhran until I was on the edge of a golden field where she stood, thumping away at the drum in 6/8 time.

I was transfixed by a vision. Her brown hair was back in a bun and she was short and sturdy, all muscle between shorts and hiking boots. I don't know, you might have seen her out there and thought she was nothing special. And you can tell me it's no great surprise to find a would-be folk musician on a trail in the Winds. To the young easterner I was at the time, Polly was — forgive me — a handwritten note from God, inviting me into the open air of grace.

She hadn't noticed me. Stowing my pack off the trail, I produced my fiddle and tuned it quietly. I'm mostly an American fiddler and those tunes are in 4/4 time, but I was able to retrieve a passable "Banish Misfortune" from some corner of my brain, to match her Irish 6/8. The field was bigger than it looked, and there was one boulder between me and Polly, behind which I paused to reconsider. In the end I emerged, keeping a distance of about twenty-five feet. I felt awkward, out of character, but I had committed to the mission. It didn't take long for her to hear me, just a few years off my life.

Her arm slowed. She cocked her head at the sound of my playing, and stopped drumming entirely. When she turned, eyes wide, I nodded encouragingly at the bodhran hanging in her hand. And then she burst out laughing. She had the brightest, prettiest smile. I hammed it up for a moment, clogging foolishly until I came to a suitable stopping point, then I bowed and said I hoped she would have a nice day, and turned to go.

Of course I found out later that I was nowhere near as far into the Winds as I had thought. I mean, I was pretty far, but not enough to outrun the friendliness that governs the trails up there. Polly had known exactly how far she was; enough that she could hope to practice her new instrument without observation, but not enough that she was completely shocked at another's presence.

Before long I was perched on a boulder by her tiny tent, eating from a gallon bag of antelope jerky, playing bits of tunes, and talking. Polly was from a small town in Colorado, originally, and lived in Jackson, Wyoming, at that time. She was an outdoors bum of sorts, and worked in an art gallery and gift shop that catered to vacationers and sold lamps made out of elk antlers, and furniture assembled from shellacked, rough-hewn trees. While I was in the 10th Mountain Division, she was in and out of college in Boulder. My trip to Somalia did come up, but there honestly wasn't that much to say about it. I had missed the fight in Mog. We did our best not to get shot, and to make sure people got fed. It was a blighted place — everything stripped, everything burned out and destroyed. We steered the conversation in more amiable directions, the usual stuff people in their early twenties probably talk about. We'd both read Gary Snyder.

Polly was easy to be around and some of

the time we didn't feel the need to talk at all. Here we were in a spectacular place, a place new to me, and I felt new myself. She had never known me as bashful, or boring, or poor or unworthy. I had just returned from a place of despair and starvation, and was ready to be free and have my fill of everything light and good — it was hard to imagine leaving her giant smile or the tiny gold stud that glinted on the left side of her nose.

I don't think she got tired of me, but she did seem glad when someone else she knew from Jackson approached us from farther down the trail. A tall, skinny guy named Will with circular glasses and a mop of hair under a purple bandanna. He seemed nice. I was immediately jealous, and told myself get used to it, Henry, because you're going to be alone for the rest of your life. It got worse when Will took out one of those backpacker guitars that never stays in tune, and wanted to play. But I could see the idea made Polly happy, so we thumped through a few 1-4-5 folk songs before I packed it up, claiming a need to reach a particular distance before setting up my camp.

"Okay," Polly said slowly, "maybe we'll see you on the way out." She made no attempt to stop me other than — she'd later inform me — a look, a "smoldering" look. I caught it but didn't, you know?

In a way I was glad because, had I lingered into the evening, she'd inevitably have worried for her safety with a stranger, a veteran and a vagabond. That was the romantic way I saw myself. Best to leave her with earnest, kindly Will and press on. As I hiked out of that field, my heart was bursting so far out of proportion that I had to laugh to keep from crying. I walked it off, or so I thought. Hours later I collapsed on a windswept summit above a cold mountain lake with just enough light left to put up my tent. Some perverse impulse made me stay in that spot a day longer than I had planned without enough food, just so it would be even less likely I'd see her again on my way out. I was surrounded by vast beauty and the smell of my own chickenshit.

After a trip to northern California, I decided to forgo the American Southwest for another pass through Wyoming on my way back East. I found Polly in Jackson, in the store she'd named. She smiled so big when she saw me that I knew love right then, then and for all time. I think about it when I need to.

I had gotten some sleep, finally, and on the

crisp morning that followed I was en route to a well pad. Outside of Midhollow, Pennsylvania, a village in western Holebrook County, DiverCo had been drilling and fracking in an easterly line, with an eye toward connecting every well they dug to a major pipeline running south. It was nice country out there. They had drilled back from the roads and on hilltops surrounded by woods, so the scenery wasn't entirely blighted. Their service roads dug deep into the slopes, often in wide switchbacks, and the gates shutting the citizenry out were equipped with video surveillance and often were manned by a roughneck guard. The whole area resembled a kind of industrial gated community.

Sheriff Dally had asked me to meet him at the well pad's entrance, which was just inside the western border of Wild Thyme Township. He explained that Ben Jackson was getting his head and ear looked at and Hanluain was patrolling the Heights, leaving Lyons to hold down the office. We were paying a visit to this particular crew because of a man named Gerardo Contreras, a maintenance mechanic who fit the description of our John Doe. Contreras hadn't made it home to Texas for Christmas, and his wife had filed a missing persons report in Elmira, New York, where he had bunked between jobs. The Elmira PD was able to turn him up once, in a roadhouse between Waverly and Elmira known for its drug trade. He'd disappeared again soon after that, and though his family and employers believed Contreras was alive, a DiverCo representative thought of him anyway when Dally asked.

As we arrived, a worker stepped out from under a canopy and spoke into a walkie-talkie before unlatching the gate and swinging it open for us. The service road was wider than anything in the township, including the paved routes. We curved into the woods on the ridge. Hundreds and hundreds of tree trunks, stripped of their tops and roots, lined the road in stacks twenty high; these had been bulldozed and would probably be pulped, as they were too small for lumber. On our way up we passed three white tractor-trailer cabs in a line heading back down, having dropped off whatever they'd been hauling.

After wending through the trees, we emerged onto a well pad the size of three football fields, ringed by forest. A mass of tanks, tubes, and storage units filled up much of the space, and out of it rose a rig ninety feet into the sky, painted red and bright blue. The rig and the pad itself were surrounded by a number of pickup trucks, all white, drones in a swarm of white king cabs with out-of-state plates that had descended upon us.

It took my eyes a moment to get used to the scale before I could pick out the workers, perhaps twenty in blue hard hats I could see scattered about the site. We approached the data van. It was a kind of custom RV with stairs that folded down from a door at midpoint. In the window I could see several men seated at computer stations, the screens of which showed colorful, almost old-fashioned representations of — presumably — what was happening underground. Dally had barely put his foot down on the first step when the storm door opened and an unsmiling man thumped down to greet us, subtly steering us away. He was about fifty, windburned, sporting wraparound sunglasses and a goatee.

"Bill Huff," he said, shaking our hands in turn. "Rig manager here. Pleased."

Dally and I introduced ourselves.

"Good to meet you." The manager had a foghorn voice, probably from years of making it carry over the noise of the rig. "Listen, I know you're here about something else. Just quick, who would I talk to about trespassing? We've been seeing teenagers, people in the trees out next to the pad, on the trails, beer cans . . ."

Dally turned to me. I said, "Any vandalism? Damage?"

"No. Not yet. But I'm just a little concerned. Not so much about vandalism."

"No?"

"There are some elements out there determined to prove this" — Huff swung an arm in the direction of the rig — "is bad for the earth. And these elements been known to resort to sabotage so they can be right."

"Sabotage."

"You know what they do? They loosen fixtures and cut lines to spill fuel from our equipment. They've got to; ain't no other way anyone's going to find dirty water. Not from our crew, not from the process. I'm only just saying."

I couldn't answer right away. For the best part of two years I'd been trying to ignore the fact that hydrofracking had followed me home from the West. Seeing it up close again wasn't easy. I stayed quiet until I could trust myself to speak, looking out at the mass of tubes and tanks sprawled on the flattened hilltop, longer than I wanted. I managed, "You can just call me at the station, bud."

Dally looked at me funny, but didn't step in to soften my response.

After that, Huff seemed to understand he didn't have an entirely sympathetic audience. "So, Gerardo Contreras. Wherever he may be. I'll be happy to tell you what I told the Elmira police."

"They didn't share too much with us," Dally said, a white lie.

Huff nodded once. "The first thing to know is, the work is concentrated around periods of drilling. There are long shifts, and we operate twenty-four/seven. Then there's downtime as the next pad is cleared. Once the wellhead gets put on, that time can be a windfall for some, a pitfall for others."

"Right," said the sheriff, "they've got a paycheck, free time, they're far from home . . ."

"That's why we hire the best, but it's almost as important that we hire family men, men of faith. You know what I mean. We can't make mistakes." Huff gestured about him, not at the well pad but at the surrounding woods. I assumed this was for my benefit. "Look around us. We need to leave this perfect. Well, Contreras brought some . . . predilections with him that we didn't know about when he was hired."

"For instance?"

"This will be in his personnel file, so I don't mind sharing. Some of the guys have a hard time cordoning off the rest of their lives from the work. They need some help getting through a shift. We had to reprimand Contreras for amphetamine. Can't imagine where he'd get such a thing, not knowing anybody out here. Must've brought it." At this, he paused to let his implication sink in. "We gave him probation, sudden death if it happened again. Shit, if we have to, we'll fly out another mechanic rather than have one that's going to do something we can't fix."

"So, drug use."

"Yeah. Alcohol too. There was some other talk, but I'm not sure it's germane. Shit, I'm sorry I brought it up, it doesn't seem fair to the man, but . . . we are out here in barracks. And it's not as if it's a major metropolitan area. The rare guy will, will . . . start to miss . . . sexual companionship. Maybe too much."

"Ah."

"That could have been a problem for Contreras. But it's just talk."

We walked slowly along one side of the operation, while Huff gave a vague explanation of the process. I interrupted him.

"Where's your pond?"

"Pardon?"

"Your frack pond."

"I see. We ain't at that stage yet. We're still drilling. But anyway this lease doesn't allow —"

"Good. Where are your compressor stations going?"

"Again, this particular lease don't allow that." Huff made an effort to meet my eyes. "This is safe, Henry. Trust me, I wouldn't be doing it for fifteen years otherwise."

Huff led us to an RV strewn with Styrofoam coffee cups and crumpled napkins. The sheriff and I are both tall, and sitting there in the undersized chairs in the undersized room felt a little like playing house. The rig manager then left to round up a small group of technicians and roughnecks who'd known Contreras best. Dally and I waited. He asked was I all right. I nodded. Then I gave a weak smile for his benefit and said, "This shit gives me the creeps."

"I can tell. We're here about John Doe, let's stick to that."

I stood and looked around in the trailer, but all I could see in my mind was the rig reaching to the heavens. "Hey, how's Jackson?"

"I'm hoping it's not a concussion, but it probably is. Direct hit to the base of the

skull. The ear is the least of his worries."
Dally continued, almost to himself, "What
am I going to do? Down a man, in the
middle of all this shit."

I shrugged and, when Dally wasn't looking, checked my own eyes for dilation.

In the hour that followed we saw five low-
level technicians and roughnecks, some
white Okies, some Mexican-American, none
of them too put out by the questions we
asked. Not one knew where Contreras
might be. To a man, they seemed to be
distancing themselves. As a finale to each
interview, we showed a photograph of our
John Doe's face. It was the cleanest photo
we had, taken on the examining table, but
the kid was still blue and wasted away, missing an eye, with nothing alive about him.
You could see the workers stiffen as they
looked.

The last man Huff brought in was another
maintenance mechanic, a little Okie guy
with a blond mustache and skin the color of
tomato soup. Vernon Yeager. He wore bright
red coveralls. Sitting, Yeager smiled with
evident discomfort and little warmth, revealing a snaggletooth. It took a couple attempts
to explain that I was Wild Thyme municipal
police, and the sheriff was the sheriff, and
that neither one of us worked for the other.

Yeager's eyes darted back and forth between us, as if waiting for some trap to be sprung. He maintained eager body language and a defensive grin through the usual series of questions: How well do you know Contreras, did you see him much outside of work, when was the last you saw him, do you know where he is. I sat back and listened as Yeager answered in polite Okie cadences, putting his *h*'s before his *w*'s and not telling us anything. Dally laid a head shot of the corpse on the little plastic table between us and Yeager, and slid it across. The roughneck's smile became vague, then uncomfortable, and then disappeared as he looked down at the photograph, then quickly back up at us.

"You saying he's dead?"

"Take a close look, please," the sheriff said. "Sorry about it, don't want to upset you."

Yeager took another look. "I . . . it ain't Gerry. Can't be."

I cleared my throat and smiled kindly. "You're saying that because you want it to be true, or . . . ?"

"No, no. I mean, the face is . . . messed up. I can't tell." Yeager looked trapped. He turned and appealed to me. "Look, what in hell's going on?"

"We just want to know is this Contreras," Dally said. "In your opinion. It's nothing to do with you, right?"

"Right." Yeager peered out the window to the sky, as if looking for aid, and back to the photo. "I don't think so. Hope it ain't."

"Okay. You let us know if you hear from him." We each gave him a business card, same as we gave the others, and he put his hard hat back on and left.

Dally and I stayed put in the RV, discussing the men we'd seen. The first four had given us nothing, but the strength of Vernon Yeager's reaction had tripped wires for both of us. As we left the RV, the rig manager Huff had been waiting for us. He caught our eyes and nodded once, almost not at all.

Leading us back to our vehicles, he thanked us for coming and said, "So please let us know what you turn up. I'd hate to think it's Gerry. I'll be honest, he wasn't my favorite, but he was one of my guys."

We thanked him, said we might be back, and left.

Since Dally was going to be in the township that morning, he had scheduled a stop at Camp Branchwater as well. Pete Dale, the owner, had arranged for Barry Nolan to show us around, and we were already late.

The camp was spread over the crest of a ridge and down a grassy slope to a small private lake surrounded by forest. In my youth, I'd always heard that since the lake was so lightly fished, the bass and steelheads with which it was stocked grew to legendary sizes, with only pike and muskellunges and the odd eagle keeping them honest. That afternoon as I stood on the crescent drive in front of the camp's main office, gazing at the stretch of lake visible through the trees below, I had a flash of recall: me and my sister, dirty kids in the summertime, staring from the hemlocks at the far side of the lake as campers in gray uniform T-shirts practiced fly-fishing casts. Though the camp forbade it, we two little Robin Hoods had planned to bait-fish an easy breakfast before the sun was over the trees, but we hadn't been early enough. It was my first time seeing fly-fishing, and I remembered thinking someone ought to tell those boys they were making things too easy on the fish.

Now the camp was empty: no boys shouting, none of the loudspeaker announcements you hear wafting over the hills in summertime. Nolan stood in the driveway beside a four-seat gator with an open trunk in the back. The sheriff and I parked one behind the other and got out.

"Sorry, Nolan," said the sheriff. "Tied up elsewhere, you can imagine."

"It's all right." He started to get in the vehicle's driver's seat, then stopped. "Just missed another shift, that's all," he said.

"We'll write you a note," I said, and gave him a look that the sheriff couldn't see.

"Forget it, don't worry. So, what do you want to see?"

We took muddy paths through cedar-shake cabins and barns sided in hemlock, the ATV skidding on the turns, the sheriff riding shotgun and me in the back. Behind me in the bed, loose hand tools and a charred grate for cooking over a campfire bounced, clinking. Every now and then we crossed the remnants of a snowmobile trail.

"How often do you patrol here?" The sheriff shouted over the diesel engine.

"I take a turn around every couple days. Nothing ever happens."

"The snowmobile tracks, they yours?" I asked.

"Yeah."

We took a wooded trail that wound around the lake, and ended up back in front of the main building, where we'd started.

"Listen," said Dally, "I hope that's all we'll need." I could tell he was eager to get back and discuss Contreras and what we'd learned on the well pad.

"Anything else, let me know."

We left Nolan sitting in his ATV and raced to town.

Back at the courthouse we didn't have much time to debrief. Kevin Dunigan was waiting in the hall with Paul Wendell, a silver-haired lawyer specializing in real estate and divorce. In the past year Wendell had done brisk business as a go-between for the gas companies. The pair didn't get two words out before Dally asked them to wait a moment. We left them in the hall and stepped into the department. Krista handed the sheriff a while-you-were-out telephone message from one of the county's judges. He looked at the message in his hand, then in the direction of the hall, and muttered a curse. He disappeared into his office. Before long, Dally quietly asked Krista to bring Dunigan and his lawyer in. They each nodded to me as they passed, and there was a look of triumph on Kevin's face.

I kicked around the department for a while, leaning on Krista's counter and chatting with her, Lyons, and Ben Jackson, who had returned to the office against the doctor's instructions. It took maybe ten minutes before Kevin, Wendell, and the sheriff emerged. Dally told them, "We'll bring him on out to your car, just go ahead and sit tight in the back lot. He'll be out." When the other two left he said, "Hope to Christ the reporters are gone."

"Springing the old man?" Deputy Jackson asked.

Dally seemed put out. "They got me on the six-hour rule. He's released to Kevin and Carly's supervision, and he's to submit himself to a physical and mental health evaluation sometime in the near future. Down in Scranton, most likely."

"Sheriff," I said, "the guy didn't kill anyone. And he's sure not going on the run."

"Yeah, I know what you think, Henry. Well, let's keep an eye on him out there, all right?"

In five minutes, I watched as Aub plodded stoop-shouldered down the hall, still wearing the same set of work clothes his distant cousins had bought him two days earlier, flanked by Dally and Lyons. Dally placed a gentle hand on Aub's arm, and was brushed off.

In Dally's office the sheriff, Jackson, and I sat down to talk about the well pad. We raised the possibility of sending for Contreras's wife to identify the corpse — it'd have to be in person, as the facial features were so degraded that just seeing a photo risked a false positive — or to give us something of her husband's to match DNA with. We decided against it then, not being far enough along yet to inflict the kind of pain those requests would cause. The sheriff said he'd ask Elmira PD to beat the bushes for Contreras again.

And we'd both smelled something on Vernon Yeager, but Dally felt we couldn't put screws to him without knowing for sure Contreras was our JD. Deputy Jackson disagreed.

"There's nothing stopping you," he said. "For all we know and for all he knows, that is Contreras. Act as if it is. You may get nothing. You may get something Elmira can use."

The sheriff nodded. "Let him stew for a while, maybe, then ask him to come in. He was a nervous little son of a bitch."

"Some people naturally are," I said. "But I agree, he's got a quality about him. He in the system somewhere, I wonder?" Sometimes you can spot a man who has done time. There were obvious hardcases, and converts holding to strict beliefs to keep from being swept back into their old lives, and garrulous types whose eagerness to please masks a kind of corrosion deep down. Yeager struck me as belonging to the final category.

Krista called one of Dally's FBI contacts, who did a review of Oklahoma and Texas for us, turning up nothing there. He did find a grand larceny conviction in Arkansas, for which Vernon Yeager had done a year in the Texarkana Correction Center. He'd stolen electronics from the dock of a big-box store, in broad daylight, right under a security camera. I could see the effect this news had on the sheriff. To me, it seemed like the crime of a stupid man who maybe had a habit to feed. Not nothing, but not murder, either.

Dally asked me if I'd mind looking in on the various sites at the ridge. Though I was eager to get back to the Heights and track down Jennie Lyn, that would wait until closer to night. It was a blue-sky day and my hiking boots had dried. I headed back over 189 to the Bray horse farm. Mrs. Bray — Shelly — seemed pleased when I asked to use her dirt lot as a base; cell reception was better there and I had hoped it would allow me to speak with Tracy Dufaigh again. Unfortunately, Dufaigh wasn't there.

"Yeah," said Shelly, leading a mare into a

215

corral, "she left early yesterday, understandably. Haven't heard anything from her since. Is this about your deputy?"

"No, no. No," I said. "Just wanting to check on her. All right. Headed up to the ridge."

"Have a good one. Oh, hey, Barry Nolan stopped by this morning. Said he wanted to call on me, let me know he was around. Given everything." She slipped a bridle off the mare's head. "He also asked what you'd said to me."

"How well do you know him? You friendly with his wife, by any chance?"

"No, she was on her way out by the time we bought this place. Summers I teach riding at Camp Branchwater, so we have that in common. He's decent enough."

"Is he well liked at the camp? I only ask because —"

"He's not the likeliest guy to be working with kids?" She laughed. "Yeah, I know. He doesn't anymore. He taught survival once."

That, I hadn't known. "Huh."

"Yeah, he loved that, it was his calling. There was some trouble with the management, and they turned the course over to a regular counselor," Shelly said. "These counselors are all well-off kids working for the summer. You can imagine. College kids.

He brought it up to me a couple times, said he got railroaded. I don't know, it might have been his way of asking me to advocate for him with Pete Dale. It came off a little bitter, but that's the way he is, kind of."

The late morning sun was high enough to warm the steep southern side of the ridge. I picked my way through the woods to the site of our grisly discovery, in a straight line over the ridge. The snow had disappeared from almost everywhere except the hollows shaded by boulders and fallen trees. I walked once around the police-tape perimeter, seeing nothing unusual, and headed back down the south side again. My heart leapt along with a startled doe as it vaulted away from me.

The wind hushed by, hinting at spring, and places I'd never seen, and being young. I would have enjoyed it had I not been aware that we'd found John Doe in the woods close behind. A befouled place.

I wended my way back down to the stone wall that skirted the edge of the forest and followed it east, looking for any natural point of ingress from the south, something that might lead from 189 to the ridge without too much difficulty. In the midst of some spindly birches and ironwoods, there was a tall stand of hemlock trees, trunks close together, forming a kind of half blind. Deer like those places, and so do hunters; I stepped between trunks and kicked aside some damp deer scat and a beer can and sat where I was partially hidden by a log and had a good view to the south. I listened to the wind murmuring again, this time sounding like my mother's voice, and conjuring vividly my threadbare clothes snapping on a line. I could feel the rough wood of clothespins in my hands.

I heard hoofbeats. Thirty meters to my south, a horse picked its way along the trail. Shelly Bray was the rider, and she scanned back and forth as if looking for someone or something in the trees. I took off my glasses so they wouldn't reflect, and laid low and waited as she passed. She had to duck under a branch, and in so doing turned in my direction. I could have sworn she saw me but she acted as though she didn't, and was soon out of sight and earshot.

Solitude and sun-dappled air is a kind of magic, a drug, like music. Before long, the township's finest was curled up with my fondest early memories of hunting for caves never found, and the smell of fresh-caught fish on an open fire. I'd taken my belt off, .40 and all, and it lay coiled in the crook of my arm. I'd grown used to having the other pistol strapped to my ribs. The hemlocks swayed and sang me to sleep.

A branch snapped. An unnatural silence. Before I was fully awake, the .40 was out of its holster and in my hand. Not twenty feet to my right, footsteps retreated east, breaking the silence suddenly and definitively. I slipped out of the hemlocks and ran in the direction of the sound, throwing the belt over my shoulder and gripping it there. Careful footfalls became someone moving through undergrowth, with me following. How close, I wasn't sure. There are times a chipmunk can sound like a man in the woods. I'd stop to listen, and pick up the trail again, sometimes waiting until my quarry decided to move. Couldn't see anything through the trees, which clicked in and out of focus, and I suspected the person I was chasing was in camouflage. Once I splashed across a stream, but there were no bootprints I could see, and we were headed uphill where the ground was dry. My head began to pulse.

He turned north, into the ridge. His movements became sporadic and cautious. I followed as best I could, trying to keep track of the distance and glancing up now and again at the sun to check direction. He was leading me northeast. In a mile, maybe more, we'd hit the swamp that bordered Aub's land, and I'd have him pressed up against it. Once, just once, I caught a flash of earthy color disappearing behind a distant stone fence. Otherwise he was just sound.

I came to a clearing surrounded by stands of young saplings growing densely together, a kind of bowl leading to the edge of a bedrock outcropping and a boulder field that tumbled into the western edge of the swamp. It was reputed to be a coyote den in Father's day. A little deer path cut down the middle of the clearing, and connected to a logging trail somewhere above me.

Nothing moved. My head began to spin. I asked myself if I had lost him, and felt a watchfulness in the silence. Pressing through trees no thicker than my arm, growing close together as bristles on a hairbrush, I headed for the rock, slowly, trying to stay in what cover there was. Through the trees, the swamp was gray-white where the ice remained, and sunlight sparkled in blue-brown water where it had thawed.

In the outcropping there was a kind of side door into the rock, a man-sized gap where, over thousands of years, the shale had been pried apart by time and ice. I crossed ten quick feet of open space and was inside. The sound of my own breathing reflected back from the rock walls. The crevice soon opened up to let more light in from the top, and I came to a place where I could either go right into another narrow passage, or down. I chose down.

The shale opened out into a kind of chamber exposed to the sky, with a fire ring, a rusted lawn chair, and a wire strung between two rock faces. Bits of dried flesh and fur clung to the wire. I poked through the black wood and ash in the pit. It still smelled faintly of smoke. Prodding the leaves and debris on the ground there, I uncovered a beaver trap, snapped shut, and a larger one that had likely been used for coyotes. Squatting there, I listened. The wind rattled dried willow in the swamp below. Nothing more. I listened. Nothing. Then, behind me in the rocks, the click of a gun safety.

For the second time that day I had the .40 in hand without thinking. My options were few, and I gave myself no time to figure out how I'd been flanked, or by whom. I could clamber up and try to tumble sideways out of the rocks, and catch a round in the head as soon as I popped it up. I could wait for my new friend to move in, hoping to get him first, knowing there'd be no way to get the drop if I followed procedure —

identifying myself as police and asking him nicely to put his weapon down. It took a moment to find a third way. In a small alcove that had looked like a dead end, there was a short passage leading toward the swamp. A slab of shale had broken off from a larger boulder above and formed a kind of roof over two pieces of rock. I slipped across the open space I was in and, bent double, backed inside. Inside the tunnel was a scattering of dried shit; little pellets from a porcupine, coyote scat laced with fur and bone. Peering over my shoulder, I moved cautiously toward the triangle of light at the eastern end.

The tunnel led to a flat semicircle at the swamp's edge, ringed by chest-high boulders. There was no way out — other than the way I'd come — but over the rocks or into the swamp. On the ground, a brown tangle of grasses and sphagnum, and to the right was a briar patch with wicked-looking thorns. From my new position, I risked a glance up the boulder field and was halfway satisfied with the view. With my back to the water, and high shoulders of rock on either side of me, I was still about pinned, but at least I would sense his approach from almost any angle. I took cover and listened, taking split-second glances back at odd intervals.

After minutes of stillness, I heard something I didn't expect: the steady trot of a horse, far up the hill. The hoofbeats paused in what I reasoned was the clearing above the rocks, and its rider, I surmised, was Shelly Bray. I didn't move, or do any other thing that might get us both shot. Silently I willed her to move on. She didn't, or at least I heard nothing. After a moment I couldn't stand not knowing, and risked another look; there was no horse, no rider, nothing.

I took cover and called out. "Stiobhard?"

Nothing.

"Stiobhard, you there? Talk to me."

No answer. I looked out over the swamp, which was busy thawing in the sunlight and didn't care what we two men were doing with our guns. I needed to move. Crawling to peer out over the eastern side of the space, I put my knee down on a thorn that was a half an inch long. As I mouthed some cusses and pulled it out, I noticed yellowed and crinkled scraps everywhere below the briar patch, like tissue paper: rose petals that had fallen probably six months before. That's when I started to see the place. Brambles that tough should have taken over everything in sight by now, and there was a reason they hadn't; nearby was a rusted hand scythe, its blade half buried in the earth. Someone had been gardening. I holstered the .40. Staying low, I brushed aside the grass, still not sure what I was looking for. First, a chipped white vase with blue flowers glazed on it, tangled in the weeds but still standing, some brown stems protruding from its mouth. And just above it, a flat square of shale. I yanked vegetation away. There was no name, only a rough cross hand-chiseled into its surface. A gravestone.

I listened. If my friend was still there, and if he was capable of ending my life, he might. He might. If he was going to, it almost didn't matter what I did, except I didn't want to be sunk in a swamp. So I'd have to get out somehow. Starting on the western side, I took what low running start I could, threw myself over the eastern rock face, and flailed into the saplings beyond. Flush with the ground, I watched and waited. The sun climbed higher in the midday sky before I could convince myself I was safe. I stood. Far as I could tell, I was alone. As I shook my head and began to wonder if I hadn't always been, I heard the sound of footsteps to my left, and turned in time to see a split-second glimpse of a shadowy figure slip into the woods far above me. My vision phased in the sun, and I spent a moment bent over with my hands on my knees. Every bit of my heart wanted to continue the chase, but my head called it a draw.

At Holebrook Courthouse, Krista let me back into the sheriff's department. I found Dally at his desk with a lunch laid out before him. I told him what I'd found, and mentioned the figure I'd heard in the woods, but left out that he might have been a phantom from my struggling brain. He wasn't too pleased with my news.

"Christ," he said. "At least the grave's marked. Maybe there's a record of it in deaths and burials. Could be a dog, for all we know."

"Yeah, maybe. It didn't feel that way."

Dally looked pissed off, and then something dawned on him, something he tried to disguise. "You want to handle this one, Henry?"

"Uh, sure."

"Have Krista take you up to records, to deaths and burials. Maybe there's something up there that spares us digging it up. Maybe Aub will be so kind to tell us what that stone is doing there. Maybe we'll catch a break just this once."

"Wait, digging it up? Sheriff, this grave looked mighty old."

"That's why I'm sending you after a good explanation. If we can't get one, then what we have is an unrecorded grave not a mile distant from a murder victim, on land belonging to one of our only two persons of interest. In which case, we have good reason to request Detective Palmer's services again. Maybe another trooper or two."

Krista and I climbed the grand staircase to the courthouse's third floor, to an attic where paper records from the 1860s to the 1970s were stored. These had yet to be digitized, and probably never would be. The room had a high ceiling but few windows, and the few it had were small and circular, like a ship's portholes. Black filing cabinets lined the walls and made up several rows about five feet high. There was a pile of cardboard boxes in the corner, presumably to be filed one day. A dead bird lay in the shaft of light below a near window, mummified by the stale air.

"I wouldn't tell the clerk you were up here alone," Krista advised. "I'm saving you some trouble not putting in official requests. He'll keep you waiting weeks."

"I appreciate that. Any idea how this is organized?"

"Alphabetical, I guess. Horrible hunting." She retreated downstairs.

I found a cabinet marked D and pulled open a drawer.

It took a couple hours. But between several different cabinets and a box or two, I put together a serviceable record of the Holebrook Dunigans, including births, deaths, and marriages. Like most of us, they are buried in St. Paul's Cemetery on Route 153. Everybody was accounted for in Aub's immediate family. If there was a beginning, there was an end — except for Aubrey, of course. And he had never been married, or there was no official record of it. I put everything in rough chronological order in a manila file and headed out.

Kevin Dunigan's auto shop was on the way, and I stopped there first. Kevin put on a jacket and led me out of his waiting room and around back, to a trash-strewn lot bordered by a creek. He seemed uncomfortable as ever, and this was probably the most private spot he had at his place of business.

I told him about the grave site and asked him if he knew of any relatives buried on Aub's land, anyone at all. He looked alarmed at the question but told me no.

"Generations back they were wild people," he said. "Half wild anyway, and all to themselves. Not . . . not American, really. God knows what that place is."

"We may need to dig it up."

"For Christ's sake, Henry, can't you leave it alone? We're talking about something very old. Maybe we missed a relative somewhere. It was olden days, records weren't so good. Is it so wrong to just let it be?"

"I need to talk to Aub."

Kevin looked away. "You can't." I waited for him to elaborate. "Our lawyer has advised us against it. And we've got to take back our permission to search Aub's land."

I stifled a flash of irritation that got my head throbbing. "I have to say I disagree with that advice, Kevin. It'd make sense if Aub had done something wrong, but he hasn't, and we both know that. It only looks bad."

"Well —"

"Our warrant lasts a week. We don't need your permission. And even if we did, it's not your permission we'd need; it's Aub's. And in any case, I'm trying to save you some trouble, so just let me talk to him."

Kevin raised his voice. "I say how it is now. You've seen the shape he's in."

"Yeah, I have. You have power of attorney?

Has he signed anything? Has a judge? Has he had his evaluations yet?"

He snorted. "Aub signing something. He's a mule. He won't sign anything we put in front of him." Kevin shook his head impatiently.

"So. What've you put in front of him lately?"

Kevin looked away and breathed heavily through his nose. "You want to talk to him, fine. But you're not taking him from our home. Dally released him to our care. I'll call Carly and tell her you're coming."

"No need."

"Yes, there is."

I followed Kevin to the front lot. He gestured for me to remain outside. It took him longer than I expected, and when he returned, it was without his jacket. There were bright spots of color on his cheeks, and he smelled sharply of sweat. "It's what, four now? How about coming over at six? You'll be done by dinnertime."

"Kevin." I met his eyes. "How about now?"

"He's sleeping."

"I'm trying to help you out. To help Aub. If I have to, I'll park in your goddamn front yard and blow my horn."

Dunigan raised his head and squared his

shoulders. "He's not there."

Four or five cars passed on the nearby road before I could speak. "What?"

"He . . . ran off. We have him bunked in the basement — it's a nice basement, carpeted — and, you know, locked in for his own protection. We took precautions, but he must've found a tool or something. He's gone. He walked away."

"Jesus Christ." I fought through the fog in my mind. "You have guns in the home?"

"Of course, but —"

"Jesus Christ."

"Of course, but they're locked up in my gun safe. What happened to 'he didn't do anything wrong'?"

"You stay here in case someone sees him and calls. Tell Carly to stay home and wait."

Evening was already coming down. I placed a call to the sheriff's department and the answering machine picked up. I didn't want to be overheard on the radio, so I drove ahead.

At Kevin and Carly's house, Carly stood in her doorway in what I took as a defensive attitude. She didn't invite me in. I was curious to see how their house was kept, but didn't press it. At my request, she went off to check that the household's firearms were all accounted for; I still didn't believe Aub to be consciously, naturally violent, but I was still learning how much we didn't know.

There were small windows set into the ranch house's foundation. Somewhere in the basement a light was on, and I squatted to check the room out; it was well appointed and clean. A sheet and a hook blanket lay unmade on a sofa, and there was a small television, and a door that could have led to a half bathroom. But if he'd been locked down there all alone, wondering why he couldn't go home . . . I became aware of Carly Dunigan standing on her front stoop, watching me. I stood.

"They're all there," she said. "We didn't ask for this, you know."

"I know." I turned and walked toward my vehicle. "How much of a head start has he got?"

She shrugged. "A couple hours?"

As I scoured the nearby roadsides and knocked on neighbors' doors, I reviewed what I did know about Aub Dunigan. He was an old man, but one accustomed to using his two feet, and presumably to finding his own way around without a car. Fieldsparrow Road was miles away. But it was where he'd turn.

On a dirt road, I took a curve too fast in the gathering dark, and wound up face-to-face with a caravan of trucks hauling water tanks. We stood idling for a moment, then crawled past each other.

There was no sign of Aub on Fieldsparrow. As I broke the yellow tape and turned onto his property, my headlights caught the wine jugs in the tree line; in the driveway, the snow had melted, leaving only white footprints where our steps of the last couple days had compressed the snow. His house was dark. I parked in the yard and checked the corncrib, calling out to Aub as loudly as I could manage, hoping not to surprise him. He wasn't in the outhouse either. On the doorway leading into his kitchen, the police seal between the door and frame was no longer intact. I flipped open the holster on my hip. On the floor beyond my feet were a few small puddles of meltwater. Someone was here now, or had been not long ago. I stepped inside.

It says somewhere in the Bible that you shouldn't talk about the old days and how much better everything used to be, but I find I often do, because when I was a kid I could buy a car from a junkyard for a hundred dollars. And I did. But anybody looking around in Aub's home would be cured of that kind of nostalgia pretty quick; it was next to abandoned, and smelled like creosote and bat piss. In the kitchen stood a table with a plastic cloth on it, scattered with bags of cheap bread and tubs of butter the size of my head. The refrigerator was ancient and unplugged. A cast-iron stove was there to provide what heat there was, though the pile of firewood next to it looked too scant for the weather. Old shopping circulars and cracker boxes stuffed into an ash bucket, for starting fires. Nothing in the pantry, and somehow there were still mouse droppings. It just didn't smell like a house in there. It didn't smell like normal life. No matter where I looked, I couldn't see a sign of anyone other than Aub.

I took care not to touch anything. Kerosene lamps were screwed into the walls, their founts drained to slicks of yellow oil. Some bare lightbulbs in ceiling fixtures, some empty fixtures. His TV set was at least twenty years old, and might have worked had his electricity been connected. A rotary phone of black Bakelite hung on the wall. Using a handkerchief, I picked it up and checked for a dial tone. Nope.

I found the cellar door, opened the old-fashioned latch, and ducked in, twisting on my Maglite. The cellar had a dirt floor uneven enough to form mud puddles. I shone my light into one and dislodged a salamander about six inches long, black with yellow spots. It fled to the next puddle and stayed there.

The cellar wasn't tall enough to stand up straight in. Aub had old wooden doors stacked up, two rocking chairs with the caning blown out, a bunch of wine jugs, a roll of rotten pink insulation. The foundation was of blue shale stacked tight, much like the walls in the woods. As I cast my light about, the beam caught little glimmers in between the stones. I stepped closer and found more turquoise insulators, maybe two dozen. A few glass bottles of different colors here and there, real old, real small, all on the south-facing wall. Some of the pieces of turquoise glass that had been nestled into the foundation were now scattered on the floor, some of them broken. Police wouldn't have done it. On the floor I found a cigar box and opened the lid: one chain of cheap gold that had been pulled in half. I headed upstairs.

A set of narrow stairs led up to a corridor connecting three bedrooms, two empty, one containing a yellowed mattress, the smell of old man, and clothes scattered on the floor. Wallpaper had peeled away in every room, revealing crumbling plaster and rough beams coated black. Everywhere you went you could hear the snowmelt dripping off the eaves.

The upstairs hall was shadowy and the dark green wallpaper further darkened the space. Above where the kerosene lamps were fixed to the walls, soot stains had spread on the ceilings, black toward the middle, yellow at the edges. Before stepping into Aub's room I took a mental picture of where everything was so I could leave it that way. As I sifted through the crumpled plaid shirts, work pants, and long johns with one hand, keeping the other hand over my nose and mouth, really what I was looking for was anything new; new would be out of place. Nothing under the mattress. Again I was struck by the lack of anything to read.

The other bedrooms were bare down to the shelf paper in the closets. Given Aub's presumed age and the traces of brogue in his speech, I figured he was second generation. I had to imagine that the further back in generations you went to the first folks off the boat, the closer you kept your valuables, not in a safe-deposit box and certainly not out in the open. I looked down at the floorboards squeaking gently beneath my feet, and remembered seeing an iron grate in the top stair, where it made no sense to have one. I shone my flashlight in, stuck the blade of my jackknife between the metal and wood, and the grate popped free. That opened a compartment in the stair, and in that compartment, a crumbling cowhide portfolio.

Carefully I unwound the ribbon that held it closed, and slipped out a folded document. Printed in that old-timey way of all different letterings and sizes, it was a certificate of U.S. citizenship for William Dunigan dated 1858; he'd signed it in tall right-leaning loops. That had to have been Aub's grandfather.

There were also photographs. I sat on the landing and examined them by flashlight. The first was a hazy portrait of a narrow-eyed patriarch and straight-backed matriarch, surrounded by offspring ranging from infancy to teenaged. The men and boys out of short pants wore high collars and frock coats; the women and girls were held in place by their dark, buttoned-up dresses. In one of the girls' laps was a baby swimming in a white gown — impossible to tell whether boy or girl.

Next was a somewhat less stern photograph of a couple on their wedding day. A note on the reverse named William Dunigan, Jr., and Jennifer, 1896. I assumed these were Aub's parents. They were each more striking than handsome, in that way that reminded you how different everyone looked back then.

From that I was able to follow William, Jr., and Jennifer into a later photograph surrounded by six children, and I wondered which kid was Aub. Probably the youngest.

The last of the bunch was a studio portrait of a young woman with dark hair, holding a bouquet of lilacs — a glamour shot that approached our modern age in a way that the others didn't, even as it was unmistakably from another era. Something about her eyes — it was in black-and-white, so no telling whether they were blue or green — caught the light, and caught you. They were so pale and alive that they kind of spoke to you across time. I found no name anywhere, and no resemblance to anyone in the other pictures. I put them back where I'd found them and knocked the grate into place.

Downstairs I reattached the broken door seal as best I could, and drove to a high point a couple miles away where I sometimes got cell reception. I dialed my station's answering service number to see if I had any messages; there were several hang-ups of increasing length. Tim Ellis left a message saying he'd arranged a small service for George the weekend after next. George was going to have his ashes poured into the Susquehanna River. In conclusion, Tim said, "So . . . two weeks." This both simplified some things for me and made me downcast; as township police, we didn't have anything like dress uniforms to get buried in. Still, I would have liked to see George all cleaned and pressed in a coffin. I admit making his face look good would have been tough, but still — it would have been nice to know his work meant more.

I also got a message from Robert Loinsigh, husband to Mary, whom I had fined for snooping around the crime scene. He requested an appointment with me, and I thumped my hand on the dashboard.

The final message, after one more hang-up, was from a man's voice rasped by cigarettes. There was bar noise in the background. "Henry," the man said. "This is Peter Spivey down at the Loyal Sons. You missing anybody been in the news lately? I'll keep him here as long as I can." The Loyal Sons of Hibernia was a half-legal bar of long standing outside of Midhollow. I say half legal because since their inception they had made a practice of skirting the liquor board, claiming they were a private club dedicated to the furtherance of Irish-Americans, and that one had to be a member to enter. The implication was that you also had to be of Irish extraction to get in, but they sold membership cards at the door, to almost anyone, at different levels of monetary commitment. You kept the card in front of you on the bar until your commitment was gone, and then you went and got another. Sometimes, when the county needed money, the sheriff would set up a sobriety checkpoint nearby and always get a couple hundred bucks out of the guys leaving that place drunk. It wasn't anybody's first choice of bars except a dedicated few. George had passed time there on occasion, and I'd met the usual bartender, Spivey, at a cookout the year before.

It took about twenty minutes to get there; the workday was just over for most people and the route was busy, plus it was happy hour, and the curse of the patrol truck is to follow drivers white-knuckling it at the exact speed limit. In a gully, surrounded by pines, the Loyal Sons' outdoor light cast the green-painted cinder-block building in a dirty glow. The exterior paint was flaking away, exposing white primer beneath. There were three cars and two motorcycles in the lot. A hand-lettered wooden sign hung above the front door, and the club's one window displayed a neon sign in the shape of a shamrock.

I pulled open the metal door. Near the entrance, a fat man on a barstool waved me inside. Smoke hung in the air. A laugh track erupted from a mounted television behind the bar, which was playing a syndicated sit-com. Whether my arrival discouraged conversation, or there hadn't been any before, I couldn't tell. Two bikers hunched over shots-and-beers at the bar, and a middle-aged man in muddy work clothes winged darts at a board from his barstool across the narrow room, a cigarette clamped in his lips. When the TV quieted I heard an indistinct muttering coming from the end of the bar, where Aub Dunigan sat, a small mound of coins in front of him.

Spivey stepped out from behind the bar and pulled me aside. He was bald on top, with a copper beard and a nose full of veins. "Sorry, Henry," he said. "He looked like just another old-timer to me. Doesn't talk much. Certainly didn't grasp the membership concept here. Justin recognized him." He indicated the man at the entrance. "I might have served him a few before we caught on."

"It's okay; I appreciate you calling." I moved as if to go past him to the bar.

"Crazy, what you boys found out there.

Hey, you got a line on whatever son of a bitch did George Ellis? I can't even believe it. Here in this county."

"We're taking care of it."

"Let me know if we can be any help."

I sidled up to Aub and took a seat on the barstool two away. I watched as he counted his silver, then lost count and began again, quietly warbling all the while, not making words or tunes.

"Aubrey," I said to him, gently. "Are you sure this is where you want to be?" He looked at me and I caught a glimmer of recognition before he turned away. "Come on," I said. "You got your cousins worried." I stood and placed a hand on his shoulder.

"Ah. I was just starting to have a good time." He shook me off.

"Let's go. It's about dinnertime; you're expected at Carly's."

The old man made a face. "I won't go back there. You taking me home?"

"Afraid I can't take you home. But you can't stay here."

"I won't go back."

I looked at Spivey, who shrugged. "All right," I said. "I'm going to go home and get something to eat. You want to come with me?"

He appeared to think for a moment, then

gathered his pile of change with shaking hands and put half in each hip pocket. He stumbled getting off his stool, and Spivey caught him, saying, "Whoa, who moved the floor?"

Outside, Aub balked at getting in my truck, but agreed when I held the front passenger door open for him. I told him twice to put on his seat belt before giving up. We set off. Though it was a small county, Midhollow was not within walking distance of Fitzmorris. I asked him how he managed to get from Kevin and Carly's house all the way there.

"Fellow stopped and picked me on up." He hummed aimlessly, his hands on his knees.

"You must be tired," I said. "I'm tired."

He didn't speak the rest of the way. Back home, I led the old man to an easy chair in the living room, then pulled a container of venison barley soup from my freezer. I zapped it for a few seconds until the frozen block of soup could slide out of the Tupperware, and then I put it in a pot over low heat. I called to the other room. "I'm going to make coffee, you want some?"

"Got a drink?"

Ignoring that for the moment, I put some English muffins in the toaster oven and joined Aub in the living room. We sat in silence, each looking at the other and away. Then he gestured to the shelf near my head. "Bring the fiddle on down."

"Man, you don't want to hear that noise."

"Bring it on down. Haven't heard fiddle in many year."

I figured okay. I was in G and I gave him a quick "Shove That Pig's Foot Further in the Fire." He nodded matter-of-factly when I was done. When I started to put the instrument away, he objected, so I tuned up quick and gave him "Red Haired Boy" in A. He smiled and called out something that sounded like "Beggar Boy." Staying in that jaunty, half-Celtic-sounding vein, I moved into "Billy in the Lowground," and his foot began to tap. Soon I had to put the fiddle aside and check on our dinner.

From the kitchen, I listened with mounting alarm as Aub wangled my fiddle into some offshoot of A with the bottom two strings skewed down. But then he began to play, slowly and in mixolydian. If you don't know mixolydian, then maybe you've heard a tune that seemed to move between major and minor without settling on either one, a tune that maybe made your hair stand up. That could have been in the mixolydian mode. Aub had the fiddle tucked low into his abdomen, and at first I thought it had to be "Hail on the Barn Door" or "Squirrel Hunters," basically the same tune with different emphases. But coming to the end of the B part, he tumbled down into a lower, much darker figure than I'd expected. It was a melody I felt I'd always known, though I hadn't heard it whole before. He finished the tune and I asked him what his name for it was.

" 'The Still Hunter,' " says Aub.

" 'The Still Hunter.' Huh. Any words to it?"

"Don't recall. You got a drink?"

"Come on," I said. "Let's eat something."

We sat at the table and I let him finish his soup in peace. Since he didn't have all his teeth, I figured he'd appreciate eating something soft. He spackled his English muffin with butter and then dropped it whole in his soup bowl to soak. He ate efficiently, looking around every now and again.

I stood and pulled my bottle of scotch down, poured a small glass for my guest and one for myself. "Been a long day," I said. We drank in small sips. Aub, probably used to sweeter spirits, coughed a bit. He finished quickly, and pushed his glass toward me across the table, in a clear request for more.

I obliged. "That's all, though," I said. "We got to get you back to your cousins'."

"Ah. Take me home. I don't want to go down there."

"I would. Except we don't like the idea of you up on that farm all by yourself."

"But I ain't."

"Ain't what?"

"Helen been coming on up the ridge sometime."

"Helen."

"Seen her hanging frocks down by the water." Aub brought the glass shaking to his lips. "She leaves me jug wine."

"Helen. You talk to her? Talk to Helen?"

He nodded. A long moment passed, and he spoke. "I see her voice, like lightning in the sky. I try to keep her. She goes where she will."

I couldn't follow. "Aubrey, where does Helen live?"

This seemed to confound him. He didn't answer. He drank.

"I was up on your land today," I said. "On the southeast corner, there's a wild rosebush. You know it?" This seemed to bring him back, but then he turned away from me, like a child. I pressed him. "There's a rosebush and a headstone."

"Never mind about it," he said. He refused

to meet my eyes.

"You've got to tell me, Aub. Something so we don't have to go back there. Otherwise we're going to have to go see for ourselves. To dig."

The old man's eyes widened. He stared into his glass a moment, then swept it off the table and raised his voice. "Never mind, that's all! Never mind! Let her rest!"

"Who, Aub?"

"My love," he said, and began to cry. He heaved awhile, eyes and nose dripping. I asked him questions that he didn't answer. He had wrapped himself in some ancient grief, and was gone.

The ride to Kevin and Carly's was dark and silent, with the old man's gaze fixed in blackness. I had time to think. But I was stuck. The thought that kept my mind spinning was, the water had risen. Over so many years, the swamp had crept up the bank, likely not noticeably at first. But steadily. And then one day Aubrey Dunigan, dressed in his finest shabby clothes, would have paced through the woods to tend this hidden grave. He would have moved carefully down the trail he'd worn into the slope, past the rocks where they rose out of the earth, and he'd have found that the path to that grave had been drowned. I thought about the very first time he would have put a foot in that cold blue-brown water to get to the love he had buried there. Had he taken off his boots and socks, and rolled up his trousers like a boy? How long before he found the secret way through the stone, and crawled like an animal?

I shook my head to clear it.

Getting from my truck to his relatives' front door, Aub wanted none of me, and neither did Carly, who thanked me perfunctorily, but fumed when I suggested that a man who isn't locked up in a basement has less of a reason to escape. "We're putting this behind us," she said. "First step is getting him tested in Scranton. Doing it tomorrow. You can rest easy, Officer, Aub won't be in our care for long." The door shut, not exactly in my face, but nearly, and I was content knowing that at least Aub didn't die in a ditch. Though I wished he'd been able to tell me more. We'd have to dig. I idled in the driveway long enough to leave a message with the sheriff's department.

I pulled away and drove into the gathering night. Yes, I wished I'd been able to get an answer. Then again, I know what it's like to lose a person you love, and I don't often want to talk about it either. Almost as bad is when you lose a place you love, which I expect was much on Aub's mind. I knew about that too.

So. Before I got hired to police Wild Thyme Township, Pennsylvania, I served Big Piney, Wyoming. Small town, Big Piney. Pinedale was the biggest nearby town, a town I'd grown to love for its associations of romance and freedom, and just everything. Much like Wild Thyme, nothing too much happened out in Big Piney. Domestics, burglaries, and drugs.

Polly and I had bought a little house on the outskirts. It was a one-story cabin-style home you often see out West, newish and not beautiful, but meant to sit in the landscape as though it had always been there. We couldn't afford much in the way of land, but open space meant a lot to both of us. The place we found had five acres of grass and sage, a stand of aspen, and part of an irrigation ditch, complete with a winch-operated gate and water rights. The house was on a wide rolling plain with just a few other homes in view. We could afford it if we both worked, and the first time the wind came over the grass, well. We thought we'd hit the jackpot. Best of all, it had a partial view of the Winds, the kind of view you could fit in your scope: neat, chiseled gray. Perfect. We bought it.

Never mind that over the rise where we couldn't see was a natural gas wellhead. The drilling had long been completed and the frack pool filled in, but there remained a white storage tank like a wedding cake as big as Jesus, and a compressor station that sounded as bad as an airport some nights. It was what we could afford and, we reasoned, someone had built there and lived there, so we could too.

Poll and I would often hike in the Winds. She loved those mountains. Me, I liked when you reached the summit with a view spread out, and you couldn't help feeling something pulling you farther in, to the next peak and the next. I sought that the way I enjoyed working up an appetite before a big dinner. What Polly liked was the in-between, driving or walking in the foothills where you felt cradled in the folds of land with sage and lodgepoles and aspen, all that green and washed-out red and yellow rising into the sky. She often said the in-betweens didn't get enough credit compared with the peaks. It was on such a hike that Poll collapsed sideways against a fallen tree, her face gray, her lungs heaving but never seeming to pull enough in, and we noticed she had a problem.

This was around the time that the Mexican cartels were beginning their push east, taking over the methamphetamine business in rural areas. Yeah, Mexican cartels. They're out there, and they're not the kind to leave revenue streams untapped. And they're still coming east, by the way, so Holebrook County get ready. Back then, in Big Piney, I was pulled into a coordinated effort with the DEA and attached to the Sublette County Sheriff's Department. But I came to find out that it was just to do the usual shit that they no longer had time for — patrolling, speed traps, issuing summonses, and the like — now that they were part of this task force. I remember it as a frustrating time: too many hours, too many night shifts, boring work, but enough money to keep ahead of the mortgage.

Poll and I began to argue about the place. In the daylight hours, when she spent the most time out-of-doors, she would complain of splitting headaches. In bed she'd dry-cough all night, cursing the compression station. I'd urge her to go to the clinic, which she did many times, with no answers or positive results. Once, she got lesions from her hands all up her arms — open sores the size of nickels that overstayed their welcome by a week and then disappeared as mysteriously as they'd come on. I suggested it might have been an allergic reaction to something she'd touched in the wild, poison oak maybe.

You see, I felt loyal to the cabin; we'd made a commitment to it and it felt like the home I'd dreamt of since back when I was sweating my balls off in the 10th. And while I was unsettled by my wife's ailments, to me, that's all they were, a series of separate symptoms with no pattern. Secretly, I'd wish she would handle them a little more stoically. The doctors were turning up nothing, and the temptation was, in my most secret thoughts, to feel Poll was being overdramatic. Because she was unhappy about me, or something else. This is hard to talk about.

Night had fallen, drawing me into the Heights. There were long threads to tug on up there, and some of them were bound to lead to George. Tracy Dufaigh's disappearance made me uneasy, and Jennie Lyn's suggestion of a killer close to George had me wondering. I meant to find them, one or both. The gauntlet of staties guarding Old Account Road had long since been sent home, and I jounced my way into the ink-black forest with no interference.

Number 1585 Upper Sloat was tucked back from the road in a little depression in the thick of the woods. The lawn was neatly landscaped, almost finicky, with a long line of carefully placed stones marking the border of the forest and a small statue of the Virgin Mary looking over a decorative pool. On one side of the house was a prefab shed and a garden patch enclosed by chicken wire. How anyone managed to grow anything in the shadow of those trees was a mystery. Nothing about the tidy little home suggested the presence of a party girl like Tracy. There were a couple lights burning on the first and second floors. I stepped up to the front door. Hung on the frame was a knocker in the shape of a woodpecker perched on a tree trunk; you pulled a leather cord and its beak knocked on the piece of wood. I tried it but got no answer. I rapped on the storm door and a dog bellowed once, and was silenced.

It was not Tracy Dufaigh who answered, but a large man with white hair. He wore an undershirt that showed off faded tattoos on both arms. One of them looked like the insignia to a fire company. His index finger was tucked in the middle of a paperback novel. He tilted his head back and peered at me through half-glasses on the end of his nose.

"Evening," I said. "Looks like I may have the wrong house. My name's Henry Farrell. Looking for Tracy Dufaigh."

"Good luck with that. Francis Dufaigh," he said, indicating himself. "Tracy's father."

"Pleased to meet you, Francis. And sorry about the hour —"

"What's she done?" He spoke softly, with a hint of something fierce.

"Nothing," I said. "I just have some news. I'd like to check in."

"She's not at home."

"Any idea where she might be?"

"Listen, my wife's already in bed."

"I'm sorry about the hour. I'd love some help reaching her. If you have any idea —"

"You said she's not in trouble?"

I shook my head no and opened my hands. The man sighed and I caught coffee breath. He checked behind him, in the direction of the staircase. "Come on in." He led me through a living room decorated with framed needlepoint sentiments and hook rugs in brown and orange. The stereo's dial glowed green and a country record spun on the turntable, its volume low, the Nashville Strings weeping. We passed into a small kitchen where a dishwasher rumbled, and a mastiff lolled on a plaid dog bed, its head on its front paws. The kitchen smelled like dog. Francis pulled out a chair for me at the table and took the one opposite.

I opened my mouth but Francis stopped me with an admonishing finger. His voice was quiet, almost a whisper. "My wife," he said. "Upstairs. Can we keep it down? She doesn't want to hear it."

I nodded. "Tracy's not in any trouble," I repeated.

"Listen, she showed up a few weeks back to collect her boots and clothes, a couple other things. She's gone."

"Any idea where to?"

"I'm telling you I don't know. Ain't seen her. Don't know if she's alive or dead."

"She was alive and well as of yesterday."

"Oh? How'd she seem?"

"Fine."

"Fine. You know more than I do."

"Look, Francis, with respect, I wonder why you asked me in, if you have nothing more to say than that. Whatever it is —"

A flash of exasperation crossed Francis's face. " 'She's not in trouble.' Sure. What do you know? She's out with these hillbillies, taking crystal and . . . carrying on. Her mother and I tried. Whatever's keeping her out is stronger than we are. She's been a grown woman for some time, but she ain't a grown-up yet. And you. What do we pay taxes for, the kind of hogshit going on up here?"

I ignored that. "Any particular friends that you know of?"

"Yeah," he said heavily. "Fellow named Pat McBride is the latest. You know of him? In your professional life, maybe?"

"Yeah." McBride was the guy we had a warrant out on, whose lab had been in the way of the SERT team and the sheriff. The connection was unexpected. "Somewhere out on Westmeath Road, right?"

Francis looked at his broad, lumpy hands on the table. He showed them to me. "In another life," he said, closing his hands into fists. "Hey. Maybe the last thing I'll ever do in this one . . ."

"Let's not get carried away," I said, knowing I couldn't rush off at that moment, but feeling a terrible urge to get moving. I looked at the aging man across from me. "It's not for me to say, but . . . I don't know, Francis, it seems like Tracy had a good upbringing."

He nodded. "Yeah. Well, it wasn't always the palace you see here. And I, I spent some time away from the family. When Tracy was growing up. Several years."

"Everyone can have a new life," I said, even as I made a note to look up Francis Dufaigh's record. Everyone has something they don't tell, and his sounded like a big one. "Everyone has the right to start over."

"I hope that's true. For her, I mean."

I hoped so too. But I said it more to be kind than because I believed it. We stood and Dufaigh showed me out; I bade him good night at his front step. He closed the screen door gently and disappeared back into his home, just as an older woman in a nightgown appeared on the stairs inside.

I stopped above the power-line cut where I'd been the night before, and picked my way down to the spot where Jennie Lyn Stiobhard's upturned ATV would have been. It was gone.

I drove to Westmeath Road. The sheriff had described McBride's trailer as "derelict." I wondered if there was a special word for a trailer that a fallen oak tree has crumpled at the midsection, because that's exactly what had happened to this one. Standing in the yard, with the bare treetop reaching out to me like a drunk lying in the gutter, I tried to imagine what kind of life made this place a home. I walked all the way around the clearing, through some swampy woods full of beer cans, garbage bags, and junk too bulky to fit into garbage bags. There was newly charred wood in the fire pit out back. The smell of it was not enough to mask the cat-piss odor of a lab.

When I stepped under the yellow police tape and got next to the single-wide, I found that the tree formed a natural border between what had been the meth lab — until SERT and Dally had busted and collected it — and a tiny crash pad. McBride had duct-taped blue tarps over the wound in the structure, effectively sealing one side from the other. On the back end of the trailer a garden hose snaked from a kitchen window to one on the lab side.

I yanked open a door that barely fit in its misshapen frame. Flipping on a light switch, I found that the electricity was still hooked up. The living side of the trailer was about what I expected. Its denizens had not been big recyclers, and empty tallboys of cheap light and ice beer littered the kitchen, along with dead soldiers of schnapps. There was a couch heaped with stained sleeping bags. In the bathroom, orange mold crept up the shower walls and stained the sink. At the far end was the bedroom; the bed had been removed, presumably to make room for more people to crash out. Blankets were heaped along the walls and the room smelled strongly of cigarettes. I opened the door to a built-out closet. In a set of coveralls hanging from a hook on the door, a life-like rubber dildo protruded from the fly — probably a nasty little jolt for the SERT team who first searched the place. Atop a pile of dirty men's laundry, I found a woman's bag with toiletries and clothing inside. The clothing was on the larger end, about Tracy's size. There were several pairs of women's boots and shoes on the floor. I remembered Tracy Dufaigh tending to horses in her canvas sneakers. In a paper sack, there were several pornographic DVDs and a glass marijuana pipe.

If Tracy had wanted, she could have returned for her things almost anytime. We didn't have the manpower to watch the place day and night. She hadn't, and I figured McBride had holed up somewhere and taken her along. Nobody was home, and nobody would return while I was around.

My car passed cobbled-together homesteads. Dogs leapt from their houses and bounced short at the ends of their chains. Groups of people on porches and in yards paused their conversations to follow my progress, cigarette tips glowing. As I rolled by a larger gathering of men in full camo, a crushed can pinged off the side of my truck.

Westmeath Road was sparsely populated. I passed a burned-out farmhouse whose one remaining barn had gone so far diagonal it looked like a dog on point. Around the bend I could see where I was going, in the glow of a bonfire reflected against silver trees. I pulled to the side of the road and turned off my headlights. Some dangerous people were up ahead, folks I called the People of the Bus. In daylight, the turquoise school bus looked like a relic of some 1960s adventure. Why else, you might ask, would anyone have painted it that strange color, if not to roam the country in psychedelic regalia? In fact, the bus was at one point the hunter-green of Midhollow High School, had been bought for a song, and simply faded where it stood, disused among more conventional automobiles, also long abandoned. A metal chimney protruded from the roof, leading down to an old woodstove. In what might be termed the front yard, an iron hand pump marked the location of a water well.

I don't know exactly who first made a domicile of the place, presumably a son or nephew of the absent landowner. Over the years someone or perhaps several different people had taken out the seats and installed bunks, hanging old sheets over the windows. I'd seen Jennie Lyn, or her car, a number of times when I passed by in my own pickup — not the township police truck — on my own time. A lot of observation I do has to be that way. I rolled down my window and listened. Men's voices clamored over each other, rough-sounding and half frantic. I couldn't make out any words. I sat and took deep breaths.

With methamphetamine you can't assume that any of the usual rules are in place. Everyone knows it destroys the people who take it, but it also has destroyed plenty who don't. It's not a peaceable drug. Best not to go startling it, I reasoned, especially so outnumbered. I rolled up my window, flipped on my headlights, and began a slow roll around the bend.

They'd stoked the bonfire to about six feet high, and the flame danced off the glass in the windows of the bus and what was left of the other cars, made cavern walls of the surrounding trees, against which the shadows of the men in the yard were black cave paintings that came alive. The shadows went still as my vehicle came into view. Nobody ran. Some remained standing where they were, and two or three lounged in bus seats around the fire. At the edges of the clearing, a thicket of spirea and crabapple separated open space from forest; it had grown in and around a fleet of dead cars and appliances. A few ATVs and rusted pickups looked to be the only working vehicles there. One of the trucks had its doors open and was blasting metal from maxed-out speakers. I unzipped my jacket and stepped out of the truck.

Standing too quickly caused blood to race from my head. As my vision corkscrewed shut, I focused on the one thing that remained, the bonfire, flickering alone in the black. Something approached, loud and primordial, in a different register from the violent music. Unseeing, I tucked the open jacket back to expose not only the .40 on my hip, but the one holstered under my arm.

My vision cleared enough to reveal one of the men moving in my direction. He didn't stop until his face was about six inches from mine. It was a face lined and hollowed, old before its time but still patched with a young man's beard. His eyes vibrated in place. It was Kyle Leahey, my old friend from the county drunk tank. I swallowed the affront of his closeness and aggression, and stepped to the side. He stepped with me. I was thinking about where and how to hit him when a man called out from the fireside.

"You're a little far afield, ain't you, Officer?" As Kyle turned his head at the voice behind him, I stepped past and approached the fire. He snorted in anger and I heard him coming up behind me. I flipped open my holster, but with a glance and a sharp whistle, the man lounging by the bonfire kept Kyle at bay. "Have a seat," he told me. I remained standing, and followed my would-be attacker across the yard with a look.

"Making my rounds," I said. I picked out two women among the men, one skinny with a grown-out dye job, the other plump and blond, neither of them Jennie Lyn nor Tracy. Everyone seemed to defer to the man I was talking to, so I kept my attention on him. "You having a good time tonight?"

"Was."

"Do I know you from somewhere?"

The man smiled. The creases in his face stood out black, and I could hardly tell his teeth from his gums. In my mind, I saw him slide his knife back into his boot and disappear into the woods by the Stiobhard place. An ATV rider from the night before. "You know you do. And I know you. We been having all kinds of company this evening."

He turned his head in the direction of the bus. He lowered his voice. "You might find someone you're looking for. Then you can continue your 'rounds.' "

I searched the man's face for malice, and found amusement, the kind I've seen turn dark in an instant. I stepped to the door, turning several times to watch my back as I did. At the main entrance — a bolted-on storm door, not the original sliding thing — I drew my .40 from the shoulder holster, concealing it from the yard with my body.

I pulled open the door. There was a sharp bang from deep within the bus. I spun out of the doorway and flattened myself against the side of the vehicle, scanning the crowd and readying myself for a dive under the front bumper. It didn't sound or feel like a gunshot, but there are all kinds. The man by the fire shrugged theatrically. There was another bang, and one of the bus's rearward emergency windows fell to the ground. A person slipped out and hit the ground running. I took off after him. He was headed for the road, and he was fast and wild as a rabbit. Like a rabbit, he chose a path through the thicket, but like a man, this slowed him down. I took a line through an

263

unobstructed part of the yard and reached the road about the same time as I expected the runner to. He wasn't anywhere. Trotting down to where his exit point would have been, and beyond, I scanned the road on both sides and worked my way back in the direction of the yard.

In the darkness, I moved into the brush. There was no hope of taking anyone by surprise. I attempted reason. "This is Officer Farrell. Come out with your hands where I can see. If you don't, when I find you, I swear to Christ, I'll break a finger for every minute you make me wait." I didn't mean it and it didn't work.

I was at a disadvantage. He could hear me and probably see me, but not vice versa. If he moved I'd be able to pin him down. The junkyard pulsed up and down in time with the throbbing in my head.

Stepping and pausing to listen, I made an arc to where I had seen the runner go in, and found his track of broken, brittle stalks, which led straight to a sedan that was so sunken in the cover that I hadn't seen it from the other side. Taking three deep breaths, I rushed in, leading with my .40 through the glassless passenger window. My man was crouched inside. He scrambled for an exit through the open windshield, calling out, "I'm unarmed, I'm unarmed!" I opened the door and caught him by the ankle. Holstering my .40, I got my other hand around his leg and dragged. He kicked with his other leg, getting me a few good ones in the ribs until I could trap the loose foot between my body and my arm. I pulled. He whanged his face on the dashboard and got a hold on the steering column until I shoved him face-first into it, then hauled on his legs again. He yelped as some part of him caught on an exposed spring in the passenger seat, and then he was out on the ground, heaving on his hands and knees. In a moment of anger I slammed the car door on his ribs, then pressed my .40 into the base of his skull. Snapping a cuff on one wrist, I yanked it around to the other, flattening the runner on his front. Once he was secured, I shone a light in his face.

"Hello again, Officer," said Vernon Yeager, wild-eyed and wincing. He wore a too-large camouflage jacket, and his neck was gashed from collarbone to chin. The slightly built Okie mechanic lowered his voice to a whisper. "Get me out of here. I can help you. I know where he is."

I stood there stupidly, wondering who "he" was, not feeling very well and needing to be still.

Yeager spoke again, this time more urgently. "You all right? Drag me out. Hit me if you have to. Just get me out of here." I made to put away my weapon, and he hissed. "Keep that piece handy."

There was movement in the brambles a few meters to the right, and Yeager fell silent. I took his advice and moved. When we got to the edge of the brush, I shoved him, hard, so that he popped out of the waist-high cover like a lemon seed and fell on his face. The onlookers by the fire cheered derisively. I pulled him to his feet. He sold the bit, repeating, "No no no," frantically as I half walked, half dragged him to my vehicle. He resisted all the way, like a child.

Kyle Leahey waited with an elbow on my hood. I showed him the gun in my hand; he looked at it as if it was a toad I'd caught. What got him to move was Yeager lurching forward and puking at his feet, as if on cue. Before I was able to shut Yeager into the cage, the man by the fire had joined us.

"Vernon," he said. "Remember what we discussed, now."

Yeager nodded and I shut him in.

"Listen," I said quietly, turning to the thin man. "If Jennie Lyn shows —"

Running a hand through his long hair, he

said, "See you, Henry." He stooped to pick up a piece of deadfall to drag back to the fire, but never turned his back to me until I was on my way.

On a clear hilltop beyond the Heights, I uncuffed Yeager, sat him on my front bumper, and dressed his cuts in the headlights. He sucked in a breath at the peroxide I poured down his neck. Other than the beads of sweat on his face and some slight tremors, he was hanging in there. Hanging in, but suffering for want of a fix. I taped a gauze pad over his neck. He picked at it.

"Am I under arrest?"

"I don't know yet."

He felt in his back pocket. "They have my wallet somehow."

I pulled on the collar of his camouflage jacket. "Looks like you got something of theirs too."

"Cold up north. Got a smoke?" He hunched over, his hands squeezed between his thighs, and his eyes began to close.

I lifted his chin and smacked him with an open hand. "Talk."

He shook the surprise off and began. When he had finished, I got on the horn to the sheriff's department.

■ ■ ■ ■

Not twenty minutes later, Yeager was back safe and sound in my vehicle's enclosure, cuffed and hidden in the foot space between the seat and the grille. We were near the New York border, parked in the trees, in a patch of skunk cabbage at the side of a mud track leading down to January Creek. Patrolman Hanluain's car had beaten me there, and I had pulled in behind him. The stocky policeman and I stood on the track, listening to the occasional car swoosh by on 37; the temperature had dropped enough that ice was forming in a sugar-thin crust over the ground. Soon it would be thick enough to announce our presence as we approached. We had Dally's blessing to go ahead, and it would only get tougher the longer we waited.

Three hundred yards down the track, a pop-up camper stood on a bank overlooking where January Creek got big. It was an angling spot of some renown, one of those local secrets everybody knows, which is probably why Father and Mag and I had tended to avoid it, preferring to catch our fish deeper in. The camper had been there, in and out of use, for over fifteen years. It belonged to nobody and everybody. Adjacent, the shape of an automobile glinted in the starlight that reached the clearing.

Our breath puffed out white against the dark woods.

"Guy didn't get too far, did he?" said Hanluain, taking a last look at the photo he'd brought with him, then showing it to me.

"Let's get going."

We walked slowly and softly down to the edge of the trees, sidearms out, making no sound and keeping covered anything reflective on our uniforms. The closer we got, the more the creek's rushing helped to muffle our steps. We stopped facing the rear of the camper. I checked out the windows with my field glasses: no light, no movement. The automobile we'd seen was a compact, and I was impressed it had made the journey down that muddy road. We were just about to circle around and meet at the front when a door creaked; stopped; creaked again and clicked shut. A bundled-up figure crept toward the car, glancing back at the camper. An arm swung out, and something heavy splashed into the deepest part of the creek. I tried to mark the spot, but it was dark, the creek was fast, and I feared whatever it was, was lost.

I gestured for Hanluain to get in position and ran for the car as quietly as possible, down low, badge in one hand and gun in the other. I was noticed, and the person took off for the car, not ten feet away. A hand rose toward the door handle, and I crossed the distance just in time to clutch it in mine. There was surprising strength there. I looked down into the broad, harried face of Tracy Dufaigh, held a finger to my lips, warned her with my eyes. In a long moment, her shoulders slumped and she looked toward the camper once, then back at me. "He's in there," she whispered.

"Armed?"

"He's got a buck knife but ain't fit to use it. You better cuff me. I want him to see that I'm cuffed too, if he's going to see me at all." She shook her head, and said, to herself, "Best this way." She began to shake, and I wasn't sure it was from the cold.

I got her fixed in restraints and pointed to a flat stone on the lee side of her car. "Stay down until we give the all-clear, okay?"

"Henry, he's —"

"Just do it, please." I turned away, then back. "Where were you headed?" I asked.

Dufaigh looked up at me. "I don't know. Not home. Maybe the Brays, sleep in the stables? Cold as shit out here. I'm tired of it. I was going to call it, call it in." Her right leg was working an imaginary sewing machine at a furious pace, but her tone was falsely light, as if it were completely normal to be in handcuffs, taking cover behind a car in the cold and dark.

"Call what in?"

She shrugged.

I pressed her. "What'd you throw in the creek?"

"Trash," she said.

I shook my head and took a deep breath. "So you're what, just along for the ride here? We've got some talking to do. Stay down."

"Don't worry about me, Officer," she said. "I'll be good."

Hanluain kicked the camper's door half off its hinges and we rushed in, shouting the usual, but the resistance we'd expected wasn't there. Pat McBride was out, curled in a sleeping bag up to his eyes. The air smelled faintly rotten. I placed a hand on the unconscious man's chest and pulled the sleeping bag's zipper down, while Hanluain patted his body for guns and sharps, finding none. We each picked up a long end of the sleeping bag, using it as a kind of litter, and, once outside, set him on the hard ground of the bank. There was a steady flow of clear mucus from his nose. His breathing and his pulse were regular.

"Jesus, what happened to him?" said Hanluain, as McBride opened his eyes quartermast, seeing nothing.

The patrolman headed back into the camper as I rolled McBride on his side to put his cuffs on. He'd shat his pants. A watery shit. I did myself a favor and pulled a pair of latex gloves from a coat pocket, and called to Hanluain to do the same. "Ahead of you," he said.

I heard movement from behind and turned to watch Tracy push herself standing against the car. She surveyed McBride lying with his face slack against the river stones. "All clear?" she said.

"What'd he take?"

"He got mixed up, didn't cut it right. He ain't OD'd, though?"

"Go back over to the car and sit on the hood and don't move."

In the camper we found chocolate bars, two empty bottles of crème de menthe, potato chip bags, and singles of American cheese. Also a large stash of what we were pretty sure was methamphetamine, wrapped in a gallon bag and stuffed in a vent. In with the crystalline powder was a smaller bag of finer white stuff; given McBride's condition, we had to assume it was heroin. The aforementioned buck knife was lying out on a counter. Hanluain took a number of interior photographs with a disposable camera, opened every drawer, and examined every dark place he could get to. I had hoped for firearms, but that hope was settling somewhere in the deep part of the creek. Hanluain wanted to linger and pull everything apart, but I led him to a window and showed him McBride lying out on the bank. He hadn't moved, and it was hard to tell if he was even breathing.

I said, "Eamon, this guy's in rough shape. We need to get him back to the station, get a doctor to look at him. That's first. We don't, he's nothing more than a lawsuit for your department."

"My department?" He sighed and nodded. "So, you take McBride and I take Dufaigh?" he said, all innocence.

I laughed. "I can't put Yeager with either of these two, they'll know he talked. Sorry, you've got to handle both."

"Aw, my back seat. Shit."

"Yeah, sorry about it."

We bagged and labeled the stashes and put them in a duffel, then carried McBride between us up the trail, his feet dragging in the mud. Tracy Dufaigh walked in front of us, eyes on the ground and saying little. We buckled McBride into the cage in Hanluain's patrol car; his head flopped back against the seat, and then made a slow rotation forward. Heavy fluids drained out of his nose and mouth.

When it came time for Tracy to take a seat in the car, she took issue. "What, you're going to keep me cuffed? Where you think I'm going to go?"

"Get in the car, miss," said Hanluain.

"What'd I do, that you're keeping me in handcuffs? What if you need me to look after him? How am I supposed to do that?" She continued to protest, but allowed herself to be maneuvered into the back seat. As the door shut, I heard her say, "Oh, goodness," as she caught a whiff of McBride.

"So," said the patrolman, "meet you at the station?"

"I got to take care of —" and I jerked my thumb in the direction of my truck, where Yeager was stowed. "Tell you what, I'll call Liz Brennan, tell her to meet you over there to get samples and do an exam for you."

"Ah, good."

"If you can't wake him up, you get his samples and the product before a judge in six hours, so we have them on possession, at least. Call Dally if you have to."

"Right."

"I want a chance to talk to Dufaigh — to both of them."

"I hope you get it. Ain't up to me."

Yeager had fallen asleep or passed out, and his breathing was slow and deep. I drove toward Wild Thyme, and when my cell phone connected with service I pulled to the side of the road. After three rings I raised Liz, filled her in, and asked her to check in at the sheriff's department.

"I'll check vitals and take blood. County gets the bill."

"That's all I'm asking, just make sure this asshole is going to live until tomorrow. And there's one more thing." I asked her to meet me at the clinic.

Liz waited a moment before saying, "Clinic's closed, Henry. What is it, ten?"

"I need a favor. I got a guy who can't be seen by the others. I just want to be sure he's all right."

"Jesus Christ. All right, see you there."

It was close to eleven-thirty by the time Liz showed up in her station wagon. Hanluain had had to call the sheriff, and the sheriff had to raise a judge, and the judge had to get down to the courthouse. I had been waiting with Yeager — who was still asleep — in my vehicle, with the heat on and the radio low. It had been hard to stay awake myself. Yeager was just a little guy, so I slung him over my shoulder. He'd pissed himself and maybe more, so I held his thighs away from my chest. My legs complained as I climbed the stairs to the second floor. By coming here instead of to the distant state trooper outpost in Dunmore or an actual hospital, I'd already made my bet that this guy was a relative innocent. Putting him in restraints meant I'd dicked up the chain of arrest, but that didn't matter if all we'd ever have on him, at best, was possession. He hadn't said everything he knew, and I wanted everything. He wouldn't have enough to lose if I put him into the system now.

Liz had prepared a gurney bed in an examination room, with a waterproof conduit sheet and blankets close by. I laid my charge on his side, uncuffed one of his wrists, and shackled him to a rail. "Is this normal?" I asked.

"Hell if I know. I mean, some people when they're in withdrawal — I gather this is methamphetamine — just shut down. It's a natural defense against overstimulation or physical stress."

"Well, it's not a very good one."

"It's working for this guy," she said. She drew blood from a vein in Yeager's wiry arm. He stirred a bit when the needle went in, but settled back into slow, rhythmic breathing soon after. His vitals were normal, with an elevated heart rate masked by his placid exterior. "He's fine. If I know anything, he'll need a smooth-over tomorrow morning. He'll try to work you. Probably try to get away. Watch him."

"Thanks, I — he's not my first crank . . . he's not my first user."

"No, of course not." Liz looked in my eyes. "Woah. You feeling all right, bud?"

"Me? Fine."

"Take off your coat. You have some dilation. Let me check you out." She led me to the other examination room and bade me remove my hat. The light she shone in each eye produced a stabbing pain, which I tried not to show. "Any blurred vision, ringing in your ears? Headaches?"

"No."

She extended her hands to either side of my head, and then ran them through my unwashed hair and over my skull. It felt good. Safe. But when she reached the pulp right-rear of my head, the place I'd dared not touch for two days, my vision closed in. I heard her say, "Jesus," from a distance, as if she were standing in another room. I turned my head to the side, moved off the exam table, found a wastebasket, and threw up the soup I'd had for dinner.

I came back to myself hearing Liz say, "It's okay, it's okay. You're going to be fine." Her hand made warm circles on my back.

I looked up at her guiltily.

"Any memory loss?" She rattled off a phone number, and asked me to repeat it. I did so, missing only two digits. "That's right," she said. "That's your own phone number. You've got a concussion. I'm going to get ice for your head, but what you need is rest."

"Yeah, right."

"I'm not kidding, Henry. You need a day off." I must have still been shaking my head, because she bent down to look me in my whacked-out eyes. "I will bring Ed in and we'll strap you to a gurney. I'll call Nicholas. Don't make me."

She took away the wastebasket and came back with a freeze-pack wrapped in cloth and a coffee mug that turned out to be full of water. As I held the ice to my head, she bustled out again and returned with a sheet and several cushions from a couch in the waiting room. She laid them out on the floor. "This is the best I can do for a bed,"

278

she said. "Your friend's got my other one, but you might need it as bad as he does. Shoes off. Belt off." She held the sheet open for me and flapped it.

"Come on," I said. This was undignified.

"You need rest and it can't wait. I'm going to watch you close your eyes."

"I thought you weren't supposed to sleep," I said. "If you have a concussion."

"Are you a doctor? From the look of you, you haven't slept in at least three days. You're dehydrated, too. You should smell your breath. Drink the water."

Embarrassed, I pulled off my boots and gun belt, stowed the belt and the shoulder holster in a low cabinet where I could reach them easily, untucked my shirt, and lowered myself into the makeshift bed. Liz took a chair by the door. The fabric of the cushions was knobbly where it touched my skin, but my eyelids began to droop and I took off my glasses.

"How's it going out there?" she asked.

"I'm not sure yet," I said. "We might have broken it open today. Some part of it." Saying as much aloud got me worked up again, but I let Liz think I was still going down.

"You being careful?"

"Always." I closed my eyes.

"Any word from George's family?"

"Yeah. I've got two weeks. They're going to . . . burn him. Send him down the river."

She asked me no more questions, and I let my breathing deepen. When enough time had passed and Liz was convinced I was asleep, I felt her hand smooth the hair from my brow gently. It was motherly, but there was something else in it, something she wouldn't have done in front of Ed. That gesture set me back a few hours of sleep. As soon as the clinic's front door clicked and she drove away, I opened my eyes.

I wasn't worried about my memory. I was just tired. While I couldn't exactly recall my phone number — or my address, I tried — I knew I knew how to get home, I could see the roads right there in front of me. As long as I hung on to the things I couldn't forget, a country boy can survive.

I don't know if you've ever had squirrel pie. There were times growing up when Father would shake me awake when it was still dark, hand me a round, and say, "Bring back dinner." And it wouldn't be any hunting season; we'd just have nothing in the icebox. You just go out and get whatever was in the woods.

Here's how you make squirrel pie, and it's not bad: Once your squirrels are skinned and dressed, you boil them. It can be done over an open fire. In my case, it was atop a woodstove. After Poll died, I returned to Pennsylvania in late summer and early fall, and oftentimes I'd tramp to a field on a nearby farm and forage some feed corn to throw in the pot. Maybe if you find a wild onion bulb to chop in there. I kept boxes of dried peas and instant mashed, or I'd dig up live-forever tubers to mash. You separate the bones from the meat, and spread the mash over the mix of squirrel meat, re-hydrated peas, and corn. I'd put it in a little baking pan and hold it in the hot woodstove to crisp up the top. It's not bad fare. You can substitute rabbit, grouse, any other small game, but a squirrel or two won't be missed. I've had porcupine.

I guess I don't eat squirrel much anymore for associations with that time, when I returned to Wild Thyme with no job, no Poll, cleaned out. What it felt like. I had nothing but some gear from the 10th and a .22 rifle with me — I'd sold everything else to pay Poll's medical bills, and then to af-ford her service, a small one for her family's benefit. I'd already scattered her ashes in the Winds, per her wishes. And then I mounted a campaign against the gas opera-tor that had put in the pad over the hill from our cabin. Every day I changed my idea of what I needed to live, in order to pay for a series of tests on the water, the land, trying to convince a lawyer somewhere there was a case. In the end it got too much and I let it, and everything else in the cabin, go. There was something snared and struggling in the back of my mind. I didn't mind dying, but I'd seen the way Polly went and I didn't want that. Didn't know if it wasn't already too late. I'd outrun it if I could. The old gray dog took two days to run from Idaho Springs to Binghamton; I kept the rifle broken down in my pack and wrapped in a towel.

Luckily, my parents were holding out for a more favorable housing market at that time, though they had long since moved to North Carolina to be near my sister's family, so the tiny house on the tiny piece of land where I grew up was still for sale and vacant. My key worked. Everything inside was gone, but I didn't mind that. In fact, I preferred it that way, at that time.

I guess people driving by had been seeing lamplight in the window of my parents' house, and someone wondered aloud to the sheriff who I might be. Maybe a neighbor made the call, maybe it was the realtor who hadn't shown the place since I'd been there but drove past every week to make sure it wasn't going to pot. Back then, the township had no police, and the sheriff's department did the enforcement for that part of the county, along with the state on weekends. That's when I first met Sheriff Nicholas Dally.

I'd seen him around in years past, but never face-to-face. He came to my door a little before suppertime, when I was cleaning a piece of game, and before I could greet him, I had to wash my hands off from a jug — the water had been turned off, so I had been lowering a bucket into the well. I admit I was a little ornery in those days. There was nobody in the world I felt I needed to please, including myself, and only one person to answer to, and she was gone. I yanked open the door and stood staring at Dally, saying nothing. He was pleasant enough but I saw a moment of alarm cross his face when he took in my appearance. After a few weeks of the diet I was on you could see my skull beneath my skin, and I was not a little blood-spattered. I gave him my name. He asked for identification, and I stood there staring at him. "Just trying to make sure you are who you say," he said genially but firmly. "Since your folks aren't around to keep an eye on things." I dug through my bag and found my military ID, which was out of date, my Wyoming driver's license, and my police ID. He thanked me for my service, and asked me was I planning to stick around. I said I didn't know. "Let me know," he said, "if you need a ride to the DMV. I'll send a deputy."

He never did send a deputy, because I never asked him to. What life I saw ahead of me didn't involve driving anywhere. He did contact an old teammate from my high school football days, Ed Brennan. I was a safety and on special teams, and he had been a left guard. We weren't particularly friendly back in school, coming from different backgrounds. Growing up has a way of smoothing these things out. Ed visited and seemed pleased to see me, and brought a twelve-pack with him, but three beers after being dry for months, with little in my stomach from day to day, and I was weaving in the backyard. I cursed him and his family. He still busts my balls about it, and I'll have to take his word that it happened because I simply don't remember it. He was back in a few days, that time bearing a container of spaghetti and meatballs, and a pie made by his wife. I thanked him but found I couldn't eat more than a bite or two, and had no freezer to save any of it.

A week of no luck hunting followed, and

consequently a week of no luck eating. I remember it in washes. It was euphoric, simple. The moonlight and the wind in the silver leaves began to feel like nourishment to me. Once I spent over twenty-four hours lying in the same spot in the yard, gazing into the sky, willing someone or something to take me away. I could sleep without sleeping, exist without getting stuck in the mire. High times. On occasion I'd hear my parents talking in the house, just for a minute, and their conversation would dissolve into nothing because they weren't there. I kept smelling something like the barracks latrine in Fort Drum in the early morning, or the high school cafeteria when it was newly cleaned and empty. Later I realized it was my body feeding on my muscle, as there was no fat left. In the end, no stag stepped out of the mist to sacrifice himself for me, no spirit animal concerned that I should eat, no. In the end — in the beginning, I should say — Ed stopped by after visiting a construction site he had going in the area, and found me passed out in the backyard with my rifle lying atop me, the muzzle tucked under my chin. Unable to wake me, he laid me out in the back of his pickup with the buckets of tools and scraps of lumber.

I woke up in a clinic bed with an IV in my arm, which I removed on my own. There was a bowl of chicken soup with rice cooling on a stand next to my bed, and a banana and one piece of buttered toast. As I was getting my second leg back into my trousers, Liz — whom I hadn't yet met at that time — swept in, saying, "No, no, no, honey. Into the bed with you." It didn't take much muscle to get me there. Her firm hands on my shoulders were the first I'd felt in months. I wanted more. "Let me go," I said.

"As soon as you eat what's on this tray. You're starving, Henry. I can see through you."

"I feel better."

"Uh-huh. I just got you full of fluids."

My head began to clear. "You know my name?" This was wonderful to me.

"I'm Ed's wife, who brought you in? Liz Brennan's my name." She smiled, and the angels sang.

"Oh. Thanks for the supper you sent." I felt bad about not eating it. "It was good." She stood up straight and I saw her baby bump where it was framed by her white coat. At that time she was pregnant with their second child, it turned out. "You look great," I said, and burst into tears.

Anyway, she nursed me back to health and

saved my life. Two different, but related, undertakings. She let me be around their family, encouraged our friendship, made me feel as if I had some value to the world. The charity of it wasn't obvious to me at the time but it is now, looking back, and I just live with it.

A distant metallic rattling woke me. It took me almost a minute to figure out where I was, as the blinds in the examination room were closed and I had been dead asleep. I buckled the .40s on and laced up my boots. There was a patch of hard, salty cloth where my shirt had been trapped between the gun and my side. I walked to the adjacent room, rubbing my face. Behind the door, I heard Yeager make a low panicked sound that rose in pitch and volume. When I entered, he quickly composed his face and relaxed his body, but it was clear from his raw wrists what he'd been trying to do. "Morning," he said. "I don't feel very well."

"Then you're in the right place," I said, unhelpfully. I looked at him in his dirty clothes and his desperation. "What am I going to do with you?"

I unlocked Vernon and had him take a shower. While he was in there I stripped our beds and dropped the sheets in a neat pile;

his soiled jeans and jockeys I tied in a trash bag and stuffed in a can. In Liz's office there were a few pairs of clean scrubs. I laid a pair of green ones out for him.

We bought him cigarettes and went to the drive-through doughnut place on the route out of town; Yeager looked at the menu like a begging dog, and I gestured to him to get what he wanted. In a nice way, a not-noticing way. He ordered the largest, sweetest coffee you could get, and four frosted chocolate doughnuts. I almost warned him not to throw up in my car, but held my tongue. I wouldn't envy anyone in his condition.

We parked on a ridge overlooking Fitzmorris, with the courthouse's cupola poking up bright green over bare treetops below us. Beyond, hills rolled south. I thought Yeager might appreciate a look in the direction home. He held down three doughnuts fine, and wrapped the fourth in a napkin and pocketed it.

"Where you go from here is up to you," I said.

"I have nowhere to go."

"You have your job."

"I doubt that," he said. The wind whistled over the rise.

"Can I ask why you ran off, Vernon?" He

was silent for a while, thinking and taking sidelong, appraising glances at me. "Before you ask for a lawyer," I said, "believe me, I'm not about making your life any more difficult. I want to know what you know; that's all. This is off the record."

"You give your word?"

My word meant nothing legally in that moment, but I gave it, and meant it.

"I can't," he said. "I can't talk about it. I want to help."

"Just start somewhere. What about Contreras?"

"Shit, Officer —"

"Henry."

"Shit, Henry, that's . . ."

"Was it him?" Meaning the photograph he'd seen of John Doe.

"I said I don't know."

"What's your relationship to Contreras?"

"That's what's . . . hard to talk about." He fixed his eyes on the dash and waited for me to catch on.

"Oh."

" 'Oh.' " Yeager rubbed the back of his head and then pulled his hair in a recriminating way. "Gerry and I used to get high. He had a connection to the guy I led you to, McBride. I had a need. Gerry had needs. I love my wife. I love my kid. But they ain't up here."

"I think I understand."

"There's always something around. Whiskey, weed. Some guys can find a cathouse in a one-street town. You look the other way. But some things ain't allowed. I'd been getting a feeling on the job. Looks, you know. Especially after Gerry ran off, and I was . . . I felt uneasy. Then you two showed up saying he was gone. To me, it . . . I realized it was in the open. Had been, and I couldn't stand the guys knowing. It wasn't just about losing my job, which I'm sure I have done by now. I have what you might call a past. One I can't go back to."

I nodded. "Were you Contreras's only . . . only friend on the job?"

"Yeah. Far as I know, and I'd know."

"You hear from him? See him?"

"Once, maybe. We — me and a couple guys — went to a bar toward Elmira, late January, I believe. It was a crowded place with a band. I thought I saw him standing toward the back when we walked in. Mostly talking to a fat — an overweight woman. Thought he saw me. Well, I followed him out the back door, and he was gone. Came back in the bar and the woman had a look on her face, like she was — like she knew all about me, but not about me and him. I can't be sure." With some encouragement, he remembered the name of the bar.

"Jesus Christ, Yeager, why didn't you say any of this when we first talked to you?"

He looked at me like I was an idiot.

"We're talking about lives, here," I said.

"Yeah," he said. "Mine. Listen, I did try to call you. Several times. You need a secretary or something. What happened to that deputy of yours, he can't pick up a phone?"

"Come again?"

"Big cranky son of a bitch, red hair, beard?"

"George Ellis."

"Maybe. He stopped us once heading out of McBride's old place, the trailer with the tree down on it? Took what — what we had, all our cash, Gerry's gold cross, said it was civil forfeit. Said next time it'd be Gerry's car and we'd be in county." He shook his head. "I don't believe there was anything to that. He was looking for a woman."

George had left no record of this stop, or of ever encountering Contreras or Yeager. Dismayed as I was by George's piracy, my ears pricked up when Yeager mentioned the woman. "Why?" I asked. "Why a woman?"

"Because he wasn't half pretending to want to take us in. And because he said so.

Asked us who was there, if there was a blond woman there that night, or ever. If we were there to, you know. Visit her." Yeager's feet began to tap. "I told him no. Didn't stop him from haunting the roads along the pipeline, following us on our downtime, you know. After Gerry left, he seemed to lose interest. Anyway, ain't seen him lately, your deputy."

"He's . . . no, he isn't around." I took a hard look at Yeager.

We stepped outside so my prisoner could smoke. He put his back to the wind and inhaled one gratefully, then lit another, pulled his coat tight, and took in his surroundings.

"I have to ask," I said. "Did you love him? Contreras."

"No!"

"Why I'm asking —"

"I know why you're asking. I love my wife. I'd never be jealous of Gerry or any other . . . guy. Just don't work that way."

"Then did you hate him? Feel taken advantage of?"

"No. It just . . . was, and then it wasn't." Yeager rolled his eyes, as if asking himself how it had come to this. When he looked around him, I don't believe he saw hills and sky; rather, he was looking at a very small room that he'd built for himself, and regretting that there was no door.

"So," I said. "So how is it you fetched up on the school bus?"

"Jesus, the school bus. We went over that last night."

"Not how you got there, or why."

"I hitchhiked for some, and walked. I'd been out to McBride's trailer before, you know. With Gerry. Thought I might get a line on him there. Imagine my surprise, it's all shut down and sealed. So up the road I went, and bam." He turned his head away and made his tone light. "I don't remember what-all went on there."

"You were ready enough to leave by the time I showed," I said.

"Yeah, well. They didn't treat me very respectfully, I remember that much. I heard them talking about what to do with me: something about a bullet to the head and a trip to the swamp. It could have been a sick joke. I was in the bus. I was afraid to go back out. That's where I was when I overheard them talking about McBride. McBride and the girl in a camper on January Creek. But you got him, right? So . . ."

So I owed him one. Thinking about what Yeager had told me, in context, I doubted that the bullet they'd been discussing was

293

intended for him. It sounded like McBride had worn out his welcome on Westmeath Road, or had something they wanted, something that was now in the county's evidence locker.

Yeager eyed the woods behind us. "Okay if I take a shit?"

"We're not done yet."

"With respect, I don't want you changing my drawers twice in a day. And I'm sure you don't either." Yeager tossed his cigarette butt aside, hopped the ditch, and slipped through the trees.

I listened, but there wasn't much to hear and soon the ringing overtook my ears and threatened to escape my head. The sun gained the eastern horizon.

"Goddamn it," I said, and went in there after Yeager. There was no sign of him at first. The woods were smaller than he may have anticipated, leading down to a ravine. On the other side of the ravine was a dense row of ranch houses on a busy road. I made descending arcs from tree line to tree line until I spotted him hidden in the lee of a boulder; the bright green scrubs were a giveaway, even half covered with leaves. He must have heard me coming, but made no move to run.

"I want to get off this merry-go-round,"

he said, looking up at me.

I extended a hand to him and he pulled himself up. "You can stop now. You need to stop. If you're telling me the truth, you've got nothing to worry about."

"I'll remember you said that."

We walked back to my vehicle. "Listen," I said, "you ready? It can't be as bad as you say."

"If you take me back to the well pad," he said slowly, "they'll shitcan me and give me bus fare home. At best. What am I going to tell my wife?"

I thought a moment. "Well, you can't leave the county yet."

"Aw, Jesus —"

"Listen, if they try to send you home, call me. We'll work something out."

"You ain't the easiest to reach, Henry."

I gave him another of my cards, with my cell phone number written on the back, and we headed for Yeager's job site. To get there, we passed through a cellular dead zone. At the gate, I steamrolled the man standing guard with my badge. Climbing to the top of the ridge, I got a beep that told me I had a voice mail; could've been the portable communications they have up there on the pads that got me the service. Yeager and I idled in the truck for a moment while I

checked it. It was from Dally. In the recording, he grumbled a bit about the condition
of his new prisoners, but grudgingly thanked
me for tracking McBride down. At the end
of the message he said, "Well, we've one
less thing to worry about, and many more.
Elmira PD found Contreras last night, alive
and kicking. Check in when you get to your
station."

The message ended. I looked at the
phone's display without seeing it, and
laughed though nothing was funny. I turned
to Yeager.

Back when Gerardo Contreras was dead, I didn't have reason to feel one way or another about him. Now that he was alive, and not our John Doe, I didn't care for him at all.

The Elmira Police Department had pried him out of yet another roadhouse known as a drug market. His room, which he'd shared with a local woman — possibly the woman Yeager had mentioned — had been littered with the remains of a focused period of use. Contreras wasn't my problem anymore.

As to the unmarked grave on Aub's land, it appeared I was in for some digging.

"I called Detective Palmer," the sheriff had told me on the phone. "He can get up this afternoon around two. That give you enough daylight?"

"Am I going to get to talk to McBride?"

"You don't worry about that. Let me worry about that."

297

"What about a diver in January Creek? We got anybody in the county? Pretty sure Dufaigh tossed a gun in there."

The sheriff made a thoughtful noise, and said, "Noted. We'll get one if we need to. If we can."

"Pretty sure it was a gun, Sheriff." Dally responded with silence. I looked out the window at a low morning sun dispelling the mist. It promised to be a sunny, warmish day, so I could at least hope for a few inches of thawed ground. I told the sheriff two o'clock would be fine and hung up. I needed some hands with shovels, and had an idea of where to get them.

As the garage came to life that morning, I was thinking with my stocking feet up on the desk. I hadn't gone home, and had been in the office since seven-thirty. In the peace and quiet, I lost track of the time; eight-thirty had come and I was supposed to be open to the public. There was a knock on my door, and it opened without invitation. The man who entered was dressed in a brown tweed jacket and soft woolen pants; his tie was fixed to his shirt with a narrow gold pin, and his white hair was brushed straight and hair-sprayed into place. Dr. Robert Loinsigh held a plate covered in smooth tinfoil, which he set down on my desk and, after looking around, wheeled George's chair over and sat across from me.

I hadn't gotten up to shake his hand, but I did him the courtesy of removing my dirty socks from view and sitting up straight. He extended his hand across my desktop, and I took it. "Mary made those," he said, referring to the covered plate. "Butterscotch."

"Thank you. Tell your wife thank you."

He smiled. "Any news?"

"Just what's on TV."

"Yeah," he said. "I saw. I'm beginning to appreciate your situation here. So, the investigations? You have all you need?" he pressed.

"They're proceeding. Dunmore lends us a couple troopers here and there. We're getting somewhere."

"Yeah." He looked about him at the little office that to him must have seemed dreary, but to me was just right. Apart from George's empty desk.

"Tell your wife thank you," I hinted.

"About that. We . . . you understand, we have standing permission to be on Dunigan's land. We've hiked his woods for thirty years. Watched birds in his woods for thirty years —"

I could tell what he was working up to, and cut him off. "I understand, but you weren't up there to watch birds. The citations have been issued and I'm not taking them back."

He sat stunned for a moment. Then he stood and said, "You've got plenty to worry about. Sorry to intrude."

"I understand. Don't worry. Actually, you've done me a favor — please sit — I had been meaning to pay a visit, ask about what you've heard or seen on the ridge."

He sat, still looking aggrieved. "No," he said, "it's shocking. I mean, are we safe?"

"We have a pretty strong theory about . . . who is responsible. Their world and yours probably don't mix. What about Mrs. Loinsigh — she see anything these days?"

"There's nothing that happens in her life that she doesn't tell me about. In detail." He chuckled. "I'm at work during the day —"

"You're a, what do you do?"

"Ear, nose, and throat specialist. Over the border. Anyway, Mary would have said."

"And you mentioned that you have permission to be on Aub's land — what kind of relationship do you have with him? Seen any changes lately?"

"Aub is Aub, always has been. I'd say our relationship was neighborly. For years. Long, long ago, when he was already an old man, and I was still young, he found out I was an MD. So, early mornings maybe twice or three times a year he'd come over the ridge, sometimes with fresh eggs or a piece of deer meat, sometimes an old medicine bottle — I collect them, for my office — and he'd have a complaint. A sore throat, a cough, something. There wouldn't be anything seriously wrong most times. I think he just thought, free checkup, free doctor. I'd see him in the garage. Once, and this was maybe fifteen years ago, he needed hospital care. Something to do with his plumbing."

"You say he was healthy?"

"For his life, for what he was. His nutrition was poor. He drank too much; that was obvious."

"When was the last time you saw him?"

"I couldn't say. He stopped visiting some years ago."

"And you never checked up on him?" It sounded more accusatory than I'd intended.

Loinsigh paused a moment, and said, "Each man has his own life, Henry."

"Uh-huh. Look, I didn't mean . . . I know it's not your job."

"Exactly. Dealing with indigents is more in your line, no?" After another cold silence, the doctor said, "Well, if there's nothing else?"

"Tell your wife thank you. Stay in touch."
As Loinsigh put his hand on the doorknob,
one more thing occurred to me. "Doctor," I
said, "Aub was always alone, far as you
know?"

"Yes."

"Never married?"

Loinsigh shook his head and scoffed, and
left.

I looked out the window. The sun had
taken its place in the sky, burning the mist
away. I walked next door to the garage,
where I found John Kozlowski underneath
a raised fire truck, banging its frame and
chassis with a rubber mallet; flakes of rust
rained down around him and settled in his
graying hair and all over his coveralls. When
he noticed me, he emerged from under the
truck. "Goddamn thing," he said. "This
truck ain't worth fifty bucks. We only keep
it around to give kids rides at the Field
Days. Fuckin thing." He patted a red fender
with affection. "What's up?"

"Would you say you owe me one, John?"

He shifted his eyes, then nodded in the
affirmative.

"And would you say," I continued, "that
your buddy Nolan owes me one?"

"He may not see it that way, but okay."

"Well. Make him understand. I've got

some county business this afternoon. I need a couple strong backs and it can't wait."

Nolan's house was closest to the unmarked grave, so we gathered in his driveway at two p.m. John had followed me in his truck, with Detective Palmer close behind in an unmarked Crown Vic, and Wy Brophy back in his maroon pickup, wearing a tweed cap.

The four of us — me, John, Palmer, and Wy Brophy — stood outside Nolan's house, waiting. Me and John carried picks and shovels and packs full of heavy-duty garbage bags, jugs of water, and sandwiches. I had a thermos of coffee. Brophy carried a metal case and had a camera hanging around his neck.

Palmer slapped my shoulder in a friendly way. "Farrell, you've got to stop turning up bodies. Or I'm going to have to buy a trailer out here in Pennsyltucky, huh?"

"You could do worse," John said.

Nolan's back door opened, and out came the man himself, hulking and droopy around the face. Unshaven, with a pair of waders slung over his shoulder, he thudded down the steps without greeting and seized his own pick and shovel with one hand. "Snow White and the five fuckin dwarves," he said, looking at all of us together.

"We appreciate your help — Finbar?" Palmer said.

"Yeah," said Nolan. "Yeah. It's Barry."

Our group complete, we set off for the trees about an acre back from Nolan's house. We passed a pond with a small dock, and continued on a trail that skirted the edge of the swamp.

On the way out, I found myself walking next to Nolan. "Busy up on the ridge these days," I said.

"Yeah."

"I was over to the Grady place. They said they used to get visits from Aub Dunigan, through the woods. Odd hours."

"Sounds like him." We walked along. "You talk to Ron?" he asked.

"Yeah, Ron and Evelina both."

"The old lady knows a thing or two. I was friendly with Ron Senior. Not sure about the son."

"Oh?"

"He's been putting the pressure on Evie to lease," Nolan said. "It's unpleasant."

"What does he care? He can lease his rights, can't he?"

"She owns it all. Ron's been pressuring me too. Trying to set up a parcel."

"You interested?"

"Maybe. Can't do it without at least Aub

304

and Evelina, at any rate. And I know Shelly Bray don't want to."

We reached the clearing and slipped down the slope toward the rock pile.

You ever dig in a cold swamp all afternoon? Wear a back brace and join a union is my advice. After a couple hours I felt two inches shorter and partway folded into myself like a rusty jackknife. Wy Brophy took numerous photos of the site in its undisturbed state, and even took a turn with the pick. His pleated pants were streaked with dirt where he'd wiped his hands. For the earth we were digging up, we'd sectioned off as much room in the little grotto as we could spare; per Palmer's instructions everything had to be saved, and could not be hucked out into the swamp. Between the four of us working — Palmer refrained, citing a bad back — we dug a good-sized, neat hole by the headstone, though one that was lined with a seeping pool of cold swamp water. From time to time, Brophy knelt and examined the exposed soil layers.

Unasked, Nolan stepped into his waders, and then into the cavity, and flung muck over his shoulder. At one point he leaned on his shovel and looked up at John and muttered, "Thirsty work." He was pale, and sweat beaded on his face. John palmed him a steel flask.

The afternoon wore on. Chickadees sang "tee-hee" from their perches far above. Repeatedly hammering pieces of shale with a pick had produced high-pitched clinks that traveled up my arms and resonated with the ringing in my ears. My head felt a little better when I took a break. As the sun made its slow vault across the sky, I tried to position it to my back. Coffee was keeping me moving, and though I'd had very little water and felt dried out, eventually I had to relieve myself, so I clambered over one of the boulders that hemmed us into the site and stepped into the woods. From my vantage point, I could see most of the clearing and the tree line surrounding it. It was bathed in light, and I couldn't look for long before my vision blurred and doubled. Scanning the trees bit by bit, I caught movement high and to the northwest, and . . . something. Beyond naked undergrowth, some color slightly out of place. A jagged, eight-foot tree stump marked the spot.

Shovels sliced into the muck, and muffled voices carried over the swamp's surface, to my left, where the others dug. Detective Palmer had a Glock in a shoulder holster, but I couldn't call to him without drawing attention. I stood there, not moving myself, waiting for a sign. Nothing stirred. And then, a slow shift, and a naked sapling danced out of time with the breeze coming out of the northwest.

I must have been gone awhile, because when I returned to the dig, four silent, expectant men were waiting for me.

"Where've you been?" said John.

"There's something down there," Palmer said.

Wy Brophy bent over his open case, sorting through equipment. Nolan squatted beside the open grave, using a shovel for support, his nose dripping sweat and his face ashen. "We hit wood," he said. "It's soft. You can't see it now, the water keeps coming in." The earthen wall facing the swamp had been seeping since we'd dug about two feet down. The deeper we got, the more that side of the hole crumbled like a levee on the verge of collapse. I moved to the edge of the pit and peered into the pooling water in its depths, water that reflected the robin's-egg sky. The others joined me. I pulled Palmer back for a moment and told him we were not alone. He nodded without meeting my eyes and without belief.

Brophy instructed John and Nolan — gently, gently — to find the edges of the casket and clear its surface of water. As the two large men slid down into the pit, I pulled on Palmer's coat again, quietly. "Something's up there too," I said, and nodded toward the tree line above. "I chased a man to this same spot yesterday, and I'm telling you, I saw someone up there. Let's work up either side of the clearing —"

"Easy," said Palmer, "I'm not doing that."

"We could have the shooter *right now,*" I said. I turned to find John and Nolan watching us from below.

Palmer put an arm around my shoulder and turned me away from them. "Listen," he said, "we've got something right here. I think you can see that. I'm doing what I was called in to do. Whatever's up there, frankly, I'm not going to crash through the woods after it. Not on your word alone."

"Why not?"

He sighed. "Sheriff mentioned. Your doctor friend? She told him. You need rest." Palmer patted me on the back and joined the others.

Feeling betrayed, I resisted looking to the tree line, then took a breath and stepped to the pit's edge. John and Nolan were at pains to work together in the small space, and after a misplaced foot and an ominous crunch, the coroner cleared them out of the hole and slid down himself, scooping away

308

earth with his gloved hands. He exposed a narrow coffin, its wood barely distinguishable from the soil surrounding it. There were no handles visible. Brophy raised a hand and asked for a hammer. Using the claw, he knelt and eased iron nails out of soggy wood; the coffin lid folded in half like cardboard.

Another age gazed up at us.

The face was dark as mahogany, its eyelids sunken into sockets that had emptied long ago, its mouth forced into a wince as the facial tissue tightened into leather. And still, its features were delicate, discernible. It. Her. And strange to relate, her face, turned slightly to the east, seemed to reach out to us from somewhere.

"Jesus," said Brophy, scrambling to his feet. "Jesus."

A film of cloth swam around the body, stained the color of iron-rich earth, its floral print still visible. Around her collarbone, lace had shriveled and turned the same red-brown. A black weal of what looked like damaged skin encircled her throat.

Brophy asked for his camera, and Palmer handed it down to him. After taking some photos, Brophy held up an end of rope, about an inch in diameter. "This is in with her," he said. "It's around her back and

309

under her arms; it was laid out here, on her anterior abdomen. Maybe she was lowered with it?" Or killed with it, I thought. He took another picture. As he cleared around the body, we saw a sodden dress clinging to hipbones, hand curled around skeletal hand. All the while, the swamp crept in.

"Wy," John said, looking at the rising water level, "she's going under, there."

"What do you think's been preserving her all this time? She'll last a while longer." The coroner took samples of water and soil. "This bog, this . . . this area here. Amazing. Never seen anything like this, guys."

"So she's what, she's mummified?"

"Pickled, more like. It's chemical." Brophy climbed out of the grave and pulled Palmer aside. As they conversed, Brophy gestured at his own neck, as if demonstrating something. Palmer nodded along. I turned to the tree line, trying to scan for my figure on the sly. My gaze came to rest on Nolan as he drank from John's flask of whiskey and let his eyelids sag in relief. He noticed me looking, and raised his eyebrows in what was the closest expression to a smile I'd ever seen him make.

"Does no good in the bottle," he said, and held the flask out to me. I declined.

After further conversation, Brophy went

to his kit and produced a body bag. "Here comes the tricky part," he said.

We cut down and stripped two saplings, then buried their narrow trunks below the coffin and heaved up, two men to a side. The box lifted free of the mud with a sucking sound, and red-brown water poured from its seams, soaking us from the thighs down. "Shit. Jesus," said John. Nolan paled but otherwise remained impassive. All I could smell was earth and swamp and something sulfurous; there was no odor of rotting flesh, not even up close. As we slid the coffin onto dry land, its sodden wood fell apart in my grip.

We gathered around the body. She looked vulnerable, smaller out in the big new world. I had an irrational protective impulse as we stood in silence, offering the woman a moment of respect before the indignity of a body bag, then transport to some lab, there to be cut and pulled open and scrutinized. It felt wrong, taking her out of there. But that's what we did.

As the others carried the body out, I broke off the trail. Palmer saw me go, and said nothing. I picked my way north through the saplings around the periphery of the clearing. The shade in the woods soothed my eyes, even broken as it was with blades of white light. A silent step, a listening pause, a step. I climbed the slope and willed my eyes to focus, to peer beyond the trunks and the thicket. With the swamp spread out below me, I reached the place I'd seen almost without realizing. The silver tree stump I'd used to mark the spot was unmistakable, though, and had been gouged to a fare-thee-well by a woodpecker. There was a faint scent of tobacco on the air. I scoured the ground at my feet and found the butt of a hand-rolled cigarette nestled into a patch of club moss. My chest tightened in frustration. There would be egress from the ridge in any direction but one, from there, and my friend remained more than a few steps ahead. Whoever he was, he had moved on.

We set the woman in the shade beneath Nolan's deck, where rolls of deer fencing and a stack of hay bales were stored. For a moment we stood awkwardly in the dirt drive, and then John said what was on all of our minds.

"You got any beers in that house?"

Nolan nodded. "Be right back."

"Can't we come in? Cold out here."

"Like that? No, you can't."

"What, who's going to care? What do you care? We'll take off our shoes."

Nolan snorted. "Jesus Christ, John, I don't want goddamn mud all in my house. Leave it alone."

When the door slapped shut behind Nolan, John turned to Palmer and Wy with a wink. "He's a divorcée. A sensitive plant. You should see it in there, it's like it never happened, all the décor she picked out, everything is still there. As if she's going to come home any minute. Poor fuckin son of a bitch."

Brophy's eyes widened. "How long ago was this?"

"Aw, no, that ain't her," John said, referring to the corpse lying under the deck. "His wife just married some blowjob up in Sidney."

While we waited, I tried raising Sheriff Dally on my cell, but had only one bar, and that winked in and out. Nobody else's reception was any better, and though the air was cooling quickly into the low forties, Wy kept looking over at the body bag. The body inside needed to get where she was going. For that to happen, we needed to know where that was, and how she'd be transported.

I mounted the steps and stood at the back door, which opened into the kitchen. Our host wasn't in sight, so I knocked lightly and let myself in, shucking my boots. The kitchen curtains let some light through, but the other rooms were dark.

I had the landline phone in hand, and had just finished dialing the sheriff's department, when Nolan passed in the hall without seeming to see me.

I heard a door open, and footfalls descending an interior staircase. I placed the phone gently on its cradle and padded in the direction from which he'd come. Nolan's living room contained a wicker bookcase with a few books on the top shelf, including a worn copy of *The Tracker* by Tom Brown as told to William Jon Watkins, and a field guide to animal tracks and sign. A row of *National Geographic*s filled the bottom shelf. The case was otherwise empty save for one framed photograph that had fallen over; it was a shot of a handsome, burly teen in a rented tux, at the prom with his date, who was plain and overweight, but sweet-looking. I set it down. On the western wall, a flight of brass ducks passed over a little Jøtul woodstove in a bricked corner. A pair of oil paintings pictured a buck at attention, and a doe and a fawn, respectively, in each case the surrounding woods a little too grand for our area.

Among a mosaic of photographs hanging

in the dark hall I picked out Nolan crouching with a buck so freshly killed his eyes had yet to glass; Nolan and the woman I presumed was his ex-wife; Nolan with his arm around the boy from the prom photo, who was in football shoulder pads, his face alight; and a dark square of wallpaper where a photograph had once hung.

The staircase groaned, and I crept back to the kitchen and pressed redial. Krista had just answered when Nolan walked into the kitchen. The smile fixed on his face did nothing to hide his displeasure at my presence. I mouthed, *Sorry,* pointed to my stocking feet, and shrugged. Nolan opened his refrigerator and pulled out a box of light beer cans. As he closed the icebox door, he seized one of the newspaper articles about his son as if seeing it for the first time in years, letting a magnet clatter to the floor. He stuffed the article into a pocket and waited by the back door.

Krista finally put me through to the sheriff, and I filled him in. Dally said he hoped she would come back as a natural death, and that he would send an ambulance to ferry our corpse to the county morgue.

"Listen," he told me. "Brophy may feel out of his depth and want to send her with Palmer to a state lab down in Scranton.

Don't let the state take her yet. It's important that the body stay here in town until at least tomorrow morning."

"What happens then?" I said. I felt Nolan's eyes on me.

"She's got a date."

"What's that mean?"

The sheriff explained what he had in mind.

When he was done, I said, "I don't agree with that approach at all. You need to be gentle with him, or he'll —"

"Just keep the body up here," Dally told me. "We'll discuss it later."

I hung up. Nolan stood by the door, waiting.

Before leaving the kitchen, I felt I should say something friendly. "How's your son been? He have a good season this year?"

"Yeah."

"Any scouts?"

"You want to . . ." Nolan gestured at the door, and tried to cover his impatience with a smile.

Outside, we sat on car bumpers and hoods and drank and shivered, and waited for the ambulance to show. I raised a beer to my companions' service to the township. John followed with a toast to George Ellis: "Rough, tough, and hard to bluff."

"Amen," said Nolan.

I deflected a couple questions from John about our investigations. Nolan's gaze wandered from our conversation and lingered on the body bag under his deck. He looked at his watch and sighed.

"You miss your shift?" Kozlowski asked.

By the time the ambulance arrived, Brophy and Palmer were negotiating over the body, and Brophy was losing.

"No," said Palmer. "You want our assistance in the field, fine. We never agreed to take anything on beyond that. It's a county matter."

"Bill, I'm in no position to take on a new subject. I just got a car accident vic nobody wants to claim. I get one more body, I've got to send one to the funeral home. Or to you." He turned to me. "Henry. She's in good shape now, but every second she spends in an uncontrolled environment, every second she's above thirty-six degrees, everything the chemical composition of that bog prevented, all that bacteria, will rush in and turn her into sludge. Now, I can keep her cold, but that's about all. The detailed examinations, the tests, the time, the man-hours, I can't do that for a subject like this. But someone should. Getting her to Scranton, now, is the best way."

Two overweight EMTs stood silently by, half listening to our discussion. I recognized one of them as Damon from the other day. He waved at me, a surreptitious hand at waist level.

Dusk was falling. In the face of Palmer's stony refusal, Brophy raised his hands. "Do what you want. I'm just asking for what's best. Never seen anything quite like that one before, so, you know." He looked me long in the face, then pulled me aside. "You ever hear of the Tollund Man?"

"No, sir."

"He was from Denmark. Lot of peat bogs over there. Not exactly like this one, but similar. And this Tollund Man was dug up in one, in a bog. He was so well preserved that people thought he might have been a modern murder victim. He had a rope around his neck. As it happens, he was from the Iron Age." His eyes shone.

It must have been plain on my face I didn't know when the Iron Age was.

"What that means," Brophy continued, "he could have been alive the same time as Christ. *That old.* People speculate — speculate, now — that he was a human sacrifice. Think about that: a human sacrifice. For all we know, he could have been a messiah, a Christ nobody ever set down in words. Can you imagine? Preserved for two thousand years." He looked with longing at the body bag under the deck. "And now we find her. I don't believe there's ever been one found on this continent. She might have been preserved for decades. Could have lasted hundreds of years more after we're gone."

"So put her back," Kozlowski suggested from across the driveway. Nolan snorted. I glared at them both.

Turning to Brophy, I said, "I bet you can handle it fine."

"No, I can't, and that's the thing," he said. "They can. Leave it up to me, and . . ." He shrugged. "We won't learn half of what there is to know."

Palmer, Brophy, and I lifted her onto a gurney, and the EMTs strapped her down.

"Not too tight," said Brophy. "I'll just do what I can do," he told himself.

I declined John's invitation to join him at the bar and got in my truck. There, in loud silence, I thought about what I'd seen that day. The woman from the bog might not have been anybody's Jesus, not in our neighborhood, but we had rolled away the stone. She was risen, and ours to deal with.

Who she had been to Aub, in life, remained to be seen. A relative, maybe. A wife the world had overlooked, perhaps common-law? The headstone was enough of a gesture that she had meant something to the old man. Whether Aub intended to keep her grave to himself or not, it *was* secret; that suggested that the woman had been something secret too. The signs weren't clear, but my thoughts of the old man were taking unsettling turns.

I was bone-tired, caked with mud, and scratched everywhere with thorns. My trousers had been soaked to the thighs with swamp water and hadn't yet dried. Even so, I knocked at Evelina Grady's, unfit to be seen and half dead on my feet.

The old lady answered. "You come by the front this time. Come in?"

"Thanks," I said, and stepped inside. Though I had tried to stomp and scrape off every bit of mud from my boots, plenty had hung on; I bent over to unlace myself. My back muscles bunched and stretched painfully. My socks were still damp and stained red, but I wasn't going to take those off, and consequently I left red-brown footprints across powder-blue carpeting. I looked back at my trail in dismay. Evelina saw it and said, "Don't worry, Henry." I followed her to the kitchen and sat while she made us instant coffee.

My bedraggled state would have made small talk absurd. The old lady knew I had something to ask or to tell, and waited for me to come out with it. The coffee she set before me tasted burnt sweet and chemical, and hot and wonderful.

"We went digging out by the swamp," I said. "Found the grave of a woman."

"On Aubrey's land?"

"Where else?"

"And you don't know who it is." She nodded, and produced a pack of cigarettes from a pocket in her sweatsuit. She laid them on the table and stared as if expecting them to get up and do something. "Aubrey is the last of a strange brood. I mean, I'm told they were considered old-fashioned even in the olden days. They kept to themselves.

"But we don't know what times was like back when he was young. We don't know what being a neighbor was, or what love was like, or honor. Faith in God. Things we laugh about now. We forget."

I kind of knew what she was getting at. I suspected that she had been drinking. There was a smell on her breath, maybe vodka. "We do forget," I said.

"I don't know who she is. Sorry. Not for sure."

"You had mentioned a sweetheart last

time we spoke. Someone who may have left Aub, jilted him?"

"I also told you what I thought of him. It's not in his character, killing a person."

I heard a hint of anger in her voice, and resisted telling her that she could never know that for certain. "I'm going out to have a smoke," she said. "Come on out if you want."

Gazing into the black woods behind her house, she lit a cigarette and smoked in silence. She wore wool socks and clogs. I was still in stocking feet, and the damp crept up my ankles; I wiggled my toes and thought, this is how Stonewall Jackson died.

"Forgive me, Evelina," I said. "It's none of my business. You're quiet tonight. Something bothering you?"

The old lady peered at me over top of her glasses. "Tell me, Henry. Out where you live, did you sign?"

"I don't own my place."

She snorted impatiently. "But would you?"

"No," I said. "Nothing against you if you did."

"Not even if you were hard up?"

"I'd figure something else out, I guess."

"But what if you were shiftless?" She leaned theatrically around me to look in the direction of her son's house.

I didn't answer.

"Sorry," she said. "Clearly I don't mean you." She looked around her, at the wild lawn, the dew caught in starlight, and the apple trees twisting themselves into the ground. "Isn't much, this. But I won't sign no gas lease. It's poison. Still, if you do or don't, there's something to poison you. It's stubborn, maybe. Pointless." She tossed her cigarette aside and muttered, as if admitting to herself, "Everybody's going to sign."

We let that drift awhile. There weren't too many people in the area left who felt the way she did. It had to be difficult.

I asked, "What can you tell me about this woman, Aub's?"

"I don't know. We're talking about old news, here. It's said she came over from Ireland to marry someone from a farm family. Like a mail-order. Aub wasn't the one she contracted with, but she wound up with him anyway. Maybe just long enough to pry herself free from her husband, then she took to her heels. Headed for the old country."

"Got a name, anything? Who was she?"

She clucked and shook her head. "I hope it isn't her you found. I don't know her full name, but her married name was Stiobhard."

Night had fallen; in my truck, the factory heat wheezed its swaddling breath as headlights from the opposite lane flooded my vision, leaving afterimages that I could not blink away. I needed to go home and I knew it.

At the courthouse, there was a light or two on somewhere deep inside, but nobody around upstairs. I had a key to the back door closest to the sheriff's department. When I first stepped inside, the basement floor was silent, and with no other sound to muffle my footsteps, it felt like I was echoing down that long fluorescent hall forever into nothingness. The feeling was comforting as a daydream. As I passed the little window set in the door to the holding cells, I picked up movement, and peered in. The side corridor glowed green. I heard voices and the sound of a shower turning off; down the hall, Ben Jackson stood in the doorway of the jail bathroom. I rapped a knuckle on the glass window. Jackson double-timed it to the door and admitted me.

From the bathroom, McBride's voice reached us like a distant chain saw: "Deputy, I know beggars can't be choosers, but this towel wouldn't dry my dick and balls." The prisoner emerged into the hall, hunched, shivering, and naked but for several patriotic and death-themed tattoos. He brandished a thin white towel like a surrender flag before tossing it to the floor. "It's cold as shit in here. I'm a health risk!"

Deputy Jackson raised his eyes to the sky. "Pick that up and be quiet."

McBride noted my arrival. "Hey! Officer! This bitch said he wants to suck my cock. Get me out of here."

"Get in your cell and get dressed."

"I lodge a complaint on you." McBride shook his head, toweled himself off theatrically, and moved into his cell, closing the door himself.

I turned to the deputy and said, "Some improvement over last night."

"Yeah. Who knows what tomorrow may bring? I should tell you he's been arraigned. Possession with intent to distribute, possession of chemicals with intent to manufacture, criminal conspiracy."

I nodded. It was what I had expected.

"Funny, what meth he had wrapped up with him was not the same as what he'd have made in his lab," Jackson said. "Looks like we're seeing the arrival of a larger supplier. There's a task force — DEA along with state Clandestine Labs Unit — that wants us to make a deal to get to whoever that supplier is. Someone's been leaning on the DA. They don't give a damn about this guy, particularly, considering what they think they could connect him to. Meantime, we braced McBride about the JD and George. Before his lawyer taught him not to talk, he swore up and down he had nothing to do with either of them."

"Where's Dufaigh?"

"She got bailed out after the arraignment. Her father showed."

"What charges?"

"Possession with intent, but they're not really after her. She'll plead nolo to simple possession and go into treatment. It's McBride they can use." We were speaking low, but Jackson dropped his voice to a murmur. "He could walk. Of course, he doesn't know that yet."

"Let me talk to him."

"Three minutes. You don't touch him, you don't open his cell, and you don't mention any plea. And," he added, pausing before his exit, "it never happened. I'll be in the john down the hall." Without another word, Jackson slipped out the door.

For a moment I stood in the green under-glow, me at one end of the hall and McBride at the other. I could hear him stir on his bunk. It was hard bringing myself to face him up close; I worried his eyes would reveal something I needed to know but couldn't bear to see.

McBride had dressed in red coveralls issued by the county, and was curled into the fetal position with his face to the wall. Something about his scalp, which showed plainly white through his buzz cut and was speckled with brown moles, inspired a loathing as pure as it was irrational. It was a head you wanted to slap, except you'd never stop wiping your hand after. The prisoner shivered and turned half in my direction.

"Sit up," I said. "Look at me."

"You're nobody." He turned back to the wall.

"I can get to Tracy."

He didn't respond.

"You must be wondering if we found your gun in that shithole. The .38? You know, Tracy did you no favors. She meant well."

"What .38? Bullshit. Just go away."

"But I'm not even here. You think I'm here building a case? I'm here so you can look me in the eye and tell me the truth, so that I know. I'm pretty sure you didn't have anything to do with that boy we found. But either you killed Ellis, or you were there when he got it. You may not have even meant to. He catch up with you, catch you with someone? You cleaning up for someone? You may have thought you didn't have a choice."

At this, he turned over and sat up. We met eyes. "I'd never shoot a cop. I hope you get the guy and string him up by his balls. Between you and me, Ellis did brace me once, maybe a month back, fractured my orbital." He touched his temple. "Ellis had the wrong idea about me and Trace — I ain't no pimp, and she ain't no whore, and it wasn't business. Not like his little operation collecting pocket change from my friends. And if you think Tracy could kill anyone, you're out of your mind." Whatever was adversarial in him disappeared. Once-hidden facets now shone forth in his eyes — fear, desperation. "You don't think it's the law I was running from, do you?"

"Good luck," I told him, then walked down the hall and exited the holding area. My head begin to pulse.

In the main corridor, Jackson asked how it went.

"He's not the one," I said. We bade each other good night and Jackson returned to his post in the cells.

I continued on and my footsteps echoed.

Somewhere in a back office of the sheriff's department a desk lamp burned, so I knocked on the glass door, then let myself in. Behind the partition, Krista's work area contained several jars of candy and very many photographs, almost all of family and friends, and one of Krista herself in desert camo, in sunlight from another part of the world. I couldn't tell from the uniform what division she had been in. I sprang the lock to the desk drawer where she kept her key ring, found the keys, and took them.

If anybody was in the courthouse with me, my shuffling footsteps up the stairs failed to draw their attention, and up in the attic room I was left alone with the dead birds and long-ago lives. In my previous exploration of the cabinets I'd found the suggestion of alphabetization, over which a fog of items, events, and documents had descended, completely out of step with the orderly passage of time. The Stiobhard section seemed to be divided between the S cabinets, in files of crumbling papers spanning old Xeroxes of documents from the nineteenth century to the 1960s, and the heap of unfiled boxes, where I found a more recent catalog, including a faded court order that had sent a young Alan Stiobhard to a juvenile hall outside of Scranton for petty theft. At issue: a few car parts pulled from a private junkyard. There were letters Mike sent in protest. Alan had been sixteen. I tucked anything that looked promising under my coat, locked the attic door, descended the stairs, returned Krista's keys, and headed home.

My house was dark, the night cold and fresh. Once again, the fires of industry flickered above the hills on the southwest horizon. As I reached my front door, I noticed a smell, and my hand had closed on the knob before I saw what was there: two pike hanging from either end of a spliced length of fishing line, cleaned and dripping blood-tinted water.

Because it was wintertime, my porch table and chairs were put away and replaced with two racks of firewood. But I had kept two chairs for sunny days, wedged into a far corner where I could look south and east down the valley. From the darkness at that far end, a silhouette rose.

"Evening, Officer."

"Alan, how you faring?"

"Faring pretty well. Got a minute?"

"Sure," I said, trying to decide what to do with his family's documents, still under my arm. "Come on in."

"I'd rather stay out; just got one rolled."

"Okay."

A lighter's flame popped in Stiobhard's hand and tobacco smoke filled the air. "I see you found my aunt today."

"Your aunt."

"Great-great-aunt. Helen, of the Kinsale Stiobhards."

"Is that who she is? Jesus."

"I believe so, yeah." Alan moved closer. He had an arm tied in a sling in order to rest his shoulder. "We appreciate you digging her up. But we'd like her back now."

In my coat pocket, my hand tightened around the grip of my little .22.

"Easy, Officer. I'm just here to tell you you've got to hand her over to us."

"What?"

"She's ours. We've been waiting years to lay her to rest where she belongs. It ain't a request."

"So even you didn't know where she was until now?"

"Sure, we had some idea. We only lacked opportunity."

"Meaning what?"

"You could ask Aubrey. Suffice it to say, we feel he's had her for too long, and she needs to come home now."

I waited for him to continue. He didn't,

and exhaled two jets of smoke from his nostrils.

"I'll do what I can for you," I said. "But you do something for me. Whatever you've got, you tell me now. The old man is suffering. I've got a John Doe and a dead deputy turning this township to rot. Your brother's on the run. And here's you walking around free as you please, talking about ancient history and goddamn aunts."

Alan shrugged. "Been putting things right in your pathway. I can't do everything for you." He shook his head. "Like I said, Helen is ours now. We're taking her back, in one piece." As he brushed past me and moved toward the steps, he paused to say, "You will not cut into that woman. Leave her as she was."

He moved into the darkness of the northern field. As he stepped into the woods, he called over his shoulder, "Roast them with butter, salt, and onions. Brain food for you, Officer."

My condition must have been improving; as I held the pike up for inspection, they looked like something I could eat. Smelled halfway decent too. I brought them inside, wrapped them in paper, and put them in my icebox.

I had a bath, and it was very human.

After washing the pike in the sink, I prepared them much as Alan had suggested — he didn't need to tell me how to cook a fish — and got them sizzling in the aged oven that came with the farmhouse. You don't want to eat pike all the time, as they are near top of their food chain and full of mercury, but they can't help it if they're delicious either, especially when caught on the young side and cooked right then. With some wild rice and green beans frozen from the garden, it was as good a meal as I'd had in days. The heat from the oven thawed me a bit.

I washed my dishes, then poured a small glass of scotch and sat at the kitchen table looking at the Stiobhard files in a stack. Below the mix of deeds and criminal records was a rich vein of photocopied documents from early in the century. Time had blurred the typewritten words, but it wasn't too long before I found what I had been seeking: a marriage license between Michael Stiobhard, who was grandfather to the Mike I knew, and Eibhilín Aodaoin ó Baoill of County Cork, Ireland. The year was 1928. It took some scrabbling among the papers at the table, and stacking and restacking, before I concluded there was no great-great-aunt among the Holebrook County Stiobhards. Helen had to be Eibhilín, our lady of the bog. I poured my whiskey back in its bottle and went to bed.

Can I tell you one more thing about my wife Polly and our place in Wyoming? She loved gardening: vegetables, but especially flowers. Our neighborhood was scrubby and dry, and it took effort to grow anything beautiful. The irrigation ditch that cut across our land meant a lot to Poll; it was a kind of anchoring presence for what she cultivated, a surety against drought and failure that not every homestead had. She planted a stretch of perennials along the far bank so we could sit on the porch and smoke a joint and survey our bright swaths of color in a gray-green ocean of sage. Yeah, we grew a bit of weed for ourselves, in secret defiance both of the law and the cartel working their way north at the time. As a lawman, I gave myself that special privilege. Anyway, the flowers: I remember the first season her salvia and Jacob's ladder bloomed together in a purple embarrassment of riches. They were not gentle nor cloudy as the lilacs we get back East, but they did the trick.

One bright morning I come home after a shift of the usual shit, waiting at DUI stops and tailing pickups, and there was Polly, out kneeling by the flower bed at the irrigation ditch. Her back was to me. It was uncommon to see her out during the day by that stage. Something about her body didn't work right in the sunlight anymore, and she got light-headed and short enough of breath that it could be a near thing for her to get back to the house. Something in the air. I was tired and almost didn't go out to her, but I did. As I got closer I noticed she was wearing something on her head. She turned slightly and I saw it was a gas mask. She'd driven out to the A to Z for it so she could weed the flower bed and be in the sun. I hurried to her side. Kneeling, she looked up at me from amid the pink and blue phlox and delphiniums, and through the mask's clear plastic, there was a smile. I remember thinking, how is it all these flowers can live here but my wife is dying?

It wasn't long after that. There were weeks of desperation as we sought treatment we couldn't afford, and nobody was optimistic; in addition to the newly discovered cancer that extended from lungs to brain, Poll's liver and kidneys had partially crystallized and her skin was opening up in nickel-sized sores that didn't go away on their own. I'll always remember the last time I saw her alive, what I would consider alive, is when she struggled out to her garden in a gas mask.

In the hospital there came a point when she was lucid and I couldn't be sure she would be again. It took some time sitting by her bedside to bring myself to say what I had to. We'd both know why I was saying it.

"Poll," I said, and couldn't go on.

She smiled.

I tried again and got a little farther. "You're the best part of this world. The only beautiful part, to me." I tilted my face back but my eyes flooded over. "Everything else is nothing compared to you."

"Shucks," she said.

I laughed at that. "I'll find you again. I can't live without you."

"But I want you to," said Poll. "Yes, you can."

Next morning I stood on the front stoop of Kevin and Carly Dunigan's place. Carly answered my knock.

"Morning," I said. "Carly, I need to speak

337

with Aub again."

"Afraid you can't. The sheriff beat you to it. They just left about five minutes ago."

"Already? Where?"

"I have no idea. Sheriff didn't say."

"What's Kevin's cell?" She didn't answer, and I asked, "Does Kevin even know about this? Does Wendell?"

"Kevin's at work. Which is where I need to be. And I assume Aub needs to be wherever he is —"

I left her standing there, slammed the door to my vehicle, and called Dally on my cell. He didn't answer, and I sped away.

I pulled around to the asphalt parking lot behind the courthouse to find the sheriff's radio car. I had arrived at exactly the right or wrong time: As I trotted to the main entrance, a siren wailed in the distance, and Liz Brennan tore up the driveway in her station wagon. She jerked to a halt a bit past the entrance, got out, didn't close her door, and hurried past me into the basement level. The siren grew louder as I followed her in, and was swallowed by the closing door and the courthouse's heavy interior.

We headed down a set of stairs to a metal door, behind which was the coroner's office and a morgue the size of a meat locker. We opened it in time to hear Wy Brophy say,

"I'm not a doctor, Nicholas."

The sheriff knelt on the floor beside Aub Dunigan, whose eyes were gently shut even as his mouth grasped — whether for words or air I couldn't tell. His right knee was raised, and his forearm flopped onto his abdomen repeatedly and with no strength. His left side was motionless. Liz swept the sheriff away, and performed what examinations she could.

"I thought we were going to talk about this," I said to Dally.

"Yeah, well," said Dally with a sigh. "As you see." He stood tall, but if you looked close enough, you could see the burden of guilt beginning to bend him.

Without turning from her patient, Liz asked for an account.

"Ah," Dally said. "Yeah. We took him down here to view a body, a body that was pulled out of his land."

"But . . . he was the one who found him in the first place, right?"

"No, a woman. Somebody new." His eyes turned to an examination table, where a corpse lay covered by a sheet. "It upset him. He pitched forward onto the examination table and ended up on the floor. I was able to, to stop his fall a bit. And here we are."

"His heart's steady, considering, but his

breathing worries me. I'm reasonably sure we're looking at a stroke. We need to take him to town." By this, Liz meant over the border to a hospital in Binghamton or Elmira. "I'll ride with him. Where's the ambulance coming from, the county? We'll need advanced life support."

The EMTs arrived and strapped the old man onto a gurney. His mouth was the only part of him free to move, wide open and gnawing at the air. They disappeared out the door, and the sheriff, silent and lost, followed them. Liz promised to call me with news that I could relay to Aub's family, and left me in the morgue with Brophy.

The coroner stared at the shrouded body on the examination table, wearing earmuffs against the cold. Coming to himself, he said, "Can I help you, Henry?"

"I'm sorry about all that," I said.

Brophy shook his head. "What a thing."

"After everything," I said. "From your point of view, the sheriff, he was pretty much on the money? He didn't leave anything out?"

"No, no. Well. Aub didn't so much 'pitch forward.' " Wy glanced in the direction of the woman's body once more. "You know, he saw her and he, he went to her. It looked like he was trying to hold her. Embrace her.

You're going to say I'm crazy, but it was romantic. More than romantic."

"So he knew her."

"Who is this woman?" Wy asked, halfway rhetorically.

"We don't know."

"Well, he was talking to her, but I couldn't understand him. And then, you know. The sheriff pulled him away, helped him up. And —" He smacked one palm against the other. We stood there in silence.

I approached Helen, or Eibhilín, or whoever she was, and drew back the hospital sheet that covered her face. She looked as human as the first time I saw her. An aspect of her lived on. It was as if she were midsentence in something that took a while to say; I waited for the message so long that Wy disappeared into his office, and came back, and I was still looking. I covered her, and the impression lingered in the room.

"While I'm here, can I have another look at the John Doe?"

Brophy led me to a bank of four morgue drawers, opened one, and slid the JD out far enough to expose his face. I don't know what I was looking for, maybe just to burn him into my mind again, or to see him in some new way. His lips shriveled back to show too much of the ruined mouth. Below the stubble on his Adam's apple, and above his black chest hair, was a constellation of chocolate-colored moles. He had no nose or ear hair, and eyebrows that were too perfect — they would have met above his nose, had they not been plucked. Once he'd been cleaned up, you could tell his haircut had taken some time and money. In more ways than one, he didn't look like someone from around here. Poor people aren't thin anymore, like when I was a kid; now they're fat on the cheap food feeding the ghost of the American dream. This kid was thin, almost extravagantly so. In the slightly more civilized setting of the morgue, I had a sense of sophistication, even wealth.

Back at the station I was reminded that what might be called normal life goes on, with or without my participation. There were voice mails from a state police dispatcher informing me of a heroin-related car accident in the township the night before, and two domestics, one violent, all handled by state troopers. Fine by me. I also had a cryptic message from my DEA liaison, as well as from Alexander Grace, owner of the stolen skid steer. His voice shook a little on the tape: "I got him, Henry. I got him here. You have to come over right away." It didn't sound good. I raced down 37 to find Grace hopping mad; a former employee had shown up claiming to know where the machine was, but wouldn't give it up until he had the money in hand. This led Grace to produce a pistol. The man consented to be held captive for a little while, then grew tired of waiting for me to show up, got in his truck, and left without being shot. Grace gave me the employee's name, and I promised to pay him a visit.

I picked up a sandwich and returned to my station. The forms were still there. There would always be a gap between what appeared on the reports and what had actually taken place. For the past few days and nights, the time sheets I submitted to Milgraham and the chronology of my work would be especially tough to reconcile, given how much unanticipated overtime it would involve. I had been lobbying for a salary, rather than wage, anyway; I don't mind staying out a little late. If done right, the reports would help my cause. Form upon form. I couldn't bring myself to begin.

I had been meaning to put in a call to the machine shop in Kirkwood where Barry Nolan worked, and finally had a spare moment to do so. After a minute of blown-out hold music, the manager got on the line, a prickly fella named Goffa. I introduced myself and explained that I was calling on behalf of Nolan. "He's had a friend die, and he's been helpful to us here in the township," I said. "I just wanted you to know that if he's missed some work, that's the reason."

"Yeah, well. That's what the phone is for. In the end . . ."

"I understand," I said, wanting to get off the phone. "I can account for second shift yesterday, and first shift the day before."

Goffa made an impatient noise. "That's, you know. Okay. What about third shift before that, and second shift the day before that? If everybody blows off their rotation —"

"I'm sorry, what?"

"Yeah. He missed four in a row. Part-timers, like Nolan, work on a rotation —"

"Thanks for your time," I said, and hung up.

I got up, put on my extra .40 and coat, had my hand on the doorknob, and then I stopped, took off my coat, and sat.

Camp Branchwater was shut up in the winter. Remote as it was, patrolled by Nolan, and offering no heat or electric, the young drinkers, vandals, drug users, and cheaters of the area let it be. I'd never gotten a call about it in my few years on the job. I needed a closer look.

There was a number for Branchwater's office in my phone book; I dialed it and got the answering machine. I left a message for someone to call me back, gave my office number and my cell, and said it was urgent. Then I called the sheriff's department; Krista hadn't heard any news of the sheriff or Aub. It took her just a moment to find Pete Dale's number in Westchester for me. I thanked her and hung up.

After a few rings, Pete's kindly wife Donna answered. Though she was surprised to hear from me, she summoned some pleasantries and questions about the township. She didn't seem to know anything of our difficulties. I made some conversation with her before asking to speak with Pete.

"Henry?" Pete's voice on the line was slow, burred by smoke, friendly. "I'm halfway out the door. How can I help you?"

"Did Sheriff Dally speak with you?"

"He did. How's poor Aub? And of course, shocked to hear about your deputy."

"Thanks. Pete, I'm calling because I'd like to see your records, records of campers and counselors from the past fifteen years."

After a pause, Dale said, "This doesn't sound like anything to do with us."

"I know," I said. "Our victim isn't local either. We saved you for last, hoping . . . Sheriff Dally, he wanted to keep you out of it."

"I appreciate it. And you have my permission, one hundred percent. Absolutely. I'll call Barry Nolan and tell him, and you can work it out from there."

I paused too long. "Is there anybody else who can let me in?"

"What's wrong with Barry?"

"Nothing. He was friends with George, and we'd like to limit his — between us, can I ask you about him?"

"He's a good caretaker," Dale said. "On the off season he'll fix a window, make sure the whole place doesn't fall down, whatnot."

"Between us," I said. "Between us, I heard there was some trouble with him a few years back."

Dale didn't answer right away. "Yeah. That was no big deal."

"Pete," I said. "Anything I should know about?"

"Nothing, a couple kids went home with black eyes and bruises. I don't know if you know, but boys do fight. How it got to where it did . . . there was a concerned parent, and it came back that the scrap happened on one of Barry's survival trips, and he didn't stop it. In fact, it wasn't the only one he didn't stop. Not saying he actively encouraged the boys to fight, but . . . people grow up with different ideas. I fired him and rehired him quietly, in a limited capacity, kept him away from the campers. It was mostly for his son. A sweet kid. You don't want to see your father shitcanned. Anyway, Nolan is reliable. He's not involved with this, is he?"

"Like I say, we're trying to give him a break. Between us, Pete."

"Oh, sure." Dale thought a moment. "You know Shelly Bray, she runs a horse farm in Wild Thyme?"

"Yes."

"We've turned over the riding courses to her. She's got a set of keys. Good luck. And Henry, remember: Branchwater is one hundred and seven years old. We've never once had need of the police."

"We're trying to keep you out of it," I said.

From the shore of Camp Branchwater's private lake, a great blue heron croaked and rose into the air, flapping its huge wings once, twice, and was gone. Winter had outstayed its welcome and spring would not be denied. As I stood waiting in the driveway, Shelly Bray pulled up in her late-model station wagon, the engine quiet as air. Waving cheerfully, she stepped out of the car in jeans tucked into high brown boots. Her hair was smoothed back into a ponytail, and she wore a puffy vest embroidered with the logo of her horse farm. Our hands touched as she passed me the camp key ring.

"Well, thanks," I said, and waited for her to leave.

"You don't want company?" Her smile faltered. "You don't have to talk about . . . anything you can't talk about."

I should have sent her away. Instead I found the office key and we went in.

The camp's main building was a large two-story house, sided with cedar shingles, that been there for at least a hundred years. The electric was shut off for the season, and dark plaid wallpaper sucked up most of the interior light; we pushed open curtains and found a waiting room with factory-made furniture designed to look antique. Under a layer of dust, outdoor magazines were fanned on end tables. I peered into a glass case and found Max Brand paperbacks sandwiched between James Fenimore Cooper and Mark Twain, along with assorted shipwrecks, kidnappings, and explorations.

Shelly watched me take the measure of the place for a moment, and asked, "Did you ever go here? When you were a boy?"

"Me? No."

"My husband did. That's partly why we ended up buying our place."

I moved from one group photograph of boys in black-and-white to the next, around the room. "You settling in, out here in the hills?" I asked.

"It's like a dream," she said simply. "I grew up in West Virginia. Before and after school, and every summer, I worked on a horse farm. I never did my homework. I thought, who gives a shit? If I have to work all my life, I might as well be around horses. Tracy is the same way; that's why I hired her. Never thought I'd have my own." She sounded apologetic. "We were dirt-poor hillbillies. Probably why it feels strange, living in that place."

"That's not what I imagined at all. Meeting you," I told her.

"What did you imagine?" she asked.

I turned away, embarrassed, but her smile was kind and if she weren't married, I'd have said there was something else in it.

We passed through a door to the offices. There, we found a hallway lined with filing cabinets organized by year; within each year, each camper had his own file, including a photo, emergency contact information, what cabin he was bunked in, and accounts of problems: health, disciplinary, and otherwise. There were about a hundred boys to a summer, divided between July and August stays. Their ages ranged from nine to thirteen. Many of them attended year after year. As I sifted through the past decade, Shelly went further back, opening drawers. I opened my mouth to stop her, and nothing came out.

"What are you looking for?" she asked me.

"I thought I wasn't going to talk to you about that."

"Here," she said. "Look at this little bozo." In a file from twenty-six years back, she found a school portrait of a boy with spiked hair and a mouth full of braces. She drew up close to me. "My husband. See?"

"Huh."

She dropped it back into the file, which she flipped through before returning it to its year.

Eight years back I found a file for Finbar Nolan, Jr. There was little in his folder other than a photograph, and on the form where contact information was supposed to be written it read simply, *Nolan.* It was the same kid I'd seen in photographs on Nolan's refrigerator at older and younger ages. In this photo he had longer hair in the back, and was sitting for a portrait against a phony backdrop of trees and sky. At age thirteen, you could see that he was already growing into a football player. I tucked the file under my arm and kept looking. In that year, most of the kids were white and Anglo in appearance. There were several African-American boys, and Filipino brothers named Roger and Oscar Villanueva. I pulled the brothers' files, compared a Polaroid of John Doe, and put them back.

Shelly stopped herself from asking a question.

I shrugged. "We have no idea who the victim is. Was. But it's just too remote of a spot to be a random drop."

"You think he was a camper here?"

"Maybe."

I passed through all the remaining rooms on the ground floor, peering at photos, looking for the year that Barry Nolan, Jr., attended. They were roughly chronological, hung over windows and between Audubon prints and vintage maps, leading into back offices, a bathroom, a small kitchen. Eventually I was back in the front room, moving up the staircase. Shelly sat flipping through a magazine.

She asked, "Can I ask why you didn't call Barry? To let you in, I mean?"

"He was close to my deputy. We're keeping him out of it."

She was silent for a few moments. "It's not — it can't be what I'm thinking. Can it?"

"We shouldn't be talking about this."

Halfway up the stairs, I found something. A color photograph of about fifty boys and counselors gathered beneath a maple tree. You could tell how dirty they were after a summer outdoors, and how alive. Without touching the frame or the glass, which already showed a recent set of fingerprints, I scanned the faces. Standing with his arm flung over Barry Nolan, Jr.'s shoulders was a smiling kid, his long black hair held down by a red bandanna, his skin deep brown from the sun. For a moment, I tried to bridge the years between the living boy and the dead man, and then descended, holding the framed photograph by its hanging wire.

Aware of Shelly observing me, I kept my face and gait calm as I made my way back to the filing cabinets. I combed the records once again with greater urgency but no more success.

"Looks like I may be a while," I called out to the lobby. "I'll drop the keys off when I'm done." I pulled the lowest drawer all the way out and reached my arm into the

filing cabinet, up to my shoulder. My fingertips brushed a manila folder that lay flat
against the floor.

Shelly appeared in the hallway without my
hearing her. She said my name and I looked
up. There was an expression on her face like
some guys would get leaving for patrols in
the Mog. I've seen it too on an elderly man
whose heart had stopped, on a young
woman whose husband had put a knife
through her ribs in a vicious domestic. The
tension of a body anticipating death, com-
peting with disbelief — a kind of involuntary
calm. Struggling to produce the words, she
whispered, "He's here. Nolan."

A second passed. She wasn't a fool. She
knew, and I knew, and she needed me to go
to work. "It's going to be okay," I said.

I pulled her down the hall and planted
her out of sight by a back door, placing her
shaking hand on the dead-bolt knob. "If I
tell you to run, stay low until you hit the
woods. Keep going until you find someone.
A phone. Don't stop." Moving to the front
of the house with a .40 out, I heard nothing. I paused at the entrance to the lobby,
checking the windows for movement. Nothing. I crept back to Shelly, who jerked her
hand back as the lock's knob began to turn,
slowly, silently, on its own.

She backed away, slipped past me, and ran to the front door, a noise in her throat on the verge of a scream. I raised my weapon. The dead bolt slid free of its housing. I waited for the door to open.

Outside, a rifle shot cut the air. Glass exploded in a thud. The report was a .270 or higher. I ran to the front door. Shelly stood frozen by her station wagon and its shattered passenger-side window. The next shot passed through her vest with a burst of goose down. She barely moved, just patted her side in confusion. I leapt into the yard and toward Shelly, sending several .40 rounds at a shadow that had already disappeared between the cabins seventy-five yards back. I pulled Shelly down, shielding her with my body. As we crawled around the rear of the car, a third rifle shot popped the near tire and the car sagged. Two more shots followed at a lazy pace after we had cover. Explosions of mud and rock. From behind the bumper of the station wagon, I saw a figure hooded and cloaked in ghillie cloth, now over a hundred yards distant, backing toward a tree line with rifle trained on our position. I sent two more shots in his direction to discourage him from getting any closer. Shelly was unhurt. We moved, bent double, to the driver's-side door. I opened it and scrabbled for the keys where they hung in the ignition. Yelling for her to stay low and climb in the back seat, I started the engine just as several rounds tore into the hood.

As I backed the station wagon down the drive and out of range, two more bullets splashed home a couple feet in front of the bumper. We moved around the bend and into safety, but not before I crumpled the open driver's-side door against a tree; the window glass shattered in on me, making me believe for a moment we were taking fire from the north as well as the southwest. Where the driveway met the road, I threw the car into neutral and stepped out. Shelly remained hunched in the back seat with her head wrapped in her arms. I called her name once, twice, and she looked up.

"Can you drive?" I said.

She pulled herself together. "I don't know, the tire's gone —"

"Drive slow. I need you to get safe, get to a phone. Call the sheriff's department."

"Okay. Okay. Fuck." She climbed out of the back and slid into the driver's seat. I tried slamming the ruined door a couple times, metal and plastic crunching together with no result. "Stop. Stop!" she said. "I'll hold it closed."

"Be careful," I said.

Shelly pulled into the road. She looked up the drive, and then at me, shook her head, and drove away as fast as her flat tire would allow.

I stepped into the woods. When I reached the place where the figure had disappeared into the trees, my eye caught a brass glint: five .30-06 shells lay scattered on the mat of wet leaves, along with a five-cartridge magazine, empty.

With each new whitetail season, I wonder why I put so much effort into killing a being that has more in common with me than the average person walking down the street. I haven't settled on the answer. One year in Big Piney there was an elk that'd been hit by a car and lived, and roamed the public land nearby for months. Its flesh had healed but its shoulder had not; the bone wouldn't support weight. Though it had a beautiful four-foot rack, a hobbled buck can't mate, can't fight, can't run, can't do anything in life. I scouted it in the fall, and the first day of the season I went out and shot it, and said thank you Lord. I like to think the elk was thankful too. With most human beings it's not so simple. We have to limp along no matter the wound.

Camp Branchwater was splayed along a

north-facing ridge; the south-facing side curled around a swamp like a sleeping dog. I headed for high ground, skirting the clearing's edge, keeping plenty of cover between me and the shooter's possible positions.

As I made my way, I passed a Studebaker abandoned beside a stone foundation, and later on, a trio of blue plastic oil drums that would likely survive long after I was gone, until the woods were all cut down around them. These were objects I happened upon without noticing until I was close by. How I expected to pick out the dull glint of a gun barrel reaching through the brush a hundred yards away, I could not guess.

I moved and stopped to look, but more to listen. Take more than a step a second and you're not really after anything. Make your footfalls sound like something else. Be something else.

Instinct and the land swung me around to the northern edge of Aub's plot. I took a long loop west, and fetched up in a patch of blackberry brambles that bordered an intersection of logging roads, and settled in there.

The shooter's hearing would be wasted after firing at least ten rounds, by my count; that was in my favor. And if he expected me to wait for police to come screaming up 189 before I went after him, so much the better. He'd be looking for an approach from the northeast, and I was going to give him something else. A long minute passed before running steps broke the stillness. They were heavy but careful. No snapping branches underfoot, no barreling through the brush. In the clearing above, Nolan moved into view, wearing shaggy state-of-the art camo, carrying a deer rifle. He turned on his heel a moment and listened. I considered a long shot uphill, and thought better of it. Then he was gone, back in the trees.

I waited a beat, two, three, and took a slanting line to follow him. In about a hundred halting paces, I caught sight and sound of him as he crossed in front of me, slipping up the ridge away from Aub Dunigan's farm. I adjusted my line and prepared to meet him. He was heading for the site where we'd found the body.

It was once just a place in the woods, open to the sky, marked by fallen trees and a scattering of shale boulders draped in lichen and moss. My eye was drawn to what did not belong. Nolan stood facing east. By then he must have known I was approaching, but only turned to look at me when I told him to drop his rifle and put his hands on his head.

"I'm glad it's you," he said. "You know. It's all for nothing. It's all a mistake."

"Drop your weapon."

"You ever do something, but it just don't seem real?"

"Nolan."

"I'm sorry about this."

His rifle was muzzle-down. He lifted it in my direction, making a lazy sweep. He wasn't angry or hateful, but helpless. I shot him four times in the chest. He fell and was gone before I reached his side.

I'll tell you what happened, to the extent that it's documented and we can believe what is set down, coming as it does from Finbar Nolan himself. He left two handwritten letters in white business envelopes pinned to his refrigerator with magnets. The first read as follows:

To All Concerned,

By now you know it was me who killed the boy you found up at Aub's. I don't remember the exact day but it was between Christmas and New Years that I found him at the camp. I meant to burn and bury him forever but could not. His name was Albert Retroz. His death was a mistake.

I am sorrier than I can say about George Ellis. He was a good man everybody liked him, even me. If it is a comfort to his family he felt no pain. I was

trying to leave the boy's car in the junkyard up in the Heights. Too late now.
You can find it at the camp.

I hope to be forgiven in the next world.

— Nolan

The following letter was hardly more revealing.

Barry,
Remember some good things I did.
Be strong.
Sell the house and land, as it will fetch
a good price now.
Take care of your mother.

— Love, Dad

Now picture a hulking, handsome young
man. He has just driven two hours from college in Bethlehem. As he sits in a back office of the sheriff's department across from
Dally, and reads the second letter for the
first time, he understands that his father is
dead. Gone too is his first love, an on-again,
off-again boyfriend in college, a wild,
wealthy boy named Albert Retroz who
would not let go of what they had, and
would not accept it as secret. Barry Nolan,
Jr., now understands why Albert fell off the
face of the earth, why the calls he made have

not been returned, and that the horror he has quietly wrestled with for months — never quite believing the worst — is real. Al is dead, and everybody knows everything, or enough. He sets the letter down and wipes his eyes with a broad hand.

We found Retroz's car, a gray German compact, in a barn at the camp, like Nolan said. We also think we found the place where he died, out front of a cabin whose cedar siding divulged to Palmer's careful eye a few splinters of bone. We never did locate his arm, or the .38, or the flintlock. Retroz's death was ruled wrongful and there was nobody to punish for it.

A bend of the Susquehanna River passes through eastern Holebrook County, dividing the town of Fitzmorris in half. On one side, the original town had been built up against the river, and then spilled its box stores, auto dealers, and fast food chains south. Two bridges spanned the Susquehanna: a recently constructed concrete four-lane, and a venerable cast-iron that the town had blocked off to automobile traffic, painted green, and left open to pedestrians.

The previous year, a flood had nearly washed the pedestrian bridge away. Some businesses near the riverbanks were still boarded up, and as I looked at the brown water roiling below us, I had to say, good thinking. Move up the hill. This year and the next and the one after that, it'll be the same damn thing.

A contingent of Pennsylvania state troopers in their dress grays stood approximately at attention, apart from the seventy-odd mourners milling on the bridge's walkway, keeping a local camera crew at a distance while a Unitarian minister presided over the scattering. The ceremony concluded with a Walt Whitman poem that I liked, that made sense to me, about all the dead getting buried and absorbed into the earth, and returning in different forms. Here's the last bit: "O years and graves! O air and soil! O my dead, an aroma sweet! Exhale them perennial, sweet death, years, centuries hence." At the minister's prompt, George's brother Tim shook out the contents of an urn. There was no breeze, and the ashes fell heavily into the river, calling to mind a backhoe emptying its bucket.

Later, I stood on the back deck of a tavern named the Barley Mow, gazing over the Susquehanna as the sun spread pink across the water, avoiding a party that had been made strange and somber by the fact that George and Nolan had run in the same circles. There were notable absences. Certain people couldn't talk to each other and nobody knew what to say to me, and I had been counting the minutes until I could steal away. Tim Ellis found me. I had come to think of him as a suburban version of his brother George, without the heft or bloodshot eyes.

Tim gripped the same wooden railing I was leaning on and gazed at the southern riverbank. He stood there a good while. "My brother. What did he die for? Did he die for no good reason?"

At the time I thought that yes, he certainly did. "That's the question," I said, "but what's the answer?"

"I sure don't know."

"I liked George. A lot of people did. He lived well, at least."

The Barley Mow was crowded and I slipped by people I should have spoken to, nodding and smiling them away. As I neared the door, Julie the blond EMT — almost unrecognizable in charcoal pants, a turquoise blouse, and a dusting of makeup — put a hand on my sleeve, looked in my eyes, and said something I couldn't hear over the dull roar. Though she appeared to expect an answer, I gestured toward the door and left her standing there. In the end, it was Sheriff Dally who caught me as I was stepping into my vehicle.

"Got something for you," he said. "About as much closure as we're likely to get on Aub and your mystery lady." He handed me a sealed manila envelope, which I tossed on the passenger seat.

"How is he?"

"Ah, not great. Can't talk, can't walk. He's in a home north of Scranton. He won't be back in the township." Dally shrugged, then cocked his head at the report where it lay. "You should read it. It says how this was a long time coming."

"Okay. I'm back to work Monday. Call if you need anything."

"You know," he said, "Krista Collins has been hoping to get out in the field. I have no openings in my department. I figured you're already budgeted for it . . ."

"I'll think about it."

"She's a soldier, a veteran. She knows what she's doing. Plus she can bring you pieces of my network, contacts in the DEA, FBI, ATF. I'll speak with Milgraham if you need me to."

"I'll think about it."

As I drove through the gauntlet of too many cars parked on Front Street, I took note of a twenty-year-old sedan parked with its nose out, whose driver was still sitting at the wheel. Hat pulled low, watching the cars and people move in and out of the slipstream of George Ellis's wake, Finbar Nolan, Jr., was undeniably right where he was, and at the same time so far away that he didn't even see me pass.

■ ■ ■ ■

After Nolan's shooting, Township Supervisor Steve Milgraham stepped in and suggested some mandatory leave, mental health treatment, and — surprise — a Fitness-for-Duty Evaluation for me. Dally supported the first two only. He appealed to Milgraham's sense of economy, and claimed that the coming investigation of an officer-involved shooting, which was obligatory, would be tantamount to an FFDE, which it was not. I could see the fight brewing between the supervisor and the sheriff over me, and while I was in no position to assert my independence, I often thought about how to make up that ground I seemed to be losing.

The first couple days I had to move around some, to avoid camera crews and reporters who had sniffed out my home address. When I'd hear anyone on my driveway, I'd slip out the back door, cross the meadow to the ravine, and either clamber down to a landing where a deep pool collected the clearest burbling water, or head up to a slab of shale beneath a stand of hemlocks, and listen to the wind move west over the hills. After a while it was plain nobody was trying very hard to find me, and I felt safe enough to drink beer on my porch and watch March turn into April.

Deputy Jackson showed up a couple times to fill me in on what I had been missing. It may have had as much to do with APA recommendations on shootings as it was out of friendship — I wasn't supposed to be alone — but I appreciated it. The first visit, he told me U.S. Marshals had spirited Pat McBride away to some special facility in the dead of night; the deputy speculated that the dealer was now a guest of the state somewhere around Harrisburg, making himself useful to a major drug case. Another visit, Jackson told me that Wy Brophy had gotten his way, and the lady of the swamp had moved out of our morgue and into a Scranton lab. In a way I was glad. I couldn't help feeling curious about her, and Aub, and how it was she had died. I was going to have a headache about it with the Stiobhards, but I was used to that.

One afternoon I heard a car pull onto my driveway, and I started for the woods, as had become my habit. Something made me stop and get a look at my visitor — I might have been hoping it was Liz or Ed. What I saw was a high-end Japanese sport utility, black, with sprays of mud on its doors. A woman emerged, shading her eyes. She was small and thin, with short silver hair. I had seen her on the news. I had waited too long to disappear; having noticed me, she strode forward with her hand outstretched.

"Do you know who I am?" she asked me.

"Yes," I said. "Please come in."

Charlotte Retroz had fine features. In fact I'd say she was beautiful, and about fifty. She had refused my offer of a drink, would not even accept tap water, and perched on the edge of my easy chair clutching a quilted cloth purse with chickens on it. "I've been over it so many times," she said. "I'm here because I need to know more."

"I'll help however I can."

"This Nolan," she said. "In your report, he said very little to you before . . ."

"Yes."

"And you had to. Absolutely."

"Yes." I had been struggling with that question on my own, but tried not to show it. In my mind, I knew it had been the only possible course. You can know lots of things in your mind.

"There's a word that appears in his letter and in your report: *mistake.*"

I nodded.

"Not *accident.* It's not the same thing," she said.

"You're asking if —"

"If this Nolan intentionally killed my son . . ." Her voice failed her.

"Can I ask what you know about their history?"

She drew herself up. "You don't need to be delicate, not in this day and age. Al came out last year. It wasn't a shock to me, but it was disappointing to his father."

"Oh."

"Successful men like Al's father, part of why they succeed is that they are less burdened by empathy. Certainly he loves Al, and he never, never attacked him, not in my presence. But I could tell it was difficult. There was a heavy silence. It was some time before we knew Al was missing.

"As far as the Nolans go, Al and the boy were friends. We encouraged it. Al's social world would have been all one thing, otherwise. They had Branchwater together when they were boys, and the summer they were sixteen, there was a camping trip with . . . the father. With Nolan. Something went wrong and it was cut short. Al wouldn't talk about it, and we figured the friendship was over. After all, their worlds were just going to get more and more different. Now I see how it was."

"Have you met with Barry?"

"He won't . . . he can't. I've tried to reach him." She looked out the window and back at me. "Sheriff Dally told me Barry said he didn't know why Al would be in the area around Christmas. That they had no plans to meet. I find that hard to believe. Don't you?"

"It's . . . Yeah."

"Officer, you haven't answered my first question."

"I'm sorry. It's because I don't know."

"If there's any impression of the man, anything you've held back for whatever reason, we won't hold it against you."

"Mrs. Retroz —"

"It matters." She drew her palms across her cheeks. "It matters if Al, who was sweet, and kind, and full of fun, died accidentally, or . . ."

I thought of what I should say, and said it. "From what I know, Nolan had his ideas, and they weren't going to change. But he loved his son. He was capable of that. I believe your son's death was an accident."

"I hope that boy is good," Charlotte Retroz said, holding back tears, her jaw clenched. "I hope he is good enough for mine."

The morning before George's service, I had

371

driven my pickup out to the edge of the woods. A large ash tree had toppled, over-burdened by an ice storm during the winter. It turned out not to be straight or broad enough to mill beyond the first ten feet. With my chain saw I sectioned what I thought might work for Ed, and bucked the rest, along with whatever other fallen wood nearby that was big enough to split for the stove but had been covered by snow all winter. The sun had risen high in the sky and I had been splitting for some time when I became aware of someone watching me. Danny Stiobhard stood there in clean work clothes.

"I followed your noise out here. Got a minute?" he said.

"You help me load this, sure."

We each carried armloads of firewood out to my pickup, then I drove him back across the field to my house.

Inside, I brewed some coffee and we sat, smelling of sweat and sawdust and motor oil, at the kitchen table.

"So anyway, I come in peace," he said, and raised his mug in my direction.

"I gathered."

"And you know by now that I haven't killed anybody."

"Very good, I'm glad."

"Yeah, so," he said. "Sorry about that night. Things could have been different. I'm going to have to work that one off. I know that." I said nothing and let him squirm. "But you think it never happens? How many guys just like me, rotting in a cell for something they didn't do?"

"I don't know of any, personally. But I can understand your worry."

"Fuckin Barry Nolan."

"Indeed."

"All over his son being, you know. With that other."

"We don't really know what happened."

"I know he was a drunk, and stupid," Danny said. "Wouldn't have picked him for this, though. He had his pants on backward about something."

"So how long did you know?"

"About the stiff? I didn't."

"Your brother did."

"Nothing in the township he don't know. Who do you think it was found George?"

"So did he know it was Nolan that killed him?"

"That I couldn't say."

Of course not. "Can I ask why were you trying to get up on the ridge?"

There was a flare-up behind Danny's eyes, but he kept it civil. "As I recall, I told you that. Kevin Dunigan hired me to clear the trails."

"He says he didn't."

"Then he's a fuckin liar and a short-assed rascal."

"You notice Aub's wheels were missing?" I said.

"I'm leaving." He stood. "All I came for was about my aunt."

"Sit down. Please." He obliged, though he was angry enough that the coffee trembled in his hand when he lifted it again. "So tell me."

"My great-aunt. Helen Stiobhard. We always did want her back for a proper burial. Guess that's out of the question now," he grumbled.

"It's out of my hands."

"Yeah?"

"Yeah. So what's the deal?" I asked. He made a dismissive gesture that I couldn't read. I pressed him. "What's the matter with the way she was buried the first time? Hey, you can tell me anything. I'm on leave."

Danny sized me up and then spoke. "The way I heard it, she took up with Aub, and we never heard from her again. I say 'we.' This was when my granddaddy was just a boy."

"Listen, I looked in the records."

"Did you? Fine."

"You don't have any Aunt Helen and I think you know it."

He slammed his mug down. "I'll tell you what I do know: we have a claim on that land."

"Aub's land?"

"Aub's land, yeah. So you need to get the dead old girl back up from Scranton so we can get a DNA sample."

"Kevin has power of attorney now, there's very little you can do. Aunt or no."

"No? What about a great-grandmother? Yeah, Daddy, he don't want to talk about it, he don't want anyone to know. Not even if it gets him the land. But that Irishwoman was his true grandmother and direct relation. She left our great-granddaddy and lived in common law with Aub for years before she got killed. That don't make a claim?" Danny stood up to leave.

"Hey," I said, my wheels still turning. "Aub was your great-grandfather?"

He scoffed, and spoke slowly, as if to a dimwit. "No. I'm a damn Stiobhard. She bore my granddaddy and then ran off, left him when he was a baby."

"Kevin know about this?"

Danny snorted. "What Kevin don't know. And I'll tell you something else: he hired me for one thing, but got quite another. Yeah. And you ask him where those fuckin car wheels went."

After the funeral I went over to Ed and Liz Brennan's for supper. It stayed light enough and warm enough that we got in a game of croquet with their kids, on their large and bumpy front lawn, before we sat down to our braised venison and roasted parsnips and carrots. I had been having trouble keeping recent events out of my mind, particularly the jolt of the .40 in my hand. In my memory, the force of the shots and the red that splashed out of Nolan's chest had become the same thing, and in my mind I was not only hearing and seeing, but feeling him die by my hand. There was very little separating me from that memory. I had talked about it with the shrink they'd set me up with in Scranton, a pleasant fellow who needed me to say something about the way I felt. I was careful to keep it to the shooting and to my feelings about George's death, and even when he asked me about my military service, which wasn't any too traumatic, I thought it wasn't safe, it wasn't smart to start talking about things it would take me too long to finish. I did enough sharing to get back to work once the investigation was over with.

That night at Liz and Ed's was the first time I'd had something strong enough to distract me, and I stayed later than I should have, drinking and calling tune after tune. Eventually, Ed passed out on the couch with his eyes open — it's alarming the first time you see it, but perfectly natural when you know it is his wont — leaving me and Liz to run through rarities in our back catalogs. She got out her fretless gourd banjo that never stays in tune, and we moved into some very ancient modal material, which reminded me of "The Still Hunter," which Aub had played for me that once.

Liz had never heard that title either. "What is a still hunter, even? Like a revenuer?"

"A still hunter goes out on his own," I said, "and doesn't have anyone to drive game his way. He knows where the deer will be. He's not actually still, he sneaks around a bit. He's on a footing with the game."

We tried the song with me in the drop tuning, and I actually remembered it; I wasn't sure I would. After running through it a couple times, Liz was able to plunk along and then it became music, and we were not ourselves but the same small part of something that was beyond everything. It's strange how the universe can open up at times, isn't it? From just a scrap of music that nobody but one old man knew, you start to think about the possibilities you have missed, and the possibilities to come.

As I stepped in the vehicle, the sheriff's manila envelope was sitting there on the passenger seat. I opened it up and found not just one report, but several medical documents pertaining to Aub Dunigan's condition, and something from Wy Brophy and a Scranton forensics expert about Helen Stiobhard, or Eibhilín Aodaoin ó Baoill, if you will. In the report she was referred to as Jane Doe. In my boozy state I didn't trust myself to make sense of them, and I took them in for Liz to read.

"His liver is almost gone," she said, after reading through them. "Where did he get the money for alcohol?"

I had some ideas about who would have liked to keep Aub drunk, but didn't share them.

"This is interesting," she said. "They looked at his brain. There's a pattern of strokes, increasing in severity over time, as they do. It's common, and it certainly would account for his dementia."

"Is that the only thing? What I mean is, we're never going to know now. But hearing him talk, I had the impression he, he had particular delusions. Strong ones."

"That might result from the strokes, or from a lifetime of drinking, or both. What delusions?"

"Ah. A woman who visited him."

Liz kind of shivered and set Aub's records aside, and looked to her sleeping husband's face for reassurance.

"What about the Jane Doe, please? What do they say?"

Liz scanned the report, which was several pages. "This is amazing. They don't know how long she'd been buried, decades. She was so well preserved that when they opened her up, they found tumors. Cancer, from her ovaries straight into her brain." She frowned. "There was also the suggestion of trauma around the throat which might indicate . . . strangulation. But they aren't sure."

"Had she ever given birth, what do they know about that?"

"They don't say. Listen, sleep here if you want, once I get this lummox off the couch." Ed raised his head, told us hello, and laid it down again.

"Nah, I've got to go." Though I shouldn't have in my condition, I drove home.

■ ■ ■ ■

Danny Stiobhard never got his DNA sample from the lady of the swamp; the state destroyed her before she could cause any more trouble. Aub died in his sleep just a couple weeks later.

One thing that has bothered me since: over in neighboring Susquehanna County, in St. Francis Xavier's churchyard, there's a woman buried who lived just twenty years, never married, had no known relatives in the area, and died in 1936. The name on her stone is Evelyn Bailley and I still wonder about her.

The psychiatrist in Scranton told me feelings of shame and depression were normal following an officer-involved shooting. I had to forgive myself because if I wasn't careful, I could turn those feelings — curdle them — into a rage that would consume me. He said it in many more words, but that was the message.

The days got longer and warmer and I kept feeling those four shots hit home in the cool dusk. I pulled over DUIs and saw Barry Nolan, Jr.'s far-off face behind the wheel of his car. I ran into old men in their formless baseball caps bloviating over coffee at the HO Mart, and I thought of Aub Dunigan, and what had made him so alone. The investigation was, after all my worry, a perfunctory afternoon in the company of the county DA and a judge in a courthouse conference room, with Dally there for moral support. Shelly Bray showed up to corroborate certain aspects. The DA and judge asked me some questions about why I didn't wait for support before going after Nolan, and I choked out an answer about the allocation of resources in the county and in my township, and reminded them that my deputy was dead. I was cleared, and Nolan's death was ruled suicide-by-cop.

It had been six weeks since Nolan, but I hadn't slept for running the film over and over in my head. I knew that someone else had to forgive me because I was in no condition to do it myself.

In the first week of June, I stumbled into the middle of Shelly Bray's marriage, and into her bed. I justified it several ways: that she'd been mocking her husband to me with subtle remarks, implying the marriage was drying up, an unmistakable preamble. That I'd been celibate so long, I couldn't let an opportunity pass. Even, Polly, that you'd told me to be happy and that I should try.

On a hot June midmorning that we both knew would end in our first assignation, when the fields buzzed with insects, and her kids were still in school, Shelly took me out riding on trails that connected her place with Aub's and Nolan's. In so doing I felt she was telling me that what had happened out there was all right, that the world —

and that ridge in particular — was a place where I could still belong. It was as much for this forgiveness as anything else that I went to bed with her. She was a decent person and wouldn't take on somebody who wasn't.

In the cool shade of the woods, we passed through where a dry-stacked wall had toppled down, and onto Aub's land. I stopped, dismounted, and moved along the stones. Soon enough I found a turquoise glass insulator, then another and another. I dislodged one and held it up to Shelly.

"Why are they there?" she asked.

I shook my head and put the dome back where it was, and managed to climb back in the saddle in one try. Actually, I have a theory about the insulators that may sound far-fetched. Aub was old, demented, and suffering strokes with no way to understand what was happening to him. The strokes and Helen's visitations may have seemed to him to come from the same place, or even to be the same thing. I think he was keeping her out, or trying to keep her in.

They say you shouldn't talk about the old days and how much better everything used to be, but my old days are still on the young side, and I often think about them. For instance, I still remember summertime out in front of my parents' home, the lime-green ranch house that looked like it could have been rolled from the department store on logs. I was three or four probably, and Ma was giving me a bath in a white plastic tub full of water that had been warming in the sun. Daylilies milled in the ditch like they were waiting for a ride. The road was dirt, still is, and the house is occupied by a new family now, with my folks in North Carolina. But I do remember that an electric-blue dragonfly landed on the edge of the white plastic tub, and those daylilies, wow! Orange, and how when I looked up everything was green, green, and big blue sky, and we seemed all of a sudden to have slipped into a slower stream of time.

You don't get very many moments like that, I find. So you have to be open to them, even knowing that you won't get many, and even knowing that when you remember them it'll only feel like you've lost something important, instead of gained something you can keep.

When Shelly and I passed close enough to Aub's place on our horses — mine a solid old-timer named Wurlitzer — I decided I would look in. The house hardly appeared any different from the outside. Just before we reached the edge of the field behind, we came across a couple of blue and white ribbons tied to the trailhead, bright against the dark green brush. We crossed the field at a lazy pace. Shelly held my reins and waited with the horses in the dooryard.

Inside the house I was confronted with Kevin Dunigan's decision to let things go. It was as empty as an abandoned house ever is. The kitchen table remained but it was bare. The refrigerator door was open and a hinge was loose. Quiet. I looked around and in the top southeast corner of the kitchen, right up near the ceiling, a milk snake had extended itself about a foot from between the walls, where a tear in the wallpaper had left an opening. The snake swayed in waltz time, smelling the air with its tongue. As I watched, it slid backward into the wall, and I was alone again.

ACKNOWLEDGMENTS

Grateful acknowledgment is made to the following friends, neighbors, and colleagues:

Lou Beach, Adrienne Brodeur, Nick Capodice, George and Jeanne Capwell, Tristan Davies, Dante Di Stefano, Brenna Farrell, Timothy Holman, Jenna Johnson, Spenser Lee, John McNamara, Margaret Mitchell, Andy Mullen, Danny Mulligan, Bruce Nichols, Ayan Babi Pal, Frank Philbrick, Becky Saletan, Andrea Schulz, and Kirk and Lesli Van Zandbergen.

Particular acknowledgment is made to:

Pete, Kate, Nathaniel, and Katherine Bouman, for their steadfast support.

Joyce Wilbur and Ed John.

My family.

Bill Luce, for hunting lore and wisdom in the field.

Chief Tim Burgh, for his valuable perspective on rural law enforcement — any inaccuracies on that subject are mine alone.

Everyone at W. W. Norton & Company whose excellent work made this book real, in particular Eleen Cheung, John Glusman, Ryan Harrington, Ingsu Liu, and Nancy Palmquist, as well as my copy editor Dave Cole.

My beloved agent Neil Olson, without whose trust, advocacy, and editorial work this book would surely have been consigned to the woodstove.

My friend and editor Tom Mayer — brilliant, generous, and in the pocket.

Barbara Jean.

And to Emily, "Always, darling."